Praise for the delightful screwball romantic comedies of
Suzanne Macpherson

"Snappy dialogue, colorful descriptions, and a sense of humor that begins at page one and holds up all the way through to the epilogue . . . She's going to be around a long time!"
Jill Barnett

"Original and fun . . . romantic and sexy . . . It's like discovering a new flavor of ice cream!"
Stef Ann Holm

"Macpherson succeeds in creating a romance that stands out from the pack."
Publishers Weekly

"Big laughs . . . irresistible romantic adventure . . . [Macpherson] will be on every reader's lips once the secret gets out."
Susan Wiggs

"No one writes humor like Suzanne Macpherson."
Rachel Gibson

"I promise you are going to laugh."
Debbie Macomber

SUZANNE
MACPHERSON

SWITCHED, BOTHERED AND BEWILDERED

AVON BOOKS
An Imprint of HarperCollinsPublishers

This is a work of fiction. Names, characters, places, and incidents are products of the author's imagination or are used fictitiously and are not to be construed as real. Any resemblance to actual events, locales, organizations, or persons, living or dead, is entirely coincidental.

AVON BOOKS
An Imprint of HarperCollins*Publishers*
10 East 53rd Street
New York, New York 10022-5299

First Avon Books paperback printing: December 2005

Avon Trademark Reg. U.S. Pat. Off. and in Other Countries, Marca Registrada, Hecho en U.S.A.
HarperCollins® is a registered trademark of HarperCollins Publishers Inc.

Printed in the U.S.A.

10 9 8 7 6 5 4 3 2 1

To James Everette,
my true inspiration

Acknowledgments

Thanks to the coolest twins I know, Kristin and Becky Gordon, and their excellent parents, Leslie and Frosty. Thank you also to the very beautiful Rita Clay Estrada, for being a true friend when I needed one, and to Marianne Stillings, for her amazing title talent.

1

Nobody Doesn't Like Jana Lee

"You want me to do *what?*" Jana Lee Tompkins Stivers bolted upright in her spa bed and stared at her twin. She quickly pulled up the sheet to cover her naked breasts. Jillian's insane request just proved that her sister had truly cracked up.

"Jana Lee, I know I don't deserve to ask anything of you, but I'm completely burned out. I can't bear facing people in my office again. I—I stood in the lunchroom screaming like a crazy woman at the vending machine because I got Mounds instead of an Almond Joy. I kept hitting the damn thing with my fists. I said terrible things to that machine. They had to detach me from it." Jillian's voice cracked.

"You should have called me sooner." Jana Lee thumped back down on the spa bed. Leave it to her sister to take whatever peace their life had and twist it until it couldn't ever be put back into its former shape.

"I'm just not ready to go back. A week here hasn't even made a dent in my stress levels. They won't give me another day off from work. I can't stay in Serenity Spa forever. Just let me have an extra week away from work. I've never asked you for this big of a favor, ever. And it's not long. I mean, after a week at that old boring Seabridge beach house you call home I'll have my sanity back and go politely back to my office."

Jana Lee shook her head. "I could never pull it off. We can't play that old switch trick on people anymore, Jillian. This isn't like the Mike and Todd boyfriend swap for the ninth-grade Sadie Hawkins dance. It's not just two dumb boys; it's your job we're talking about. Our lives are too complicated now."

Jana Lee didn't mention the *other* switch they'd done. The switch that had created years of resentment between her and her sister; the switch that had ended her engagement to Elliot the idiot.

But it was obvious that her sister really was on the edge of some sort of breakdown. It was noticeable. Jana Lee had only seen Jillian cry three times before in their entire lives. And right now she definitely heard her sister suppressing a sob.

The minute she'd gotten the call from Serenity Spa and heard Jillian begging her to join her for a long weekend at this place, she'd known something was up. Either Jillian was trying to mend fences between them, or she had personal reasons. Turns out it was a little of both.

"My job is like *four* dumb boys instead. Mike and Todd were harder than this would ever be! You did an *amazing* job of being me that night, remember? We can do it again. Don't make me pull a Bette Davis *Dead Ringer* thing on you."

"I'd rather be drowned by Bette Davis than take your place at Pitman Toys. *I'm* the one who'd have to do all the lying! You won't have to fool anyone. I'd never allow you to fib to my daughter, and Monty Python dog will see right through you. Your perfume is more expensive than mine. He'll want canned dog food on a regular basis the minute you show up," Jana Lee said.

"I can play you at the PTA or something. Wouldn't you love to skip out on some responsibilities for a while? Besides, we are *actresses*." Jillian's voice sounded so unusually desperate.

"We are *not* actresses." Jana turned her head toward Jillian to be sure she heard her clearly. "Being the Little Princesses on the Harvey the Dragon Show when we were kids does not count, dear. I can't believe you didn't call me and tell me how stressed out you've been. What is that about? I'm *only* your twin sister, for crying out loud. I thought we'd made some progress in putting things behind us.

"I knew something was wrong back in November at Thanksgiving, but you told me it wasn't. Don't lie to me about things like this anymore." Jana Lee sat up stiffly but obediently as the spa assistant wrapped the last strip of herbal-soaked linen around her boobs. She felt . . . exposed . . . and somewhat mummified. "I feel like King Tut," she sighed.

"That makes me sushi." Jillian *was* sushi. Jillian's personal spa guy had painted her with green goo and wrapped seaweed over every part of her body except her face.

"I smell way better than you do," Jana Lee said.

"True, but I'm exfoliating. I just need a little pickled ginger on the side and I'll be done," Jillian replied. "All this food talk is making me hungry."

"Try not to think about it." Jana Lee tried to relax while Sumiko, her personal spa attendant, smeared mud on her face with a soft brush. She peeked over at her sister's spa bed to see whether she was doing better at relaxing while her guy piled on the mud. Jillian didn't look very relaxed. She looked as tight as a violin string, and they weren't done with this subject, that was for sure.

"*Please*, Jana Lee, I need you to help me out. I've been gone a week already. If I don't go back, or if someone doesn't go back and *be* me, I'll get fired for sure. There's this overzealous junior accounting executive witch just itching for my job. I used my extra vacation time for this year going to the

Bahamas with that dolt I broke up with. At least I got a tan out of it."

"You'll have to tell me more about the Ron thing. I thought *he* broke up with *you?*"

"It was mutual," Jillian said flatly.

Jana Lee remembered distinctly that that wasn't the case. "I'm going to lie here and think about your request, so stop yammering." She tried to let the tension flow out of her like . . . what was it Sumiko said? Like a tropical waterfall gently flowing down upon her, while the scent of plumaria drifted around her. She was to let the images wash her stress away. Washhh.

Oh, geez, did she leave a wet load of wash in the Maytag back home? It would be a total mildewed nightmare by the time she got back from this emergency weekend with Jillian.

Maybe her daughter would drop in at home to get something, smell it, and rescue the load.

Maybe pigs would fly.

"I've left a load of clothes in the washer and they're going to mold. Everything molds in Washington." Jana Lee felt her mud start to harden up. Sumiko put a warm towel over the top of her head and several across her wrapped body, which felt wonderful. Maybe she could forget about laundry for once.

"Okay, I brought you here to help me feel normal again, and to give you a much deserved break, so no laundry or cooking or mommy-type thoughts for one weekend. Those are the rules. Besides, you needed this as much as I did, admit it. You're letting yourself get away with something at last—a weekend of pampering at a spa. You can feel guilty about it for at least the next year. Can we heap on any more guilt? Maybe you'll guilt out and help me?"

"I can feel guilty that my evil twin sister had to pay for me to come here and keep her company while she recovered from a minor nervous collapse instead of me knowing she was in trouble."

"I'm not the evil twin, you are, r-r-r-remember?" Jillian rolled her *r*'s and did her evil twin voice, which sounded a little like Bela Lugosi in an old vampire movie.

Jana Lee felt the thick brown facial mud crack at the corner of her mouth as she started to laugh. "Cut that out, I'm breaking up."

"It's true. You *are* the evil twin, and you know it," Jillian said.

"No, you are," Jana Lee replied through her pursed lips, trying not to laugh at their old joke. "I just *wish* I was."

That was true. She'd spent much of her life wishing she were more like Jillian. Jillian was pushy and brave and lived on the edge. Jillian had always had more fun and caused more trouble. She'd envied her and wanted to be more like her—if that was possible for an identical twin—that is, until Jillian had taken Elliot away from her in college, anyway.

Then she hadn't wanted to be anything like her sister anymore. But hey, Jillian had suffered plenty when Elliot had cheated on her and she'd ended up divorced. Neither Jana Lee nor Jillian had seen the truth. Elliot was an ass.

And if Jillian hadn't stolen Elliot away from Jana Lee, Jana Lee might have ended up married to him, instead of to Bill. She'd learned during their short time together that Bill was ten times the man Elliot was.

She'd learned a lot about her sister, too. Jillian had spent months with them after Bill died, helping Jana Lee get back on her feet, helping Carly deal with school. That counted for a whole lot in Jana Lee's book. They'd missed so much time together while Jillian had been married to Elliot. It felt good to see Jillian reaching out to her again instead of hiding away.

Jana Lee was actually worried about Jillian for the first time in years. Her time at Serenity Spa had only unwound Jillian a few notches, not enough to cope with her high-pressure job at Pitman Toys back in San Francisco. The truth was, Jillian was right—she was on the verge of a bad breakdown.

"I know what you're thinking. You're thinking I have more fun than you do. Well, I do. I've had so much fun I'm exhausted. That's why we're here. But the difference is I have no spa guilt. How could we have turned out so differently that way?

You know, I've never felt guilty about a facial or a massage in my entire life. How come you got the martyr gene and I didn't?"

Jana Lee waited for Jillian to answer her own question, something she did often.

"I know, I know, you're more like Mom, and I'm more like Dad. That's obvious. But you know, Bill would be happy to see you doing this. He'd want you to get on with your life. Two years of mourning is long enough."

Jana Lee felt the old familiar twinge in the pit of her stomach. Maybe two years was enough, maybe it wasn't. Jillian always knew how to push her buttons. And it wasn't that she was a martyr; it's just that she'd made different choices than her sister, and her choice had led her to being a wife and mother, and unfortunately . . . a widow.

"You should talk. You're a complete workaholic. It's just as much of a strain for you to sit still and be pampered as it is for me. Look at you, you're a wreck, and you know it. Now quit it. We're supposed to be relaxing."

As soon as she said it, Jana Lee knew she'd lashed out at Jillian just because of her own pain. "I'm sorry, Jillian. You touched a nerve." Jana Lee wiggled her toes to make sure the weird body wrap she was in hadn't cut off her circulation. She sighed and breathed in the soothing eucalyptus scent to calm herself down. She wished Jillian hadn't mentioned Bill.

She looked up through the glass-paneled roof to the beautiful California sky above her. The heat made her feel better. It thawed out her cold bones. The steamy hot wrap and hot towels helped too.

It seemed to her that she'd been unable to stay warm for the last two years; that the absence of her husband in their bed at night had left her unable to sustain any body heat at all. She often slept in her old gray sweats and his Husky sweatshirt—*Go Dawgs*, Bill's favorite college football team.

Jana Lee had kept herself silent for a while.

Jillian spoke softly. "Jana Lee, I'm sorry. You're right. And we are supposed to be relaxing. It's a rare moment for both of us, and I'm grateful we are spending time together, even if it was brought on by my nerves going haywire. I've got such a big mouth. Ignore me, okay?"

"I'm very good at that," Jana Lee said.

"I know. Actually everyone is good at it these days. Only a few people actually saw my meltdown. They all think I'm on vacation. I swear I could show up to work in a clown suit and no one in the office would notice."

"That used to work for us, didn't it? Literally. Of course Harvey the big blue idiot dragon would get all jealous and make wardrobe stitch him up a clown hat and collar. But we're not kids anymore, Jillian. There is nothing special about us now. We're not the Little Princesses anymore."

"Speak for yourself! I'm very special. I'm still a

princess at heart, even if I did get us fired off the damn Harvey the Psycho Dragon show. It's just that no one knows I'm a princess anymore."

A surprised Aussie voice came from behind Jillian's left shoulder. "You were the Little Princesses on *Harvey the Big Blue Dragon*? You're *those* Tompkins twins? Hey, Sumiko, these are the Tompkins twins!"

Sumiko said something in Japanese to Jana Lee, then grinned and started in singing . . . *the song*. Akk.

> *We are happy little princesses*
> *in the land of make-believe,*
> *we have a big blue dragon,*
> *and he will never leave—*
> *because he loves us, he loves us,*
> *and yes he loves you too.*

Sumiko knew all the hand movements, too. By now the Aussie spa dude had joined in, and the towel girl had come over to gawk.

Jillian groaned. "You can't tell me they syndicated Harvey reruns in Australia and Japan?"

"You bet! I was just a little tyke, of course, and we got the show a lotta years off the boat," spa dude said as he crossed his arms and looked pleased. Sumiko nodded her approval and agreement. As if what? She and Jillian were like—ancient old women?

"We were only five years old in the first episodes you know," Jana Lee said.

"How come we didn't get foreign rights on that, Jana Lee?"

"We probably did. Uncle Cyril probably bought that new yellow Cadillac with it." Jana Lee sunk into her herbal wrap and tried to look invisible.

Jillian must have noticed Jana Lee's discomfort. "Thanks, folks, but we just want to exfoliate and detoxify in peace here."

The staff members went back to work and left Jana Lee to simmer in her herbs. "Who would have figured they'd nail us with the dang song?" she said.

"No kidding. I don't mind that much. I guess they cut the episode where I kicked Harvey in the shins and sent him crashing into the castle set."

"I guess so. You sure packed a wallop for a kid."

"Little Johnny Hoffstater and I had been wrestling after school."

"Oh, is that what you called it? I thought you were practicing kissing."

"Haw, haw." Jillian sounded like her mud had seized up.

"Speaking of wrestling, what about that new guy you've been after at the office? A nice romance would perk you right up after the Ron fiasco. It always has," Jana Lee teased.

"Honestly, I don't think he's interested in me. I all but threw myself at him during the office holiday party. I—oh, it's too humiliating to think about." Jillian groaned.

"What? Spill it. My life is too dull for words. I have to have some vicarious fun."

"I stalked him until I caught him alone under the mistletoe, then laid a big wet one on him, complete with octopus arms and a full-frontal boob squish with my low-cut green velvet dress. I oozed cleavage all over him."

"What guy wouldn't go for that?"

"*That* one. He all but ran out into the snowy night. It's taken me five months to be able to look him in the eye again. The only good part is he wasn't in the room when I beat up the candy machine."

"Well, there's other fish in the fishbowl. You're a very good-looking woman. I should know."

"So funny." Jillian laughed. "At my age it takes more than looks. I think I'm a little intimidating."

"Tell me about it."

"Jana, come *on*, let's do it. Just one week?" Jillian begged. "I bet you could use a change."

"I could use a change, that's a fact. At least you've got work that you love. I'm really at a crossroads. I spent the last twelve years being a wife and mother. I've been trying to figure out what I can do now. I haven't got a clue. I used to be good at art, but that's not going to pay the property taxes or college for Carly in a few years. She's going to be a junior in high school next fall, you know?"

"I'll help with little Miss Carly Charlotte's education. Besides, I thought Bill left you enough to cover that."

"His life insurance was pretty good, but if you figure living expenses plus college costs for the next six years without any input from me, it's going to run out eventually. And Carly is looking at Stanford or something equally expensive.

"I told her she'd have to either get a scholarship or stay in state. She looked at me like I was sending her to a nunnery instead of the University of Washington. Her father did just fine there." Jana Lee had lost her relaxed mode again. Boy this was hard, but she might as well tell her sister everything. Jillian had been honest with her, and she appreciated that. They were making a whole lot of progress in healing their old wounds this weekend. It was good to talk to her sister openly again. Besides, she needed to talk. And Jillian needed to understand why she couldn't do what she was asking her to do.

"Carly has no respect for me anymore. I'm not sure if I have any for myself. I've hardly left my house for the last two years, and I know I haven't actually cleaned it in about that long. I just do the bare minimum, then curl up with a gallon of tea and watch talk shows.

"And talk about a nunnery, I have no idea what to do about meeting a man. I don't know if it's in me anymore. No wonder Carly wants to get as far away as possible. I'm as much of a mess as you are, I guess. I *sure* don't have it in me to do what you're asking, Jillian." Jana Lee's eyes watered up, but the tears had nowhere to go. They puddled against the mud and finally absorbed.

What a pathetic creature she was, crying into her mud facial. She didn't like quiet. It gave her too much time to think. She could shut off her head when *The View* was blaring in the background.

"Look, Jana, if you let me stay at your place, I'll clean house, wash the dog and straighten up my niece while I get my head back together. It'll be very Zen—carry the water, scrub the floor, you know? I miss the old place. I need to connect with my roots. We did a whole lot of growing up in that house.

"I feel like I've missed the boat on this family thing, and it's been too long since Carly's seen her aunt. Besides, I know this sounds weird, but if I could just see what it's like to have a quiet, suburban life, I might stop thinking about what I've missed out on and be happier. I'll probably hate it after two days."

"It's not that quiet. You'd be surprised. But I doubt Carly will even notice if I'm gone." Jana Lee's mud was getting very soggy around the eye area.

"And if you went to my office you could see what it's like to sit in a big leather chair and sign papers all day. We're in a really slow time right now at Pitman and you'd only have to go to a few meetings; but you do have to be me. Oliver, my assistant, can do all the real work. I don't want those slackers in production to think that the accounting department isn't watching them every minute. You'd be doing me a huge favor. Gawd, the thought of going back to work Monday is giving me the vapors."

"You don't get the vapors, Jillian, you've never gotten the vapors in your life. You are a tough cookie." Jana Lee looked over at Jillian, but what she saw was not a tough cookie. She noticed her sister's hand was trembling slightly, and she looked very thin, even wrapped in green goo. She also knew Jillian's job was anything but easy. "Why don't you just tell them you need more time?"

"I can't. My position at the company entails too much responsibility for them to think I'm weak. They need to believe I'm that tough cookie. And jobs like mine don't come around too often these days. It's all I've got, Jillian. Right now I'm a seaweed-wrapped nutcase. I don't want them to see me this way. Just say you'll think about it."

"I'll think about it if you promise you'll deal with the molding laundry the minute you set foot in the house." Jana Lee couldn't believe she was saying this, but something in her sister's voice really got to her.

"Yuk. I promise."

"For real."

"We'll see. I might hire someone."

"It has to be your own hands."

"Fine, I'll wear rubber gloves and a gas mask."

"That's more like it." Jana Lee laughed, then drifted off into the dreaded quiet. She tried to imagine herself at Jillian's job as comptroller for Pitman Toys. Jillian could add and subtract and create sales average graph charts. Jana Lee couldn't. But she *could* help her sister keep her job just by making a brief appearance and hiding out in her office for a week. At the same time she'd get a glimpse of what a real company in the big city was like.

It was a plain fact that she'd never held down anything besides a volunteer position in her entire life. She'd chosen to marry Bill instead of finishing college, and Carly had come along very quickly.

Even when she'd found out she couldn't have more children and Carly had reached school age, she hadn't gotten a job. Bill had always said he liked it when she was home for him.

Not that she'd minded. She'd taken a great deal of pride in having dinner on the table and keeping a home for her family. She'd felt useful, and when Bill had been away on business trips she'd always been there for Carly.

But Jana Lee remembered that she'd felt most alive when she was painting. Of course, she had no training, but the time she'd created a beautiful garden mural on her little girl's bedroom wall, complete with rabbits and birds and butterflies and a floral array worthy of Monet, had given her great joy.

Her friend Leslie had gushed and said she should go into the wall mural business. Jana Lee remembered planning it out, but in the end she just hadn't had the courage to do it.

If she hadn't had the courage then, how was she going to find it now? Where was she going to find the nerve to make a new career for herself at thirty-five? Where indeed?

But really, it wasn't the worst idea ever to try it out in Jillian's office. She was sick of being a scared rabbit. Maybe she'd shake up her life for once. Maybe she'd do it for Jillian. Maybe she'd be the strong one for a change. Jillian *had* spent months with her after Bill's car accident, helping with the memorial and all those sad details that go along with the end of a person's life. Jillian had given her the space to grieve by taking care of so many things.

And here she was asking for help herself. Poor Jillian. She really did need a rest.

Jana Lee sensed a shadow over her face, and she opened her eyes. Her sister Jillian was looking down at her with a very shiny, clean, but pale face. A face that looked so tired, Jana Lee knew she'd do anything to help her sister feel better.

"Wake up, Sleeping Beauty, the beast is here, and she's hungry," Jillian growled.

"What's the point of getting all sweaty and slenderized if it gives you the appetite of a bear?" Jillian moaned as she tried to fit a fourth "gourmet health wrap" on her plate while they stood in the lunch buffet line, only to get a glare from the catering assistant. More like gourmet health *crap*. She needed a big fat sizzling steak with a side of jumbo fries. "Don't they believe in high-protein here?"

"Shhh. This is part of the detoxification plan, and it's supposed to help you get well." Jana Lee shushed her.

Jillian picked up the wrap and looked down the end like a spyglass. "There's like . . . *horse* food in here."

"Those are wheat berries and raw oats in a curry sauce. Now be quiet and behave."

Yuk. Jillian ordered a yogurt smoothie at the end of the line with as much actual fruit as possible. None of this wheatgrass for her. She'd have them grind up a nice barbequed chicken in there—or at least replace that yogurt with ice cream—if she could.

"We are hitting Dairy Queen as soon as we're outta here for a double cheeseburger and a fudge brownie treat sundae," Jillian said.

"And undo all this health? Speak for yourself.

Of course you're the one that can eat like a horse and never gain an ounce. I thought we were supposed to be identical. What's up with that?"

"I *am* eating like a horse," Jillian whinnied and bit into her healthy wrap as soon as her butt was in the dining room chair. She chewed and made a face at her sister, who was actually making a worse face, having had her own bite. "I think it's because you had a child. It rearranges things. Not fair, is it?"

"I suppose the joy of motherhood is supposed to make up for that. But when they hit fifteen, I'd rather have my old hips back, thanks anyway."

Jillian choked and looked at Jana Lee with surprise. It was nice to see Jana Lee wisecracking. She was just too damn serious most of the time. You'd think she was the firstborn. Come to think of it, she was. By about ten minutes.

Jana Lee removed a piece of what looked like actual wheat from her wrap. "Oh my, I just thought of something. If we're really going to do the switch, and I'm not saying we are, I'm going to have to lose a few pounds and cut and dye the gray out of my hair."

"Oh yeah. I forgot. Plus you'll need a manicure for sure, and—um, I sort of got a tattoo."

"You what?"

"I didn't think you'd approve. I got it in the Bahamas."

"You got a tattoo in a foreign country?"

"Hey, at least if we're in an accident together they can finally tell us apart."

"There is no way I'm getting a tattoo, besides no one will see it anyway." Jana Lee waved her off.

"It's sort of in a visible spot." Jillian pushed her white terry robe sleeve up and revealed a subtle tribal scroll bracelet design around her wrist. "We can do yours in temporary ink. That will wear off in a few weeks."

"It better."

"This will be fun."

"Fun as in me on a treadmill sweating my extra ten pounds off in twenty-four hours?"

"You don't have to lose ten pounds. You can just tell everyone you pigged out at the spa." Jillian laughed.

"Thanks." Jana Lee stuck her tongue out at Jillian. Then she raised her eyebrow. "Of course you'll need to be putting some on if you want to fool the clerks at Central Market."

"I'll just tell everyone I slimmed down and had a makeover at the spa," Jillian replied.

"You always win. You are a brat."

"Just bratlike. We have much planning to do, sister in crime."

"Well, you don't have much to do because I never see anyone but my daughter, and she'll be glad to see Aunt Jillian, if she even notices you've arrived. And listen, I'm only considering doing this to help you keep your job, and to see to it you actually rest. Plus, I'd get to see if I actually want to enter the workforce or stay at home and take in ironing for the rest of my life. It would be sort of a test run. Can't I just say I'm me, taking over for you?"

"That's not anywhere near as fun, plus I'd still get fired. Besides, think what horrid trouble you could get me into while I'm at your place, mopping floors."

Jana Lee smiled. "That has possibilities."

"And I promise I'll get a nice rest at your place."

"Oh, I forgot, I do see someone. There are the four mouseketeers I watch for a few hours after kindergarten, and their various parent pick-ups. Did I mention I've been doing a little babysitting?" Jana Lee poked her fork into a piece of cantaloupe and gestured to Jillian calmly. "Is that going to be a problem? It's only three days. Their school is almost out."

"What? Well, I guess I can endure three days of rugrats. They can't be any worse than the advertising department." That was true. Jillian was so tired of all the office politics and ego-moments she'd endured over the last ten years that even a pack of grubby, whiney kids didn't sound bad. Not to mention that big stupid kid Ron.

What was wrong with her taste in men anyway? He'd dumped her right after their trip to the Bahamas. The trip *she* had paid for. What an idiot she was. And worst of all, she'd actually convinced herself she liked him, when really he was the rebound guy from having Jackson bolt away from her at the Christmas party just before that.

Jillian felt her hand shake as she stabbed at a bean sprout with her fork. She was actually scared at how unraveled she'd gotten. She had to get some rest. She hadn't even told Jana Lee about the panic attacks she'd been having.

Jana Lee was the intuitive one, and she usually saw right through Jillian's little white lies. This time Jillian was grateful she hadn't. She'd been to three doctors already and only managed to get a temporary medication to deal with her problem. They all talked about long-term therapy and used words like "disorder," which made her have an even *worse* sense of panic.

But truly, even though she was thinking mostly of herself at present, she'd been worried about Jana Lee, too. Nothing seemed to be able to spark her out of her mourning for Bill. It was understandable, but so sad. Jillian stuffed another piece of melon in her mouth and thought of the many ways to remake her sister's house, her ingrate kid Carly, and maybe even . . . her sister's love life.

Surely there was some cute land baron or yachtsman Jillian could start something up with and leave for her sister to finish. A little flirting, a little smile, and Jana Lee's phone number dropped in the right direction? Who knows what could be waiting for Jana Lee when she got back home.

A huge grin crept across Jillian's face, and she put her napkin up to hide it from Jana Lee. Surely she could do all that and get some rest too. Of course she could.

Jana Lee stared at her like she knew what she was thinking.

"Okay then," Jana Lee said. "I'm willing." She held up her hand, palm toward Jillian, fingers apart.

Jillian matched her hand to her sister's, like they had since they were babies. It was their secret sign. She remembered looking at Jana Lee when they were very young children, dressed the same as she was, and wondering if she was looking into a mirror or if Jana Lee was real. It was one of her first memories.

She also realized that Jana Lee hadn't offered that hand since their terrible year in college, and she knew it was an act of forgiveness on Jana Lee's part. It moved her deeply to know that. Jillian felt a tear stream down the side of her cheek. She wiped it away with her other hand.

2

Fair Trade Agreement

Jana Lee Tompkins wobbled down the hall of Pitman Toys Inc. on her sister's black sling-back Ferragamo high heels. She also had on the shortest skirt she'd ever worn, which was the longest skirt in Jillian's closet. She'd topped that with the least revealing blouse she could find. She'd strategically tied a soft yellow silk scarf at the neck to cover up her cleavage just a little more, and she'd added a short black leather jacket that zipped up the front to cover her bare arms. She wasn't used to being displayed in a sleeveless blouse. The jacket was very *Jillian*, anyhow.

She had to admit that she felt pretty. Her reflection flashed back at her from office windows as she moved down the hall. Her new dark brown hair looked very pert in the short bob Jillian always wore. She probably should have cut and dyed hers years ago instead of wearing it in that long Earth Mother braid. Their hair was thin and straight, and this was a much better look.

That nasty health food, plus the horrible things Jillian had subjected her to at the Serenity Spa, all in the name of relaxation, had resulted in a six-pound drop in her weight that actually made a tiny difference. That was lucky, because of the fifty outfits she'd tried on last night, this was one of three that fit. She'd just have to wear those three over and over again for the next week. According to Jillian, no one paid even the slightest attention to her anyway. With that in mind, she'd skipped the fake tattoo.

Jana Lee jumped and joggled her purse and briefcase as a severe looking woman came down the hall toward her, smiled oddly and said good morning. Jana Lee reassembled her load, responded and kept moving, her heart pounding twice as hard. Was she just a dead giveaway? Was the woman turning around and staring? Jana Lee didn't want to glance back and find out.

She was seriously scared out of her wits.

Jillian had a way of leaving out huge details, and even though she'd faxed Jana Lee a ten-page itinerary and short profile of everyone she might encounter, Jana Lee had that sure sense there was going to be some very big surprises around the corner.

The main plan at the moment was to get hot water for her tea, find Jillian's office, shut the door and hide for the rest of the day. She smelled the familiar scent of java and followed her nose to an open lunchroom area. Where there was coffee, there was hot water.

Unfortunately there were also groupings of employees, and she hadn't read the material enough to clue in to any names.

But she was on a mission—morning tea. She sucked her breath in, slapped on a Jillian-like smile, and tried to adopt her sister's braver-than-the-average gal demeanor while she made a beeline to the coffeepot hot water area.

"Hi there, good morning, thanks." Her three-word vocabulary got her through the short line, where she snagged Jillian's cup off the peg rack and filled it with hot water. She braced Jillian's briefcase against the counter with her legs, dug in the purse she'd brought, and found one of her special tea bags. She felt many eyes upon her.

Uh-oh. From the looks of the cup, Jillian drank coffee. Damn. Well, Jillian must have had a revelation at that spa and sworn the stuff off. That's right. Jillian now drank Red Zinger tea. She plopped the bag in the water and watched it turn a lovely deep red color. She loved Red Zinger.

As Jana Lee turned out of the line she came smack up against a very tall, *Man Zinger* of a man. Wow. He had on a pale gray suit, and his tie looked vintage forties, with palm trees on a yellow background. She hadn't seen a whole lot of suits in the room, so this must be someone important. He had that air of authority around him. If he wasn't, he sure was one heck of a hunk of a good-looking nobody. He had intense brown eyes and well-behaved, wavy brown hair.

"Good morning," she flashed a bright smile at him, shaking in her sling-backs all the while.

The man looked startled. "Good morning, Miss Tompkins." He looked her over like a prize Jersey cow, from hoof to tail, then zeroed in on her eyes.

Oh God, not already. Did he see something? She broke eye contact and moved past him. "Excuse me," she whispered.

"You look very rested after your trip."

"Thank you." End of story. Jana Lee split out of there fast. She was never going to survive five days of this.

Jana Lee made it past a truly scrutinizing stare from Jillian's assistant, Oliver Abbott. She mumbled something about not feeling well so please don't disturb her, bolted through the office door and shut it behind her. She leaned her back against the closed door, let out a huge audible sigh and hoped Ollie didn't hear it.

Jillian's office was neat as a pin. *If this was Jillian's office!* She'd just assumed that since Oliver was at the front desk with his nameplate, this was Jillian's office.

There was way too much window glass involved in this whole deal, so Jana Lee quickly rounded the room and dropped the shiny, brass-colored metal mini-blinds down. The tinny rustle of a thousand strips of aluminum dropping into place gave her the willies.

The large glass desk left no hiding place for clutter, but of course there was no clutter—only a black leather desk set that included a blotter, a pencil can with pencils neatly contained within, all black, all sharpened, a letter opener with black leather handle, a black leather stapler, and a sleek container for brass paper clips, all large, all the same size. Joining the paper clips was a slot for a large sticky-note pad, and there it was; plain white with black block lettering that read Jillian Tompkins. Whew, right office.

Next to that was a phone that looked way, way too high-tech for Jana Lee's taste, and centered on the desk was Jillian's laptop computer, keeper of all things she should know. Suddenly, she felt extremely grateful that she'd taken that basic computer class in college. She was right in thinking that whatever she did for a job, computers would be involved.

It'd been a good four years since Jana Lee had been to San Francisco to visit Jillian. Since before Bill died. It always astounded her what a neat freak her sister was. She did recall a whole lot of sister fights about the state of their shared bedroom, and how finally Jillian had insisted on her own space when they were about fourteen, and how all her socks used to line up in the drawer like obedient show dogs.

There was a large, low, black credenza with brass accents situated behind the glass desk, and Jana Lee brightened up to see there was a framed photo of her and Carly sitting upon it. She set her tea on the glass desk, then dumped Jillian's too small purse and Jillian's sleek black leather briefcase on the credenza next to her picture.

Flipping the combination locks—fortunately, the code was their joint birthdate—Jana Lee opened the briefcase and dug out Jillian's file. Even though she'd already read it twice, she'd have to make some notes. She'd have to bone up on this operation and see if she could match faces to people.

Her mind reeled with how crazy this whole thing was. She tried to remember why she'd agreed to it: to give her sister a much-needed rest before she ended up in a less pleasant place than Serenity Spa? To keep her sister from getting fired? To jump-start her own stagnant existence? To gain some insight into the work world? Right. All that.

Once she felt less like crawling under the desk she might be able to snoop around and get the feel of this big company—the great Pitman Toys Inc. This city *was* pretty exhilarating after being stuck in the sticks for so long. She spun the rod on one of the blinds and peeked out the window to see the shore side of San Francisco, so vibrant and alive.

Jana Lee peeled off the black leather jacket and flung it on an upholstered bench next to one of the water-facing windows. She slipped behind Jillian's desk and sat in the cushy leather office chair. It swiveled. She rocked and twisted and spun around. She felt like a kid.

Something buzzed. She turned to look at the phone and saw that a light was flashing. She picked up the receiver, but it dial-toned back at her. She hit a few buttons. Nothing happened. The buzz came again. Now, how would she explain her inability to answer that, whatever it was? Better think fast before Ollie nailed her. She jumped out of the chair and headed toward the tall office door.

Too late. It swung wide open, barely missing her. She caught it with her hand. The very amazing-looking *Man Zinger* stood in the doorframe with a quirky smile on his face.

"Um, phone's on the fritz," she croaked.

"Intercom," Oliver's voice called flatly from behind the hot and suited gentleman with the vintage tie.

Jana Lee stared at his tie. He stepped in without an invitation.

"What can I do for you?" Jana Lee found herself backing up to the wall looking for some kind of support.

He removed the door from her hand and closed it behind himself. "I came to return that Christmas present you gave me." His brown eyes danced with a devilish grin.

"What Christmas present?" Jana Lee had lost all ability to sort the situation out. She wasn't ready for actual office contact yet! She'd moved backward enough to hit the wall. She felt it with her fingers to be sure it was there.

"This one."

Man Zinger took three big steps forward and pinned her against the wall like a moth to a collector's board, his hands pressed on the wall next to each side of her head, his body so close it created a heat wave. He looked into her eyes for a moment, then went straight for her lips. She heard herself make a squeaking sound as he pressed in for the hottest kiss she had ever, ever tasted.

Ohhh! *Oh* man. The electricity ran a shock-line through her entire body—from the lips to the toes then back again. By the time the wave hit her brain, she started to regain her senses.

She pulled out of his kiss and gasped. Jillian had obviously left some major details out of her notes.

Without the slightest hesitation, her hand, which must be working off some primal instinct disconnected from the rest of her body, flew up and slapped her handsome visitor right in the kisser. He looked surprised. His hand flew to his face. Then he grinned.

"I'll pick you up here at six for dinner."

He then, much to her shock and dismay, turned on his heel and vanished out the office door, not waiting for her reply.

Jackson Hawks could hardly believe that was the same Jillian Tompkins who'd thrown herself and her cleavage at him during the company Christmas party last December. He'd been avoiding her like the proverbial plague since then.

She seemed so different now. She sure must have needed a rest. Her whole face looked softer. Her usual hard-edged black eyeliner and red *power lips* deal had been replaced by a much softer, earthy look. Even that cleavage looked . . . earthier. And she'd acted positively demure in the coffee room instead of oh, assaulting the vending machine, for instance.

Maybe he'd misjudged Jillian Tompkins. People did change. Why, he actually felt seriously turned on by her, slap and all. Her bright blue eyes and her short swingy brown hair had him hot around the collar and it wasn't even nine o'clock in the morning.

His love life was abysmal at the present time anyway, so why not give Miss Jillian another chance? Besides, he couldn't get her off his mind after seeing her in the coffee room this morning. He'd found that so odd. Odd enough to think up an excuse to visit her end of the hallway. Like maybe he'd needed even more sales figures for his afternoon meeting with Cavanau. But he'd come away without sales figures. He'd come away with a taste of Jillian instead. He smiled as he walked down the bright hallway.

Cavanau was such a wank; he loved pie charts. Jackson would have Oliver send them over on the computer and pile them on because Cavanau was their biggest account at present, and their last line of toys hadn't performed as well as they'd hoped, so today he'd have to convince Cavanau to keep the faith in Pitman Toys.

Which reminded Jackson of some details he had to attend to, like making sure the conference room was ready and that Olga had Cavanau's favorite lunch ordered. Check, double-check, and check again. Ever since he'd accepted the vice presidency he'd felt a heavy responsibility to keep Pitman Toys in the game.

Of course being VP of Pitman meant wearing many hats, but that was fine with him. That translated to keeping his own butt employed, and the rest of the motley crew around here, too. It was chilling out there in the job-hunt line. San Francisco had been hit hard by the economic roller coaster of the last ten years.

But at present, the thought of connecting with Jillian Tompkins seemed to be overshadowing a whole lot of other things. He'd asked her out to dinner, and she hadn't said no. Well, to be more correct, he hadn't let her. He could spend the evening staring at her new, softer look across a nice meal and see if she really had changed so much or whether it was his sex-starved imagination.

3
Trading Paces

Jillian stood out on the small back porch breathing in the fresh, salty sea air. Memories of sitting here having awkward conversations with middle-school boyfriends came back to her. It was the only place to get a little privacy in the small beach house her parents had bought when they'd moved up from L.A.

Seabridge Bay was calm and quiet. The lapping waves made a rhythmic gesture against the smooth rocks that brought back many pictures in her mind, like a scrapbook made from scents and sounds of the past that were still the same today.

But right now she was actually trying to get away from the fumes she'd created in the laundry room. Apparently two cups of bleach and half a box of powdered laundry detergent did more than get the mildew smell out of the stinking, rotting clothes she'd dealt with yesterday upon her arrival; it also made the washing machine explode. "I promised to rescue the wash, now I'm rescuing the washer," Jillian muttered to herself.

She went to the garage, found Bill's old red toolbox, dragged it inside and opened the lid.

She had to admit, she had no idea what to do about the washer, but she was going to find out. She could do anything any man could do, and in her experience, if you took something apart and put it back together, you usually figured out what was wrong with it.

It was seven in the morning, and she had hours before the munchkins arrived after school. Hours. She'd hoped to sleep in, but the sound of some freakin' happy morning birds had disrupted her enough to make it impossible. She'd just wanted to *fry* those damn birds for breakfast. Them and their seagull friends.

Now, where was the manual for this thing? Jillian dug in the upper cupboard in the laundry room looking for the book to the Kenmore washer. Hot glue gun, a box of old sunglasses, random batteries, a rubber-stamping kit: oh no, it would be too logical for Jana Lee to keep the books right next to the units. Jillian stepped back and wiped her dusty hands on the front of the old apron she'd found hanging on a hook in the laundry room. It looked like one of Mom's. It probably was.

It was a good thing she'd grown up in this house and knew every inch of it. That would make her useless hunts for everything slightly easier.

Jillian stepped in the kitchen and washed her hands, then poured herself a cup of coffee. Where the sugar and creamer were, she had no idea. Wait, the copper and tin canisters were still on the counter, just like when they were kids, and lo and behold . . . Jillian popped the lid off the old sugar can. Sugar. She'd have to use real milk, if there was any in the house. After the washer incident there was no doubt she'd have to go grocery shopping. Oy-Arse Domesticus.

She pulled the old fridge open and located a carton of milk, opened the spout, sniffed, and about gagged. Instead of subjecting herself further, she put it back in the fridge. She'd purge later.

The sound of pounding footsteps down the stairs was followed by the blur of a teenage body with some sort of hip-hugger pants, a streak of belly flesh showing, and a tank top. The blur paused long enough to grab the five bucks Jillian had been instructed to place on the counter.

"Bye."

That was it. Carly's repeat performance; one showing at ten o'clock last night, one showing at seven in the morning. Last night it was "hi" followed by a streak up the stairs to her room, and the slammed door, then the bumping beat of alternative rock and roll. Jana Lee had bet Jillian a box of chocolate-covered cherries it would take Carly at least a week to even notice her Aunt Jillian was standing in for her mother. Jillian was beginning to think she was going to lose that bet. At least she'd win the one where Oliver would spot Jana Lee in thirty seconds or less.

Not only was her niece a piece of work but this 1969 tract house was a piece of junk. It didn't even have that kitschy charm sixties houses sometimes get. Dropped plastic ceiling panels with fluorescent lights, mustard shag carpet, bad aluminum windows, and ugly, ugly brown vinyl fake brick on the kitchen floor. No wonder Jana Lee was depressed. It was a split-level nightmare.

Jillian leaned against the old white sparkle-vinyl countertop and slurped her sugary black coffee. And she was supposed to be unwinding. She sighed.

Speaking of depressed, Monty Python, the oldest golden retriever on the planet, was staring at her from his downtrodden position on the sofa in the family room. His big doggy eyes knew the truth.

"Monty, you know it's me, just get over yourself. She'll be back in a week," she told the dog.

Monty's floppy left ear made a tiny movement. She knew he'd heard her. He'd been in that exact position since last night. The sofa was obviously dog domain, and that was that. He wasn't moving.

"Just don't pee on it. You know where the dog door is."

Monty rolled an eyeball at her.

Now, to the washer. She slammed through every cupboard in the kitchen and came up empty on the manual. Well, there was always the internet. She hadn't seen any computer hooked up on the main floor, or in Jana Lee's upstairs room, so if one existed, it was most likely in Carly's room.

Jillian took off her apron and stomped upstairs, thinking up ways to search for washer manuals on Google. Her pants slid down a bit, and she pulled them back up. Geez, Jana Lee's jeans were a little loose on her. She better find a belt before they fell off. She'd put on these jeans and her sister's clean but ugly pink T-shirt and a pair of old Keds tenny runners. That was the extent of the wardrobe hunt so far. It did feel rather good not to have to get all slicked up for work.

She should have packed more of her own stuff, but she hadn't really known she'd be coming here when she'd checked into Serenity Spa. What she did pack was dirty from her spa week, and of course to *wash* it she had to fix the washer. She was in a tragic sitcom loop.

The door to Carly's room was covered in stickers and Keep Out signs. When Jillian pushed, it creaked open like in a horror movie. Jillian stood in the doorway for a moment, too stunned to move. This was obviously the gateway to hell.

There must be a bedroom here, but stinking piles of cast-off dirty clothes coated every square inch, except those inches that were covered in magazines, makeup, empty soda cans, pizza boxes and take-out drink containers with straws sticking out of them. The smell was bad, way bad. Jillian kicked through the piles and made a path.

In one corner was an old white-and-gold French provincial girly-style desk. On that desk was the flickering screen of a desktop computer. It looked like a fairly decent model. The screen saver was Justin Timberlake and Janet Jackson in her famous bare-boob moment. Well, at least Justin was cute.

Jillian located a chair and scraped herself a space at the desk. She had a deep, abiding need for charts and lists and databases. She set her coffee cup down, hiked up Jana Lee's jeans, and got to work.

In one hour she'd downloaded an entire yearly household maintenance master plan off of one site, created a daily checklist on Excel from a site by a gal called Flylady, and pulled up and printed off the mechanical specifications for the Maytag top-load washer. Being capable was a good feeling. She three-hole-punched all those and created several notebooks from binders she found stuffed around the room. At least Carly had office supplies.

In two more hours, she'd taken the entire

washer apart but hadn't located the problem. That was sort of an understatement. She couldn't really grasp how to reassemble it. Perhaps she'd overestimated her own mechanical abilities. She'd have to call a repair guy. She needed this washer in running order because Carly's Hell Room was on her list of things to do, and so was teaching Carly to wash and dry her own damned clothes.

She'd tackle her on the reentry run tonight. She'd have to forfeit the bet, though. Would Carly really have taken a full week to realize her aunt was standing in the kitchen instead of her mother? They'd never know now, because Jillian had a plan to implement and she was enlisting her niece first thing off the bat.

Let's see. If she could get a repair guy by one, he might be able to be out of here before three, when the rugrats came. Jillian went back in the kitchen and looked at Jana Lee's scribbled notes in the spiral notebook with Tweety bird on the front. She and Jana Lee were *so* different. After-school snacks. Got it. She'd go to Central Market and stock up on stuff. But how would she do that while waiting for a repair guy? Logistics.

Jillian found the phone book exactly where her mother had kept it, in an open shelf by the kitchen wall phone along with five years of outdated phone books. She picked the most accessible local book, which was about five years old but showed the most use. Maybe there'd be notes.

She opened it, flipping to the back, and noticed Jana Lee had a list of phone numbers scribbled in the back: school, pizza, handyman. Handyman. That would work. Those guys did everything. Maybe.

Let's just hope she could get this guy on short notice. While she was dialing she grabbed the old phone books and walked them to the recycle bin outside on the back porch; thankfully the spiral phone cord attached to the ugly old wall phone reached a whole twenty feet.

"Hi, is this Dean Wakefield?" she asked. He said yes, so she launched into it. "This is um . . . Mrs. Stivers. I think you did some work here once? Well, I sort of disassembled my washing machine. Can you put it back together? It's kind of an emergency."

The guy started making excuses but said he did remember her. Oh, and how brilliant was she to pick a guy that knew her sister? Wow, she really was bad at this whole thing.

"Oh *please*, I'm begging you. There's a teenager here who hasn't washed clothes for six months and she'll have to wear a flour sack to school if I don't get this thing running." She meant all that, too. What she didn't say was that she had no idea about anybody else in town, and at least her sister had taken the time to write his name in her phone book, so he couldn't be completely stupid, could he?

He surrendered and said he'd be right out. Sure.

It was almost noon. He'd come rolling in here about two—or three—or four, or never. Dean Wakefield. He was probably available because everyone in town knew better than to hire him except her sister.

Her jeans slipped down below her hips. She yanked them up again and went to find her three-ring binder organizer thingies to keep herself from becoming . . . off track.

Fifteen minutes later Dean Wakefield's white truck pulled up in Jana Lee's driveway while Jillian watched through the kitchen window. She knew because it had Dean's name written on the truck door and a cartoon handyman painted next to it. Great, she'd hired a cartoon repairman.

As he came around his truck she noticed he sure didn't look much like a repairman. He was lean and mighty good-looking. She stretched further sideways to see him through the window as he climbed up the cement stairs to the front door. Let's just hope Dean had a sense of humor as well as good looks.

"What the? . . ." Dean closed his mouth and kept his opinion to himself. What had this crazy broad done, gone wrench happy? He wasn't sure which was more shocking, the completely disassembled washer, or the extreme changes in the lady who had disassembled it. Mrs. Stivers sure looked different. But then he hadn't seen her in quite a while.

"I was trying to fix it," she said.

"I see that." He bent down on his knees and sorted through some of the parts.

She got down beside him and pointed. "I thought maybe the agitator had seized up from all the gunk."

"Might have, but we won't know till it's back together."

"I suppose."

He looked over at her and smiled. She was sitting cross-legged on the floor against the dryer, watching him. He could hardly believe this was the same Mrs. Stivers he'd seen the last time he'd been out here. He'd been genuinely sad for her, losing her husband like that, so young. And he knew what that pain was like firsthand.

Her hair was different. Everything about her was different. Sort of. She had a beautiful smile, and wild, dancing blue eyes. He hadn't noticed that at all when he'd come and replaced the sink faucet. He felt himself attracted to her, which put him off-kilter. He picked up the injector nozzle and reconnected it with the correct valve.

"Are you going to watch me the whole time?" He didn't look at her while he asked that; he just kept putting parts together.

"I have a curious nature. If I watch you, I might learn how to fix it, then I won't have to call you again."

"What fun would that be?" He shot her a quick glance.

"How much am I paying you an hour?"

"Oh, forty bucks or so."

"Are you pretty busy? You didn't seem to be."

"It's a slow day. But I only take calls two days a week." He wondered at her questions. Was she adding his fee base up in her head? Two days times eight hours times forty bucks? It didn't add up to a living, for sure.

Of course he didn't often put on his handyman hat. He'd given up his big contracting business to pursue his other hobby and only occasionally lent his services to people in need in the community. Most Mondays were spent working for his senior friends, fixing whatever needed fixing in their older houses, which was usually quite a few things.

But she didn't need to know that he'd said yes to her out of pity.

"Why not all the time?" she asked.

"I have other interests. Hand me that plastic pipe by your feet—the big white one, please."

"What kind of interests?" She handed him the pipe by doing a very yogalike move.

He raised his eyes from his work to look at her. "I'm a sculptor. I make metal art, or work in stone sometimes."

"That's cool. Are you famous?"

"I made a gate that looks like a windblown tree for Earl Johnson's north cow pasture. Does that count?" He pulled his toolbox over and got his sealing tape and D wrench. She seemed disappointed at his answer.

"This art; is it a Calder kind of thing, or a Bruce Gray kind of thing, or maybe a Horiuchi style?"

Dean looked up at his inquisitive client. "Where'd you learn so much about sculpture?" He didn't really answer her question. It was more of a Dean Wakefield thing, anyhow.

"Oh, I'm a modern art buff. Do you have a website?"

"No, now excuse me, I'm going to need to concentrate on your washer so I don't run up an exorbitant bill for you. Do you have any coffee?"

"Sure."

She gathered herself off the floor, and he watched her grab at her loose waistband. Those jeans of hers were a mite big. She must have lost weight.

"Exorbitant. There's a three-dollar word for ya," she called from the kitchen. "In excess of normal. I had to look it up once."

Dean laughed. "Make that coffee black, please. How's your daughter? She must be pretty big now."

Jillian's coffeepot froze in midair, splashing one sploosh on the countertop. She'd figured out Dean Wakefield had met her sister Jana Lee, but she hadn't thought it would actually come up. She was thinking it would have been sort of insignificant to him and he wouldn't have really paid attention to Jana Lee. Why the hell did she get herself into this by calling a repairman her sister had hired before? She tipped the pot back to pouring and finished up his cup of coffee. Now what?

"Carly is very fifteen these days," she answered brightly. "I've been out of town. I went to a spa this weekend." Now what sense did that make? She shut her mouth and brought Dean his coffee.

Dean was staring at her, probably wondering where her whole spa comment had come from. He was sitting on his heels, looking up at her. "Well, you look great," he said.

He had an extremely sexy smile and intense brown eyes. She noticed the muscles, lots of muscles: leg muscles, arm muscles, chest muscles. Sculptors must have to heave things around quite a lot. When her eyes came back up to his face, she noticed he was looking back at her. She scooted back to the kitchen and grabbed her own coffee, slightly embarrassed at herself for checking out the repair guy. The repair guy-dash-sculptor.

She parked herself in a wedged corner of the kitchen and gathered her wits. She sipped her coffee and shuddered at the lack of creamer in it. Yuk.

Here was a really good-looking guy, down to earth, artsy, able to fix a washer; Jana Lee would love that artsy part. And he could fix stuff around the house. If she did this right, not too much, just enough, she could leave a little surprise for her sister to return to.

She'd have to make up some rules. Like no kissing him. That would be really tacky. So she'd have to entice him in a really Jana Lee kind of way and just leave it sort of open for business. She grinned at her own thoughts. She really was the naughty sister.

As if he knew, Monty Python slumped off the sofa and wagged on over to Dean the repair guy. He got right in his way, in his face, and gave him a big dog smooch.

"Monty, cut that out!" Jillian plunked her coffee down and ran to drag the damn dog off the cute repair guy. She tugged at his collar, but he seemed quite dog-mule-ish about the whole thing and stood his ground. "*Come on*, dog!" she pulled at him, digging her heels in. My God, this dog was heavy!

"It's okay, he's . . ." Dean the repair guy was laughing at Monty. Then, because the floor was still wet and despite her mopping up water with at least ten towels, she slipped and landed on her ass. "Oh, geez, are you okay?" He stood up and reached down to her, still laughing.

"So *very* funny," Jillian said. She was miffed at herself, and her butt hurt. She ignored his hand and moved to her knees, then pulled herself up using the side cupboard, her back to him. Unfortunately, her sister's jeans didn't get up with her. They just slid right down to her knees.

"Ah . . . er . . . the pants." Dean was laughing harder now. He was having trouble getting the words out.

She frantically yanked the jeans up. Now why the hell had she picked the red thong today? Her only clean leftover spa break undies, unfortunately.

"Good grief, I'm such a klutz," she said. She tried to regain some dignity. Monty Python barked one dumb huge bark at her, then walked off, disinterested at the chaos he'd created. "I'll get you later, muttley," she yelled. "Look, Dean, I know this is really odd timing, but would you like to go out for a drink later tonight?"

Dean looked shocked. He was wiping his hands on a purple rag and his laughter-watered eyes on his flannel sleeve, but he stopped dead in his tracks when she finished talking. An awkward time gap appeared between them, and Jillian could actually hear the kitchen clock click seconds off. Tick, tick tick. Loud.

"I'd love to have a drink with you," he finally replied.

"This isn't just all about the red thong, is it?" Jillian laughed at herself.

"No, but it's a nice addition. I just haven't enjoyed a woman's company this much in a while, and I'd like to extend that longer."

She dusted the dirt off the rear end of her jeans. No, Jana Lee's jeans. Longer, huh. She wasn't going to be around here very long, but he didn't need to know that. "Let me check my calendar and see if I'm free, now that I blurted that invitation out. And while I'm at it, I'll hunt up a belt while you earn your forty dollars an hour, mister."

Jillian made a dash for the stairs. She had to smile on the way up. Guys out here were *so* easy. Drop your pants, and you've got a date. She'd chased Jackson Hawks for months and hadn't gotten anywhere with him except a stolen kiss under the mistletoe.

Dean watched Mrs. Stivers dash out of the room holding her pants up and realized he didn't even know her first name. Wait, it was on the callback order that Marcy at the phone answering service had written out from a year ago. He picked up his clipboard and read off the top paper. Jana Lee Stivers, 512 Hollyridge Road, Seabridge, Washington.

She didn't look like a Jana Lee, but there you go. She looked like a woman who'd been out of circulation a long time and still had a fire inside her waiting to ignite. Hence the red silk thong underwear. He smiled to himself and got back into reassembling the washer Ms. Jana Lee Stivers had taken apart. Who would have figured she'd ask him out?

She was quite beautiful, red undies aside. He thought about doing a smooth marble piece of her. The curve of her hip was round and angular all at the same time. He imagined running his hand over that curve. He hadn't worked in stone in a long time. But Ms. Jana Lee wouldn't translate well in metal, unless it was a bronze cast.

He flashed on the last time he'd done stone and got the old, sad pain back. He'd done a piece for Trina's gravesite. Maybe dating someone who had lost a husband wasn't the best idea. Or maybe it was. Trina hadn't been his wife, but being a live-in lover for over six years had almost been the same. He was grateful he'd gotten to share that short time with her and help her through her illness to the very end.

Maybe being with someone who had experienced that kind of loss herself would make things easier. They'd understand each other.

Maybe he should snap out of the deep thinking and just go for a drink with the pretty lady with the red underwear.

Jillian belted up and checked Jana Lee's notes for the day. Rugrats arrived 3:30, stay till 5:30. Nothing after that. No PTA, no quilting bee. Just Dean the repair guy over a glass of Pinot Noir. Did they have good wine in this town?

Last time she was here there had been a mediocre

Mexican restaurant, a Dairy Queen, KFC, and Mitzel's. Don't leave food to people who think lutefisk is an actual edible thing. Norwegians.

Well, if it were Jana Lee on this date, she'd leave it to Dean. Jana Lee was a whole lot more passive about such things. Come to think of it, Jana Lee probably wouldn't have asked Dean out. But it had to start somewhere.

She donned her best submissive air and wandered back down the stairs as if she hadn't just bared her thonged ass to the cute repair guy. Sculptor. Repair guy.

He'd done a damn good job with the washer. It was even looking like a washer now. So when the kids tumbled in they wouldn't think washer parts were the new Legos. Oh my God, the kids.

"Dean, I've got to dash to the market before the afterschool gang gets here. I don't know you, but I don't think there's anything valuable to steal in the house, and you just agreed to go out with me anyhow, so pick the place and pick me up at seven-thirty. I'll be ready." She grabbed her purse and her sister's white hoody sweatshirt off a peg and ran out the back door. "I'll pay you later!" she hollered back at him.

She flung open the door to Jana Lee's minivan, jumped in, found the keys above the visor, revved it alive, and peeled out of the driveway.

Maybe that wasn't exactly as demure as Jana Lee would have been, either. Oops.

* * *

Dean watched the mistress of the house burn rubber out to the main road and wondered exactly what he'd gotten himself into. She was about as high-strung as a Jack Russell terrier. He scratched his head and looked around at the cutesy floral prints and the stenciling on the kitchen wall. Modern art buff? It was all very confusing. He decided to put her washing machine back in working order instead of trying to figure it out. He got back to his tools and shifted the front panel out of his way.

She was a real puzzle. The house was very homespun and disorderly. Last time he'd been here she'd left all the decisions up to him, even down to the faucet type. Somehow, that didn't match up with the woman who'd dismantled her own washing machine and ordered him to pick her up for a date at seven-thirty.

4

Toying with Affections

"Who are you and what have you done with my boss?" Oliver Abbott draped himself on a chair and stared at Jana Lee. He was casually flipping a black pencil back and forth between his fingers, as if it were wagging at her saying *Neener, neener, you're busted.*

Jana Lee took a big shocked breath in, then let it out and threw herself face-first on her arms across the glass desktop in despair. "Augh," was all she could muster.

"Let me guess. Jillian Tompkins, aka your twin sister, convinced you to switch places so she could stay in the Serenity Spa longer. Either that, or they locked her up for an extended stay and you are here trying to save her job while she regains her balance. How am I doing?"

Jana Lee rolled her face up toward him. "Pretty damned good. We had a bet as to how long it would take you to see through me. Jillian said one minute. I said ten seconds. She promised to call you as soon as possible today. Oh, and hi, I'm Jana Lee Tompkins Stivers, idiot twin sister." She stuck her hand out from under her face, and he graciously rose up, set down his pencil and note-pad, shook her hand, returned to the chair, picked up the notepad and pencil, and reseated himself.

"How do you do, Jana Lee Tompkins Stivers. Well, well, well. What a lovely farce. I'm enjoying myself already. How is sis, anyway?"

"She's finishing her recuperation at my house in Washington. No doubt she's burned it down by now."

"No doubt. Domestic skills aren't her forte."

"Am I that obvious?" Jana Lee picked her head up and looked at Oliver.

"Only to the trained eye. And by the way, that was Jackson Hawks who came in here and kissed you. A bit of a complication there, wouldn't you say? I can tell you he's never done that before. It's not a regularly scheduled event like coffee, kiss, and back to work."

"How did you know he kissed me?"

"The gaping silence between dialogue is always a dead giveaway, plus the sound of a slap adds a nice touch."

"You are very observant, aren't you?"

"Lucky for you."

"Who is he, anyway?"

"Vice president of Pitman Toys."

"Yikes. He invited me to dinner." Jana Lee felt herself blush, with terror really. She'd slapped the VP. She'd screwed up Jillian's job in the first hour. Smooth.

"Did you say yes?"

"I . . . didn't have a chance."

"That's Jackson all over. Kiss and run. He's the bad boy of the office dating scene. No lucky girl around here has ever held his interest longer than, oh . . . two dates."

"Wow."

"Let's table Mr. Hawks for a while. I have to say, I adore my Miss Jillian and I wouldn't want anything to happen to her job. I can't imagine working for any of these other cavemen—or women, for that matter. Therefore, I've decided to help you with your little charade. But we've got piles of work to do if you're going to pass for the Queen of Comptrollers."

"The Queen of Comptrollers?"

"That's what Jillian does, you know, she's the comptroller for the company. That means she keeps an eye on the figures. Here, I'll read you her job description."

Oliver slipped a typed piece of paper out of his notebook, straightened up on the chair, adjusted the collar of his navy blue pinstripe suit jacket to lay perfectly flat, and then began to read aloud. " 'The Comptroller, or CFO, uses strategic planning and advanced management principles and skills to position the company to meet constantly changing business practices, technology, and legal requirements, including the implementation of and response to regulatory and legislative policy initiatives regarding product safety. The CFO manages a biennial operating budget in excess of 5 million dollars, oversees the collection of approximately 2.9 million dollars in revenue annually, and is responsible for the development and administration of all accounting and cash flow functions within the company.' "

"Excuse me while I go throw up. I knew she was the numbers gal around here, but you make it sound so . . . *vital*." Jana Lee moaned and rested her head on her hands again. "I can't add without a Hello Kitty calculator."

"Hello Kitty? Are you really from the same genetic pool? Jillian is your sister? The Jillian Tompkins that has a master's degree in accounting and business?"

"Don't be mean, Ollie, I've got my talents. I just can't remember what they are at the moment."

Oliver laughed. "Don't worry, I can keep a lid on things for at least a week. Quarterly reports were done in April, so let's see, when is Jillian planning on returning?"

"Next Monday. Maybe we can revamp that plan

and get her back Friday. No wonder she almost had a nervous breakdown. Who could be responsible for all that?"

"Well if we were talking the IBM Corporation here, she'd need shock treatments. But this is Pitman Toys. An infinitely easier gig."

"What do y'all do here?"

"Y'all. That's so cute."

"My mother was from Louisiana originally. It rubbed off, I guess. It slips back when I'm nervous."

"Pitman manufactures toys of questionable taste but apparently with enough appeal to the masses to result in a sizeable profit. Most likely you're aware we make the Snotz doll line?"

"God, yes, Jillian sent Carly every last livin' Snotz on the line. How could I forget? Are those still alive?"

"They breed and reinvent themselves every season now, but the last effort was a line called Byker Chikz, and shall we just say that even bad toys have an invisible line of no return. Apparently Byker Chikz went too far with their little tattoos and realistically scaled Harleys."

"Ick. No wonder Jillian didn't send those."

"Carly, I assume, is your child?"

"Charlotte really, but that's too old-fashioned for her. That was her Louisiana grandmother's name." Jana Lee spun in the chair and grabbed Carly's picture as she rotated by. "This is my daughter. She's fifteen, and she gets more like her aunt every day."

"So Jillian is in charge of the care and feeding of a fifteen-year-old child?"

"Watch it, Ollie, I trust my sister."

"I'm just kidding. She deserves a break, if that qualifies. So, where do you want to start?"

"Lunch?"

"Hours away. How about personnel?"

"Jillian made me a chart." Jana Lee handed Jillian's notebook to Oliver. "But she didn't say anything about Jackson Hawks being on the prowl. Quite the opposite, as a matter of fact. Something about mistletoe and Jackson running out the door?"

Oliver leafed through the notebook. "Ah yes, the holiday office party fiasco. Let's start there. That will be most entertaining. You know, if you wanted to, you might leave things a little more interesting than you found them for your sister, if you know what I mean?"

"The thought has occurred to me. So I guess I should keep that dinner date?"

"I would." Oliver smiled at her.

I would too, if I were Jillian, Jana Lee thought to herself. At least she'd found an ally here. If Jana Lee laid low and relied on Ollie, she might not botch this for her sister as bad as she thought she might.

She'd have to apologize to Jackson for the slap,

though. Not that he'd seemed fazed by it in the least.

At six promptly Jackson walked past Oliver Abbott's desk and gave him a passing hand gesture like an unfulfilled high five. He didn't wait for Oliver to announce him through; he just knocked on the tall, sleek mahogany door and opened it in one motion.

He heard a faint buzz from the intercom, but Jillian didn't bother to answer it. She seemed to be rearranging herself. For him? She looked embarrassed. That was a first. He'd seen her chew up and spit out cowering research and development people at production meetings.

"Hello. I was just . . ."

He glanced behind her to the wide window ledge and saw most of this year's lineup carefully arranged in groups of product age groups. Interesting. It almost looked like she'd been playing with them. Tiny Snotz girls were on their tiny skis with tiny parkas and stretch pants on.

"Adding up unit prices?" he joked.

"Um. Sure. That's it. I wanted a more visual approach, so I had Oliver get the whole set in here," she answered.

"Well, I'm looking forward to our dinner. Are you ready to go?" Jackson took a step toward her. She held both hands out in front of her, indicating for him to stop.

"Stop!" she yelled.

"Consider me stopped."

"I appreciate your dinner invitation, but we need to address our earlier . . . encounter."

"Address away," he said. She sounded scripted, and he was extremely amused. She must have practiced this speech.

"I sincerely regret my earlier behavior at the office party last December. I hope you'll accept my apologies."

"Consider yourself forgiven. We'd all had too much punch."

"And I'm sure that's what facilitated your . . . your . . ."

"Returned gesture?" He tried to supply her with a phrase, since she seemed to have forgotten hers.

"Yes. That. But if I'm going to accept your dinner invitation I'd like to ask that we take a step backward and get to know each other before we make any further . . . such, such gestures." She made a sweeping motion to emphasize "such gestures," then took a deep breath and paused, waiting for his reply, it seemed to him.

"That sounds perfectly agreeable to me, and you can tell Ollie I said so."

She looked a bit sheepish, then smiled, put her hands behind her back, and nodded. "Good. Then we're on for dinner. And I'm sorry for slapping you."

"Apologies all around. Are you starved? I am. I

found a couple of great places on Steiner. Are you up for Italian, or a big steak at Izzy's, or how about Asian?"

"Asian sounds good," she answered. She went to the concealed wall closet and pressed the surface. It popped open, and she pulled her black leather jacket off a hanger. He moved to where she was and took the jacket from her, holding it out for her to slip into. As her arms slid into the satin lined sleeves, he couldn't help watching. He moved the jacket up to her shoulders smoothly. She turned around. "Thank you," she said.

"You are welcome, Ms. Tompkins. Shall we?" He offered his arm. If she was going to do this courtship proper thing, he'd play it up for her. Besides, she looked very hot. Her thin silky blouse fluttered open at the neckline despite the scarf she'd so carefully arranged to hide her assets. Those lovely breasts of hers were very voluptuous. Actually much more so than they'd been back in December. A little weight had improved Ms. Tompkins's figure quite a bit.

They exited the office and passed by Oliver's desk. "Thank you for those figures, Abbott, and excellent speech, old man." Jackson winked at him.

"Think nothing of it, Mr. Hawks." Oliver gave him a wry smile. "Enjoy your evening. I'd suggest Lin Yen for Asian."

That devil Oliver must have had his ear to the

door the whole time. Or maybe he had a line in through the intercom. If he ever decided to *do* Jillian Tompkins on her butter-soft black leather bench or her spotless gray mohair wool carpet, he better make sure the switch was flipped to the off position.

Jana Lee and Jackson walked out to the hallway and she dropped his arm, for appearance' sake, he supposed. He let her take a few steps ahead of him, and Jackson took a long look down his date's backside, appreciating her roundness. He watched her and wondered why she kept looking up at the huge trusses that held the mostly glass ceiling in place over the Pitman offices. She acted as if she'd never seen the place before. Maybe her vacation had given her a new appreciation for their surroundings. It was a hell of a beautiful office.

The sun was still bright in the sky, the morning fog having burned off long ago and the summer day lingering on late. Jana Lee gazed at the amazing play of light through the prism-like structure of the Pitman Toy Company office. She'd been such a nervous wreck this morning that she hadn't really appreciated the architecture of the building.

When they reached the outside doors she saw the amazing view of the Pacific Ocean. San Francisco Bay, to be exact. She'd lived around water all her life, but her town was on a sheltered area of inland straits. This was . . . majestic. Humbling. The colors were amazing.

"Jillian? Can I call you Jillian?"

"Sure." She snapped her attention back to Jackson. Only the Pacific Ocean could have distracted her, really. Jackson took up a whole lot of air space. Sure, he could call her Jillian. If she'd answer to it would be pure luck.

"I've borrowed the limo. It's only a few miles, but the parking is insane, as you know. Pops can zip us down there and bring us back later to pick up your car."

Jana Lee realized a rudimentary knowledge of the city would have come in handy. She had only a visitor's sense of the town. "Great, Pops and the limo."

"Oh come on, don't start with the budget tonight. It's take-a-break-from-work night. No work talk, no worrying. From what I've seen lately, you could use a worry break." He opened the door on a white stretch limo that was smack in front of her on the street. She slid in.

Jana Lee thought back to her high school prom and how a bunch of them had rented a big stretch limo. That was the only other time she'd been in one. Not bad for her first day at work. She sat back in the soft white leather and enjoyed herself.

Faster than he would have liked, Jackson found himself sitting across from Jillian the accounting executive as she scanned the menu at Ace Wasabi's Rock & Roll Sushi. He'd picked Ace's when she'd gotten excited about sushi, like she'd never had it before. Whatever turned her on, he was game.

She'd shed her leather jacket, and her soft yellow blouse fluttered in the breeze of the overhead fan. She looked a little confused about the menu and was taking a whole lot of time to read it. But he was enjoying the view anyhow.

He ordered them two glasses of chardonnay and sat back, sipping his wine, wondering about her. She was such a mixed bag of a woman. He couldn't quite put his finger on her. Usually he'd have a woman typed and pegged and in his bed in short order. Of course he did have a tendency to steer toward rather stereotypical women: beautiful and less than brilliant. But something about Jillian Tompkins today had made him break with his standard pattern.

Ace's was usually loud and full of singles looking to make a connection. But tonight for some reason it was quiet. Still, he hoped he didn't bump into anyone he'd been with before. There was some sort of unwritten rule about not letting on if you'd had an encounter with a person if you saw them out with someone else, but Jackson could think of at least three women he'd dated who wouldn't know an unwritten rule if it bit them in the ass.

"Shall I order for us? I've been here before."

Jillian had on a pair of reading glasses, and now she peered over them at Jackson. He wondered what he'd been thinking after all. Maybe she was too smart for him. But when he gazed at her revealed cleavage, he remembered. He'd been thinking how much he'd like to get Ms. Tompkins into his bed. A sleepover. A play-date.

"That would be great. I can't decide, and I like everything. Surprise me." She set down her menu.

He planned on it. "More wine?" He tipped the bottle and started to pour more in her glass before she answered, "No, *thanks*." Her hand covered her glass, and he caught the pour just before it splashed over her fingers. He'd need quick reflexes for this woman. He was learning fast.

Jackson put down the bottle and waved at the waiter, who bee-lined over to their table. It *was* slow.

"Let's do the asparagus tofu salad, the Ahi potstickers, and a couple of Ace Wasabi Rolls to start with, for two all around."

"Very good, Mr. Hawks," the waiter took off.

"He knows you. Is this a regular place for you?"

"I've been here. It's really a small town in some ways, don't you think?" he said as he gazed at her, watching her pretty, full lips.

"It seems huge to me . . . most days." She took a big gulp of her wine and looked nervous.

"Are you uncomfortable?"

"A little. You *are* the vice president of the company."

"Don't think about me being vice president. I mean hey, what's vice president? I think your job is more complicated than mine. We're just two people, lost in that big office, looking for someone special." Where had he heard that line before?

Oh brother, who did this guy think he was kidding? She wondered how often he'd gotten away with that baloney. According to Ollie, it had actually worked on quite a few women. He was incredibly good-looking, almost exotic. His suit was sharp, his white shirt spotless, and his vintage-style tie gave him a real *GQ* look.

"Yes, two lost souls," she exaggerated in a swoony voice.

"Okay, that was way corny. I'm sorry," Jackson said. "I'm sort of surprised at myself for not taking you up on your interest in me before. Now that I'm with you, you don't seem at all like I thought you'd be."

"You were attracted to me before though, right?"

Jackson shifted uncomfortably in his chair. "On a purely physical level, yes. But, you have to admit, you did come on rather strong."

She wondered what else Jillian had done besides the Christmas kiss. But the good news was, he did find her sister attractive. She'd just have to show him the softer side of Jillian. She did have one, didn't she?

The waiter showed up with a strange array of dishes and arranged them between herself and Jackson. It all looked very different, but when was the last time she'd had an adventure—even a food adventure? Let alone a good-looking-guy adventure that might have possibilities for her sister. She thanked the waiter and watched Jackson for a clue. He took up his chopsticks and skillfully picked up a section of asparagus.

Now, chopstick use was not a skill Jana Lee had ever mastered, despite the fact that she lived near Seattle and had many Asian friends and families around her. Seabridge was not known for its Asian cuisine. Mostly for their Sons of Norway dances with a nice hunk of ham or roast beef being sliced at the end of the buffet line. Maybe meatballs, and once in a while, salmon.

She and Bill had gone often before . . . *before*. She put it out of her mind. It seemed like life had been an endless stream of chicken nuggets and frozen pizzas for the last two years. As she wangled her chopsticks, she felt a pang of guilt for neglecting to introduce her daughter to a wider array of cuisine.

The damn things just wouldn't work. She went for a potsticker, but the little sucker just slipped out of her pinch like an elusive sea creature. It *was* dead, right?

Jackson smiled at her. "Shall I get you a fork?"

"I think that would be giving up, wouldn't it?"

"I think that would be switching to the tool that can get the job done."

"Sounds practical." She set down her chopsticks as he motioned to their waiter for a fork. Pretty good sign language on his part. She sighed and sat back in the chair, waiting for her fork to arrive.

Now what would Jillian want to know about Jackson? They seemed similar in many ways. They both had an edge to them. But hopefully, Jillian's edge was softening as Jana Lee sat here, having dinner with Jillian's boss.

Her fork came, and she got right back to the elusive Ahi and hamachi potsticker. She dipped it in its sauce, took a nibble and was amazed at how good it was. And spicy. It made her lips tingle, which reminded her of the kiss Jackson had laid on her.

"So, Jackson, do you have family around here?"

"Both parents, not together, but still in the city. They divorced when I was about twelve."

"How sad."

"You know, it was. I still don't get it. I have a brother, Marcus, but he doesn't get it either," Jackson said.

"Younger brother?"

"Yes. Two years younger. He lives in Mill Valley with his wife. They have two kids."

"And that makes you how old now?"

"God, I forget. Thirty-six?"

"And you've never been married?" She'd take notes, but he'd probably notice. She tried to retain it all, but her head was getting a little fuzzy from the half glass of wine she'd consumed rather quickly.

"You get right to the point, don't you?" Jackson speared a potsticker with his chopsticks and stopped talking to take a bite. He chewed thoughtfully for a moment, then answered her. "I guess I never met the right woman."

"Not for lack of trying, I hear." Jana Lee felt embarrassed as soon as she'd said it. She hiccupped.

"Office gossip, eh?"

"I apologize. That was rude."

"I tire of the chase."

"No you don't, you love the chase."

"Ouch, woman. Stab that potsticker instead of me."

Why the heck did she keep jabbing him? She felt herself blush. Well, hey, he was dishing some pretty trite reasoning for his behavior. According to Oliver anyway. Maybe his reputation as one of San Francisco's premier Casanovas was exaggerated.

She looked at him across the table. He had sharp, handsome features, and dark brown eyes that melted right through you. He was well dressed and had an air so smooth it bordered on slick. He definitely elicited a response from the women around them, even her.

Maybe his reputation wasn't exaggerated.

She set down her fork and took another sip of her wine. No wonder Jillian had gone after him. It might be the wine talking, and it'd been a hell of a long time since she'd chased a guy, but she had a feeling Jillian had taken the wrong tack with lover boy here.

Jana Lee giggled to herself. She just *might* be able to leave this better than she found it.

"Did I amuse you?" Jackson asked.

"I am amused, no doubt about it." She batted her eyelashes, set down her glass and went back to her dinner. Jana Lee felt like she hadn't enjoyed herself so much in years.

They stood in front of the Pitman Toys office as she tried to act cool about inserting her security card in the parking garage. A few fumbled tries and the door light hit green. "I'm a little clumsy," she said.

"I'll walk you to your car. Pops will take me back to my place. I rode the cable car in today."

He walked beside her, their footsteps echoing in the empty underground garage. Her feet were killing her. A girl just can't transition from clogs to skyscraper heels in one day and live to tell about it. She stifled a groan.

"This it?"

Damned if she knew. She dug in her purse and found the key chain with the unlock button and hoped it would help her find Jillian's car. A tweaky beep-beep came from the left of them.

"There she blows," she pointed.

"You are very funny, you know? I didn't realize you had such a dry sense of humor."

"Funny me." Jana Lee bounced ahead of Jackson toward the sound of the car. When she'd absolutely claimed Jillian's Honda, she paused and turned to say goodnight. She stumbled back a little over those damned high heels, planting her rear end on the front end of the hood. Jackson swooped over to steady her. Right. He probably thought she was drunk. But she was cold stone sober. She'd had five cups of green tea and a three-hour dinner to shake off her one glass of wine.

He was as close as a breath. He held her arm where he'd steadied her and tipped her chin up with his other hand. "I've had a lovely evening. Shall we continue it?" he said.

Jana Lee saw his mouth take *the position* and his head angle in for a kiss. She grabbed his wrist and moved her face out of his grasp. She held his hand in midair for a moment. *"No,"* she said.

Jackson looked more startled than he had when she'd slapped him. He de-angled, de-readied, and stared at her. She dropped her grip on his hand. Jana Lee was surprised at herself.

"Jackson, I didn't ask for that first kiss today. Well, maybe you didn't ask for my mistletoe kiss either. So we're even. But I'd like to start fresh.

Let's keep this casual and get to know each other slowly." She stuck out her hand. "Thank you for a lovely dinner."

Jackson's face remained so stunned she wondered if he'd remain upright. He reached out for a polite handshake in a rather unconscious gesture. Jana Lee shook his hand.

"Well then, goodnight. I'll see you in the office tomorrow," she said. She wedged herself into Jillian's Honda Acura and shut the door behind her. She waved again to Jackson, who looked perplexed as he stuck his hands in his jacket pockets and walked away. She rounded the parking garage and smiled to herself. Jackson Hawks was going to be eating out of Jillian Tompkins's hands by the time she was done with him.

Boy, it was refreshing to play with her sister's life. Her car was pretty cool too. When the wooden arm popped up to release her from the garage, Jana Lee hit the gas.

Jackson had never in his life ended a date with a handshake, and that counted his first date at fifteen with Backseat Brenda Reese. At this moment, he didn't even know what to do with himself. He, the great smooth-talking Jackson Hawks had struck out?

He decided to walk home the twelve blocks to his duplex. The air would be good for him. When he emerged from the parking garage he sent Pops home, assuring him he'd be fine. The sun hadn't set yet. It was an early-summer sun that stayed up late. He walked past people sitting on their front stoops, people from everywhere in the world. San Francisco was his kind of town.

Maybe he'd play Jillian's game and do the whole flowers, candy and courtship thing. He was bound to wear her down.

But why would he want to put in that kind of effort when he could have any Babette from the Pacific Bank teller pool down the street cozy in his bed in one night's work?

True, but shallow. Maybe he was tired of shallow. Something about this woman just stuck with him. He couldn't stop thinking about her. Damn it.

5

Out of the Frying Pan into the Fire

"Give me that dog biscuit, Andy, I mean it."

"You're mean. Where's Mrs. Stivers?"

"She's on a vacation. I'm her sister, I told you that already. We're twins, remember?" Jillian slowly crept up on Andy, but he bolted.

"Aaaaaaaaaaaaaaaaaaaaaaa you can't catch me!" he yowled as he ran in circles around the living room, even across the ugly brown leather sofa.

Jillian watched in horror as the other three kids joined him. What did Mom used to do with the two of them? What the hell did her sister do with four?

Jillian backed up against a safe corner of the wall and watched, frozen in terror. At that moment, the front door opened and she saw Carly walk in.

Carly took a good look around, dumped her back-pack on a bench, and stared directly at Jillian, who knew she'd been found out. It had only taken two days! Jana Lee had underestimated her daughter.

Carly let the screaming stream of five-year-olds pass by and went directly to a drawer in the kitchen. "Who wants Kudo bars?"

"Ya ya ya ya ya yay!" they shrieked in shattering unison.

"Line up here," Carly commanded. She pointed to a spot on the kitchen floor.

Jillian couldn't believe they actually did what she said. She watched as Carly demanded they sit around the kitchen table to eat them. "Get juice," she yelled to Jillian.

Jillian jumped to the fridge, grabbed the apple juice and flung a few cupboards open till she found glasses and started to count down four.

"Plastic," Carly called.

"Right." Jillian abandoned the glass and found pastel plastic cups on the same shelf. What was she thinking, arming these crazy kids with glass? She threw the plastic cups on the table and filled them with apple juice as their little grubby hands reached in to snatch them.

Carly ran to another drawer and brought out a plastic bin of crayons, plus a pile of blank coloring sheets. "Who wants to make monsters?" she asked.

"Yay!" They all scrabbled for paper and started

scribbling. Amazingly, there was a small, minute, minuscule moment of peace as they chewed, colored, and drank juice in big gulps.

It sure felt like Miller time to Jillian.

Carly left the scene of the crime and came over to the kitchen. She smiled all know-it-ally and poured herself a big glass of apple cider. "So, *Aunt Jillian*, what the freak is going on? Where's Mom?" She tipped the glass to her lips and kept her eyes on Jillian.

"Um. Thanks for the rescue. You'd think I'd know kids better working for a toy company," Jillian stalled.

"We better get food ready. After that she sends them outside. There's a jungle gym in the backyard. Their parents pick them up at five-thirty, so that about covers it."

"I'm on it. I've got the stuff she put on her list right here. The macaroni sort of turned into paste, so we'll have to start over, I guess."

"She made you a list? And is my mother still at the spa, or did she run off and join the navy? Here's a clean pot. We'll boil some more macaroni quick." Carly rummaged in the drawer below the stove.

"She's being me at my office." Jillian refilled her coffee cup and sipped a good, strong sip. Bracing. She needed it. She set down her coffee, took the pot from Carly and started filling it with water. "We had a bet regarding how long it would take you to notice she wasn't me, otherwise I would have stopped you on your morning run out of the house. It wouldn't hurt you to look up and take notice of what's around you, Carly."

"Who won the bet?"

"I did. Less than a week."

"I'm glad you're here, Aunt Jillian. Things have been a little weird around here."

"I see that. I'm supposed to be the one getting a break, but I think it's turning out your mom needs one worse than I do."

Carly sat down on a tall kitchen stool opposite her aunt. "That's for sure."

Jillian put the pot on the stove, hiked up the burner to high, then crossed over to her niece. She put her arms around her and squeezed. "I've missed you, kiddo. I love you."

"Me too, Aunt Jilly." Carly squeezed back. Jillian could feel emotion in that hug.

"Watch out," Carly said sharply. Jillian felt something whiz by her head and spotted a green crayon as it smashed into the wall.

"Hey, monsters, no crayon throwing." Jillian marched over to the table of five-year-old terrors. Little redheaded Andy giggled. Jillian rounded the table, looking at their drawings. "Wow, kids, these are great. Andy, is that a two-headed snozwonker?"

"A what?" Andy squealed.

"Two-headed snozwonker." Jillian pointed.

"Yeah, yeah! It *is*." Andy seemed delighted.

"Lemme see," Susy leaned over.

"Very neat work, Susy," Jillian said.

"Thank you, Miss Lady," Susy smiled.

"You're welcome, Miss Susy." Jillian walked back over to the kitchen and pried open a box of macaroni and cheese. She dumped the whole thing into the water, then had to fish out the cheese packet. "Oops." A few stirs, and she picked up her coffee as she watched the noodles boil. She noticed Carly had a cup of coffee. Coffee at fifteen? What was that about? "So, kiddo, what's new in high school?"

"Sophomore year sucks."

"How's your art coming?"

"It's the only thing that keeps me sane. I placed second in the spring exhibition. What's new in the big city?"

"Burnout. I hit the wall. That's very cool about your award."

"Thanks. So you picked our house to chill in?" Carly sipped her coffee.

"Yup. Why are you drinking coffee?" Jillian asked.

"Mom lets me."

"It looks to me like Mom just waves when you pass. Give me that stuff. I'll fix it up for you."

"No way."

"It'll be better, I promise. Trust Aunt Jillian."

Carly looked at her funny but slid the cup over the counter.

Jillian took it away from her and went to the pantry for the hot chocolate mix she'd seen. At least she could minimize the effects. She used the scooper to dump a goodly amount in the cup and stirred by swirling it in the air. Then she headed for the fridge and the new half and half cream she'd bought at the market. She stirred the heck out of the whole mess and gave it a small blast in the microwave, then squirted whipped cream out of a can on top. Ta da.

She passed it to Carly. "Mocha Java à la Jillian."

Carly sipped. "Not bad."

"With a little effort, I was thinking we might change things around here. It might make your mom perk up. What do you think?"

"Like *Trading Spaces*?"

"Yeah, like that. I mean hey, this is the same stuff as when I lived here in 1985."

"My parents thought it looked retro."

"Retro would be an improvement."

"What would I have to do?"

"Work your butt off. Strip that duck wallpaper border off, paint walls, stuff like that. And honey, clean your horrible room."

"Can we do my room over too?"

"I'm only supposed to be here a week, but they make it look easy on television. And I do know how to do one thing. Hire people. I hired a guy to fix the washer today. Which reminds me, I have a date with him. Well, your mother has a date with him. I thought he was very interesting and maybe I could leave her something to come home to."

"Geez, Aunt Jillian, fast worker. But I'll have to check him out, you know. I get final approval. Can we do over my room?" Carly asked again.

"Yes, yes. But I've watched enough home make-over shows to know you've got to gut the place first."

"I've got a bunch of ideas."

"I do too. Like you doing all your laundry, because I ain't touchin' it."

"Okay, if you promise that no matter what I come up with for my room you'll do it."

"How about no matter what you come up with I'll look it over and make sure it works, and you'll do your laundry no matter what."

"Deal." Carly slurped up the rest of her mocha and popped off the kitchen stool. "I've got math homework, but I can do that fast. I'll stick a load in first."

"Deal, and I love math, so after the rugrats are gone, I get to look at it, okay?"

Carly rolled her eyes. "I'm only saying yes because you'll bug me anyhow."

"Good." The sound of a whiney female child rose in the air. "Susy, that's quite a siren you've got going there! Air raid alert! Let's move our act outside, kids. There's an Oreo in it for you."

"Aunt Jillian, bribes?"

"I bought four packs of cookies, and I know how to use them. Want one?" She pointed to the familiar cellophane package on the counter.

"You should have told me before I finished my coffee."

"We're going to cold turkey you off coffee, girl. There's a kettle on the stove and you can move to cocoa."

"Are you going to hold my room hostage and make me do what you say?"

"Now you're getting the idea."

"You are the meanest aunt alive." Carly made a face and went for the Oreos. She broke them open and took a handful, then handed the package to Jillian.

"Thanks. I try. Okay, kids, let's roll!" The kids followed like rats after the pied piper, and Jillian led them out the sliding door, over the deck, to a stretch of wood chips and a climbing structure at the back of the house.

She very much liked the blackmail-slash-bribery thing with Carly. It was working well. And making Carly her partner in makeover crime would be a great way to get to know her again. It also made Carly stop long enough to talk to her aunt. Jillian liked that.

Jillian watched the frightening four stuff Oreos in their mouths and run for the climber. Two more days of them, and she'd be a free woman. The sun shone full out on the happy bunch. Their energy level should be bottled. She didn't know how her sister did it. Kids were just . . . scary.

Jillian was exhausted from her first afternoon of kid care. She'd cleaned up and was now faced with date spruce-up. But how could anyone feel sexy in a denim jumper? And where could they go for an intimate drink on a Monday night? Maybe it was two-fer-night happy hour somewhere and the cute repair guy could save money. Or was she paying, since she was the one who'd asked him out?

Jillian was getting frantic. She dumped the contents of her sister's closet on the bed and gazed at the pathetic pile of rag-bag thrift store specials. The only thing decent was a vintage dress from their grandmother's era. 1965, here we come. She pulled it out of the pile and shimmied into it.

Back in those days they must not have believed in back zippers. She all but dislocated her shoulders, but the damn thing went on. Wow, Grandma was skinny. Jillian gazed in the full-length mirror and smoothed the dress out around her waist. The black lace of the bodice was as delicate as spiderwebs, and the peach-colored satin lining made it look like it was just lace, no lining. Very Cher in *Mermaids*. It hugged her waist and flared out into a slim black skirt. The neckline ran straight across, but the back was a bit plungy. Good grief, Granny, who was this dress for?

Still, 1965 plungy was not that indecent. Jillian wondered if she'd be over the top for Dean. She dug in the bottom of the closet and found a great pair of vintage black suede pumps with tiny bows from the same era. Jana Lee should stick to vintage stores, this stuff was cute. At least their feet were still identical even if their bodies weren't anymore.

Jillian flipped up her hair with the hot curling iron plugged in by the mirrored dresser, just to complete the look.

The doorbell rang. The dog barked. That couldn't be him. She glanced at her watch. Seven-thirty already? Damn. She heard Carly's footsteps pounding down the stairs. Oh, let her get the door. Jillian needed a few more minutes. Besides, since their talk this afternoon, Carly had been busy gutting her room. She probably needed to switch the loads around in the washer.

Jillian sure hadn't thought out this switcheroo stuff very well. The moms from the rugrat brigade all knew it was Jana Lee's sister, because Jana Lee had called each one of them personally. The supermarket people thought she was Jana Lee spiffed up from the spa and Carly knew it was her, but Dean thought she was Jana Lee. Jillian's head spun with it all. Oh, what a tangled web we weave when first we conspire to deceive. Her dad used to say that to them when they'd try to lie their way out of something as kids. Correction: When *she* lied. Jana Lee just didn't do that kind of thing.

Speaking of webs, Jillian twisted herself a few times in front of the mirror to make sure she didn't look too Vampira in this getup, then grabbed her own red lipstick and gave herself a quick painting. There. That ought to do it.

She sauntered down the stairs calmly but noticed that her heart was beating pretty darn fast. Hopefully she wouldn't have a panic attack on a date with the repair guy, for goodness' sake. She'd dated CEOs of San Francisco corporations. She could do this.

No one was in the living room. Her entrance was for nothing. She followed voices and found Carly and Dean—and Monty the dog—looking into the washing machine, talking.

"We probably should have run a rag load first. I hope it comes out," Dean spoke into the washer.

"What comes out?" Jillian looked over their shoulders.

"Some funky streaks on my sheets," Carly said. She looked up at her aunt and got a goofy look on her face.

What? Jillian thought. *Is my hair sticking up?*

"Let's run it through again. Maybe it will wash out." Dean pulled the detergent off the upper shelf, measured out a double capful and started the machine back up. He shut the lid carefully, removing Monty from his odd position, and turned to see Jillian. Dean got the goofy look too.

"You clean up good," he grinned.

She was thinking the same thing about him. Black T-shirt, black leather jacket, nice jeans. He was yummy. His dark hair and deeply tanned face made him look like he'd just flown back from the Mediterranean. He must work outside. He was taller than she remembered. Maybe because he wasn't hunched over washer parts. "So do you, Dean. What's the plan, Dew Drop Inn Tavern?"

"Something like that. Carly, are you okay with this? Run a load of those old wet towels. It should only take one time through, but don't move to the nice stuff for a few more. Jeans next."

"I've got plenty of all of that, thanks, Dean." Carly winked at Jillian over his shoulder in a very *I'm not good at winking* way, but Jillian got the idea. Dean was on the okay list for now.

"Carly, *honey*, I'll be back early. Don't forget your homework."

"Yes, *Mother*, I won't forget."

Okay, they sounded completely lame. Jillian had to get Dean out of here. "Let's ride, Dean." She grabbed her purse off the kitchen counter. "Oh, I owe you for this afternoon. Write me up an invoice and we'll do it over a drink."

"Romantic type, aren't you?" Dean took Jillian's elbow and guided her out of the utility room door, not letting Monty follow. He moved with her down the steps to the driveway.

"Excuse me, Dean, but I'm not a delicate flower.

Thanks for the elbow ride, but I can make it on my own." She turned in a rather huffy manner, took one step, caught her slim vintage high heel on a big hunk of gravel, and fell on her face. Well, more like her hands and knees.

Dean picked her up. He actually did. He put his arm around her waist, picked her up and moved her onto a grassy strip next to the house. Then he straightened her up, dusted the dirt off her knees, turned her hands over and looked at her palms. Jillian was so surprised that she let him.

"Looks like minimal damage. Shall we proceed?" He ran his hands over her palms to dispense with any remaining debris. His touch was sexy. *He* was sexy.

Dean opened the truck door for his date and offered her a hand up. She took it, and he watched her slide into place. She was pretty. Very pretty, and very spirited. He shut the door and walked around the back of the truck so he could have a moment to compose himself. He'd been stifling a laugh since she'd bounced onto the ground after the big speech. Who knew this gem was hiding in a suburban one-dog stinker of a house?

He opened up the truck door and climbed in. "Ready?" he asked.

"Ready. I'm sorry I was . . . stupid."

"You're just assertive. Nothing wrong with

that." He started up the truck and moved toward the edge of the driveway.

"I didn't used to be. I've changed."

"I see that."

"You knew me before?" she asked.

He thought that was an odd question, but she was a little odd anyhow. "You've probably forgotten I came out and installed a new kitchen faucet for you once."

"I had forgotten."

"You were still pretty messed up from your husband's passing away." He regretted saying that right away, but facts were facts.

He heard a whole lot of silence on her side of the truck.

He better make small talk, although he was pretty bad at it. "Your spa visit must have helped. You look great."

"Yes, it was very refreshing." Jillian felt like a first-class heel lying to Dean. She'd blundered in like her usual self and forgotten how hard it would be to be her sister. She herself had a great deal of pain over Bill's death, but Jana Lee's entire life had been derailed. All the more reason she should make a better effort to play her sister and get something going with Dean.

Already she figured she should have thought twice before asking him on this date. Too close for comfort. She should have played it cooler. Her sister sure would have. Then again, her sister hadn't had a date in a long, long time, so there you go. She was stuck in a corner.

Jillian looked out the window at the green, beautiful trees as they drove out on the main road. Fir trees dipping graceful bows down toward the road, alders all decked in summer leaves. "Pretty country around here." Oh, brother, this was so much harder than she'd thought. Jana Lee had been here for years.

"Yes, we forget how beautiful this area is," Dean commented.

"Being away and all, I notice it more now," she stumbled around.

"Have you ever been to Manor Farm Inn?"

"Can't say I have." Boy, was that true. She had no idea where Jana Lee had been or not been. "Is that our destination?"

"Yes. The owner is a friend of mine. She's a patron of the arts, so to speak. Her husband is the chef. I know you said a drink, but have you had dinner?"

"Well, actually, no."

"Then in the interest of not ending up loopy, they've offered to make a little dinner for us. I hope you don't mind meeting people."

"Why would I mind? Bring it on." Jillian couldn't stand herself anymore. She was wondering if Jana Lee had ever met this lady at Manor Farm. For all she knew, it could be one of the rug-rat parents. "Do they have kids?"

"Two older boys in college. They come back summers and work the farm with them. It's a few miles down this road."

"Great." Jillian shut up. She'd have to find a way to converse with this guy more like her sister would. What had she been thinking? She wasn't as good at this as she'd thought she would be. She bit her nail. A big chip of her red polish came off. Damn, being a biter she didn't have much in the way of nails anyhow. Dating was probably not on the list of things to do when you were trying to de-stress. She felt like she was going to implode.

Dean must have noticed. "Don't worry, we'll have a great time. Relax. I know first dates are weird. It's been a long time for me, too."

"It has?" *Ah ha*, she thought. She could just make him talk about himself! "How long?" she asked.

"I didn't want to get right into it, but I had a long-term relationship with a woman. She died of cancer."

"I'm so sorry."

"So, I guess we have something in common."

Jillian felt like the lowliest worm imaginable. If she got out of this date without slinking into snake form, it would be a miracle. God would get her for this. She better be careful in lightning storms.

* * *

The Manor Farm Inn was charming. The hostess and owner, Fran, was a gracious older woman, and the table she and her husband, Teo, had set for them was picture-perfect, on a brick patio covered with a rustic twig canopy, draped in climbing roses and wisteria. Dean did date good.

Teo poured them a glass of white wine. He asked her a few questions about the food, whether she liked capers, and if she was allergic to anything. Mighty thoughtful. No menu, she guessed, just a surprise. Teo shook Dean's hand again, and Fran left a warm basket of bread, olive oil with balsamic vinegar, and the bottle of wine for them to enjoy.

Nice folks. When Dean had introduced her as Jana Lee, Jillian had felt sick. She closed her eyes and let the sun warm her face as she sat back in the cushions of her wicker chair. She sipped her wine. If it hadn't been for the fact that she was lying her head off to nice people, she'd have found the relaxation she was looking for. She opened her eyes briefly and saw that Dean was drinking his wine, relaxing and watching her intently.

She closed her eyes again. Maybe she'd wake up and find herself in a nice office somewhere with a budget to balance. Maybe Dean would turn into a really horrible date and start hassling the help and acting like he was God's gift to the universe instead of being a very interesting, talented guy with great taste.

Maybe she'd just let guilt overcome her and melt her onto the brick patio in a pool of bad-girl ooze like the wicked witch of the west in *The Wizard of Oz*.

6

Sister Twister

Gloria Kissinger was not related to Henry, which would no doubt have helped her chances with the Hawks family and her relationship with Jackson. The humiliation she felt at his disinterest in her after their perfect night was more than she could stand, and yet she was still compelled to correct his thinking on that score. He just didn't realize how good she'd be as a mate. Or how much better she could do the comptroller job than Jillian Tompkins. Gloria was all about control.

But to have Jillian move in and take *both* spots was just beyond Gloria's ability to bear. Her only solace was that Jackson was prone to losing interest in women extremely quickly. Perhaps another week and he'd dump her like he did all the others.

If there was one thing her harsh, demanding father had taught her, it was that vigilance paid off. She'd been watching Jillian very closely at every meeting, every coffee break, every company holiday bash and softball game for the past two years.

Gloria had actually taken a special personal day to celebrate when Jillian had cracked up and tried to pound the vending machine into submission. But now something was up with Jillian Tompkins.

When she'd returned, Gloria had spotted a significant difference right away. No way had she rounded out that much in one week. No way had she turned all soft and nice in *one week*. Was she the only one with a brain around here? That just simply wasn't Jillian Tompkins, it just looked like her.

That made Gloria's mind reel with all sorts of sci-fi possibilities—had Jillian been cloned? Was she a robot? Gloria had always thought the term *artificial intelligence* applied well to Jillian. Gloria decided she'd been watching too many *Deep Space Nine* reruns. It hadn't taken much poking around to find out Jillian Tompkins had a twin sister. One Google search had brought up their former child-star status.

Whatever was going on, Gloria decided it was in her best interest to continue to observe and stay quiet, although it gave her a twitch in her left eyelid to know that the Tompkins office had received a huge flower delivery this morning. What had that imposter woman done to deserve that, she wondered?

The office was full of flowers: big, huge, extremely fragrant, blousy, romantic, white lilies. Jana Lee saw Ollie peering out between two large crystal vases.

"Apparently your date went well?" Ollie commented more than asked.

"Sort of. He's a bit of an arrogant ass." Jana Lee stood in front of Ollie's desk like she was in the principal's office.

"He's the arrogant vice president ass, so keep that in mind. We want your sister to return to her current position and not end up in the mail room doing ship-outs." Ollie tapped on the desk with a black pencil. "Get yourself settled in, I've got some things to go over with you. Did you get your tea yet?"

"No, sir."

"I took the liberty of having a hot water pot installed in your office, and a selection of teas brought over."

"Why, thank you, Ollie."

"You are most welcome. Fewer trips to the coffee room for you will be better all around."

"Gee, here I thought it was a gesture of kindness."

"It was. It's kinder to your sister for you to stay in this office as much as possible."

Jana Lee smirked at Ollie, but knew he was right. She had a different air than her sister Jillian. Her clothes hung differently, her makeup was softer, her whole attitude was less "killer," and an observant eye would catch that, just as Oliver had. Fortunately Jillian was right when she'd said observant eyes were in the minority here at Pitman. So far she'd gotten by practically unnoticed.

She scurried into the office and set the black briefcase in its usual spot on the credenza, then searched out the tea maker. There it was on a long counter with sleek cupboards below and above. She'd snooped into them a little and found nothing but files and fat three-ring binders with titles like Production Data 2000 labeled on them.

No wonder her sister had burned out. Her head was full of numbers. Numbers were weird. When Jana Lee had had to take over the job of paying bills and figuring out the household budget it had given her genuine headaches. There was a reason her husband had handled all that before. But she did have a certain sense of accomplishment when everything turned out balanced these days.

She hoped Jillian was getting some rest. Jana Lee had avoided calling her so Jillian wouldn't click into work mode and ask her a bunch of questions. So far, no real emergencies had turned up, just a real eye-opening first day.

Gosh, this place was sterile. Jana Lee paused for

a moment, then marched back into the outer office and grabbed a vase of lilies. She was going to pretty up that damn black-on-black office with some flowers. Ollie was on the phone and only raised an eyebrow at her.

She planted the vase on Jillian's desk and surveyed her improvements. The toys on the window ledges looked great too. At least she could be slightly useful. She made herself a pot of tea in the clever machine, choosing Constant Comment to steep in the white ceramic pot. Ollie had also left four very pretty flowered cups for her. Boy, he was good at what he did. The wonderful aroma of the tea filled her senses with calmness.

Her calmness didn't last long. As soon as she'd planted herself in the office chair and unwound Jillian's black pashmina shawl from her shoulders, Ollie knocked, walked in, and set an army green file folder down on her desk. It made her stomach jump.

"Change of plans. You'll have to Jillian up and be at a nine-forty-five meeting. It seems the numbers on the Byker Chikz product line have been less than rewarding, and they are looking at replacing it. We've got a trade show in six weeks, so we'll have to have preliminary specs and models at the very least. Pitman has to go into high gear. I'll sit beside you and take notes as usual. I've been watching the dailies—those are sales figures from across the country—so I've got a good grasp of the situation. Normally, your sister would have a whole lot to say at these meetings. I'm thinking we'll plead that you've lost your voice."

Jana Lee choked on her sip of tea. More like she'd lost her *mind*. "Works for me."

"That smells delicious. Mind if I have a cup?" Oliver walked over and got himself a cup of tea.

"Not at all. Thank you for the lovely china."

"It seemed to suit you." He returned to stand by her desk. "Don't get nervous. These people spend so much time backstabbing each other between departments they will hardly notice you. Besides, they'll be relieved you have nothing to say. Jillian usually pokes holes in all their pretty balloons with boring facts like unit cost of four-inch plastic doll heads and things like that."

"So I have a half hour?"

"Twenty-seven minutes, to be exact. I'd suggest a red lipstick. Here are some lemon drops to make you look authentic. I keep a bag in my desk drawer for just such times." Oliver reached in his pocket and scattered a half-dozen cellophane-wrapped yellow candies over the desk.

"Ollie, you're an amazing man."

"I know. Now drink your tea, and I believe you'll find a tube of Bobbi Brown Riot Red in the center drawer. I'll give you a warning in fifteen minutes." Oliver took his tea with him back to his protective front desk, which guarded her from harm. She was extremely glad she had him to trust with this whole thing.

Speaking of trust, she needed to call her sister right this minute. This qualified as an emergency. She picked up the phone, punched buttons till she got a dial tone, then dialed her own number. It might be long-distance, but she wasn't going another day without speaking to her daughter, bet be damned.

"Jillian, is that you? What is that racket?" Jana Lee heard what sounded like an earthquake in the background.

"Oh hey, we're just moving furniture. That's the sofa. The dog won't get off of it, so he's being moved too."

"Who is 'we'? Carly's in school, isn't she? You didn't give her some kind of early summer vacation thing, did you?"

"Oh no, she's in school. I met this nice repair guy person and he's helping me."

"And why are we moving my furniture?" Jana Lee drummed her fingers on the desk nervously.

"Jeez, Jana, the place needed a little pick-me-up. Don't worry, you'll love it."

"And why did we need a repair guy?"

"Oh, I had a little trouble with the washing machine. No big deal."

"For that you'd call an appliance repair person. There is a list of all of my local repair people in the back of the green phone book."

"I'll remember that. How are things at the office?" Jillian's voice got a little muffled. She must not want the repair guy to hear her.

"Oliver has me on house arrest."

"Oh, he figured you out, did he?"

"In like thirty seconds. You should give him a raise when you get back."

"Don't tell him that."

"And my daughter?"

"Second day, and that's only because your afterschool gang had me cornered."

"Tell her I'll call this afternoon."

"Will do. She's really fine. We're having fun. We make a great team."

Jana Lee felt a twinge of jealousy. She and Carly hadn't been a good team for quite a while, which was very sad. "That's nice," she said. "By the way, I have to go to some meeting this morning, but Oliver says I've lost my voice, so I'll just sit and take notes for you."

"Meeting?"

"Something about those Byker Chikz dolls not doing well in tests and replacing them with another item. You'll have to talk to Ollie about it."

"Oh God, they're monkeying with the holiday line? I should be there. He lets you call him Ollie?" Jillian sounded stressed.

"Yup." Jana Lee knew right away she should change the subject from work problems. "And excuse me; was there something you forgot to tell me about Jackson Hawks? My first day here he plants a big wet juicy one on me. Have you two re-connected since the mistletoe incident?"

"Not even close. He must have changed his mind!" Jillian sounded excited.

Jana Lee decided to toss her sister some warm-fuzzies. "He didn't have a clue I wasn't you. Even during dinner."

"You went out to dinner? On a Monday? You went out on a date with Jackson? How the hell did that happen?" Jillian asked.

"It was more of a business thing," Jana Lee lied. "We talked about work and . . . stuff."

"You went out with Jackson?" Jillian repeated.

"Don't worry, Ollie is keeping him far away from me—you—whatever. He's kind of arrogant, you know?"

"A little. He's a good-looking, extremely well-off guy with a great job. I suppose he has a whole lot to be arrogant about."

"Well, I can see the attraction, but we didn't ex-actly click." Jana Lee stared at the vase full of beautiful lilies on Jillian's desk. She felt herself blush and pulled at her long white silk scarf un-comfortably. "I think he's much more your type."

"I suppose."

"Are you getting some rest there?" Jana Lee tried to change the subject *again*, because this sub-ject led to their least favorite subject, which was what had happened in college. How Jillian had impersonated her, lied to her, and seduced her fiancé, then married him, then been dumped by him.

All leading full circle to their forgiving each other years later, but the subject of one sister having designs on a man the other sister wanted was still like walking naked into a cactus garden as far as Jana Lee was concerned. Her own pain around the subject was easily revived if poked.

"Your description of the afterschool gang should have included a self-defense lesson," Jillian said.

"Oh, they are a high-spirited bunch," Jana Lee replied.

"That's an understatement," Jillian said.

"You're just not used to kids, sis."

"Thank God for small favors."

Jana Lee was going to say something about how Jillian would make a great mom, but she paused just long enough for Oliver to stick his head in the door.

"Time to go," he called.

Jana Lee waved and nodded to him. "Oh, Jillian, I've got to go. I'll call later and catch Carly."

"I want daily updates, do you hear me?"

"I'm thinking that would be bad for your stress levels."

"I'm not talking about work, I'm talking about Jackson Hawks."

"That too. Bye, sis! Take care, take long baths, have some fun." Jana Lee hung up the phone before Jillian could reply, then she giggled. It wasn't often she got the upper hand on her powerhouse sister, and it felt pretty darn good.

She opened the top drawer and got Jillian's Riot Red lipstick out, plus a tiny black leather-bound mirror. She lined her pale pink lips and filled in with the bright red. What a ghastly color. As soon as she was done she grabbed up her sister's brief-case, adjusted the buttons on her white silk blouse to cover a little more of her more-ample-than-Jillian's bust, wrapped the pashmina shawl around her shoulders and scurried toward the door. The flounce on her red floral skirt kicked in the breeze of her rush, and she felt giddy maneu-vering in her sister's expensive red high heels. She was actually having fun for the first time in years.

Jana Lee's chances of remaining inconspicuous went out the window when Jackson came over to her, pulled out her chair for her and whispered in her ear.

"You look beautiful. Did you get the flowers?"

She glanced at Oliver as he sat down beside her. Ollie rolled his eyes and busied himself with the fancy leather binder he kept his legal pads in. Crisp white paper with black lines. He used a black pen at all times. Jana Lee wished she had that much order in her life.

"Yes, thanks," she hissed at Jackson, trying to keep her voice sounding hoarse. "Now go away, you're bothering me."

Every pair of eyes on every person sitting at the long conference table was glued on her and Jackson. She slid into place and adjusted her skirt. She was aware that every movement she made was decidedly un-Jillian like.

She straightened up and tried to look tough, as Jackson skip-hopped with his hands in his pockets down the length of the conference room, whistling some inane tune. The nerve of that guy.

He took his place at the head of the table, helped himself to the ice water positioned in front of him, set it down, and smiled at her; *directly* at her.

If she could have crawled under the table, she would have. Instead she gave him a glare and pretended to look at the folder full of papers in front of her. She opened it and studied the first sheet. It was pretty interesting, actually. There was a photo display of an advertisement Pitman had done to promote Byker Chikz.

It was easy to see why they hadn't done so well. These "girlz" were over the edge. They came with tattoo kits. She covered her mouth to stifle a laugh. What had they been thinking? Pinkie McGee and her Girl Gang of Motorcycle Mamas were tough street punks with spiked hair, studded leather outfits and questionable taste in makeup. Whoa. Just what every mom wants her little girl to play with.

"Good morning, people, I'm sure you all got my memo about the changes in the holiday line-up.

We're here today to listen to Development's ideas. Dawson, what have you all come up with to replace the B.C. collection?"

Dawson, a nerdy-looking guy with a short sleeved shirt and wide tie, got up and went over to an easel. He almost knocked it over, and Jana Lee could tell he was extremely nervous. He steadied the stand and flipped over the first big page. There was an illustration with four figures on the top row, four figures on the bottom row.

Dawson cleared his throat and took a pointer off the easel. "Of course these are preliminary, but we all know how big fantasy is now. We've got the Vampire series here on top, and the Slayers series on the bottom. These are based on a Buffy-like concept, but they are kids. There could be a book series developed around them, kind of a comic book thing, and a cartoon spin-off potential. We can use the anime team from Japan for that.

"We could release the preliminary run of eight characters for the holiday with a sort of Dark Castle thing going on, you know, and a Vampiremobile. Note No. 2 vampire, we call her Angelique"—his pointer thwapped the paper—"who switches back and forth from normal to vampire when you twist her head and push a back-located button. She's got retractable fangs and two outfits."

Dawson heaved a huge sigh, and the three people at the table next to where he'd been sitting let out a matching sigh. That must be the creative team. They looked vaguely goth-like, Jana Lee thought. No wonder.

A dead silence followed Dawson's presentation. Finally someone spoke. "Is there any more coffee?"

Several hands passed down a hot pot to the lone voice, and several cups were refilled. Jana Lee hadn't even touched hers, not being a coffee gal.

She thought she would have to go to the ladies' room to keep herself from either screaming or laughing out loud. She was new to this game, but this sounded like the dumbest idea ever. It might have some limited appeal, some dark, twisted, kids-that-should-be-in-therapy kind of appeal, but it sure as heck wouldn't boost the Pitman toy company's reputation *or* sales as far as she could see. But what did she know? She was only a mom.

"What else ya got, Dawson?" This came from Jackson himself.

Dawson stood silent for a few minutes, then flipped the large page again. A similar format faced them.

"Angels and Demons, bouncing off the whole Dan Brown thing. Top row, angelic beings armed and ready to do battle with the forces of darkness. Bottom row, demons." His pointer thwapped a few more times. "Demonmobile, several variations on weapons and powers, and the Dark Castle again. Think "Night on Bald Mountain" from *Fantasia*."

Jana Lee reached for her coffee cup. It clattered

against the saucer. She focused on the sugar and cream at their end of the table and doctored up her coffee, stirring the spoon noisily. Oliver looked at her. She could tell he had lots to say. What was the deal around here, anyway, didn't anyone have the guts to send these people back to the drawing board? She sipped her coffee, cleared her throat and set it back down. The throat drama addition was just to make Ollie happy.

Back when she was a kid, Pitman made the coolest board games, adventure sets and some truly classic old-style toys like colorful wooden dollhouses with little tiny families and playing house kinds of toys: little vacuums and brooms and pots and pans. But she guessed being domestic wasn't hip these days.

And what about stuff like . . . clay? And dress-up, and dolls that just did nothing but be your best friend? Carly's favorite toy for one entire year when she was about seven was a set of mini-cars. She'd made road ramps all over the backyard when Bill was building their deck. That, and her set of My Pretty Pony horses, which seemed to breed and multiply until they took up an entire wall of her room. Bill had made a special shelf with little cubbies just for those ponies.

Bill. The shock of her memories made her close her eyes. She'd gone so many days without hitting the pain. She put her hand to her forehead and rubbed her old images away.

When she looked up, everyone was looking at her again. Jana Lee glanced at Ollie. Obviously they all expected her sister to do the dirty work around here.

"Miss Tompkins is a bit indisposed today," Oliver said. "Laryngitis."

Jana Lee smiled and clutched her throat, nodding in agreement.

A collective rumbling murmur went through the room. Jana Lee figured they were figuratively drawing straws to see who would tell Dawson the creative department had gone over the cuckoo's nest.

Jackson's voice came from the end of the room. "Anything else, Dawson?"

"That's about it at present, sir."

Jackson slapped the folder he'd been holding down on the table hard enough to make Jana Lee and everyone else jump. Dawson backed up against the padded wall.

"What have you guys been smoking up there in Creative? I mean what, are you *high*? Seriously. Vampires? I can see it, but I think we're breaking a long-standing tradition at Pitman when we embrace the dark side. Snotz was bad enough in my opinion, even though they sold well, and I believe the problem with the B.C. line was its rather unsavory presentation. Don't you, Dawson?

"Can we get our heads out of the gutter for a moment? Or at least out of the blood-sucking realm? Do you think Disney made millions on evil? I'm thinking this is the year for comforting toys. For warmth and love, and all that sort of drivel. Do you think your crew can deal with that?"

Jana Lee felt genuine pity for Dawson. The rest of the Goth-like team looked devastated as well. Geez, business was nasty. *Jackson* was nasty. But she had to admit she'd thought the same thing. He might have put it a little more tactfully, though. Wasn't that supposed to be the executive thing to do? Diplomacy?

"Ahem, if I may," Oliver stood up. "Miss Tompkins and I discussed this earlier, and we'd like to refer to the cost analysis reference guide just past page seven of your materials. It's the stapled item."

People shuffled papers. Jana Lee drank more coffee. Even with three lumps of sugar and some cream, this stuff was bad. Everything about this meeting was going down badly.

"As you can see, this isn't the first time the vampire series has been considered. Please note the figures on the transforming retractable teeth mechanism, and the total unit cost figure. We're not seeing this item as below $14.99 retail, which, if you consider the economy and spending trends for this period in time, is a bit steep. And thank you to Dawson for giving us the preliminary sketches so we could patch together this itemized speculation on short notice." Oliver tapped his pencil decisively on the desk and reseated himself. People clapped.

"Thank you, Oliver, Miss Tompkins. As usual, you've both brought order to our meeting. Mr. Dawson, I apologize for my outburst. I'm feeling particularly burned out on the hard edges of life. Now go back to the drawing board and come up with something cute, and I mean *cute*, damn it. We'll meet again tomorrow. I'd like to see preliminaries on the four main executive's desks by three o'clock. That will give everyone a chance to crunch numbers and play with promotional concepts. Looks like we're going to be working late, folks."

The big groan went out, but when Jana Lee looked up at Jackson, he had a big grin on instead, and it was aimed at her. He looked as if he was going to corner her; there was no doubt about that. Jackson was on the pursuit.

Well, good, because she had a few things to say to him. Just because he was VP didn't mean he had to be such a bully! Poor Dawson was huddled with his black-haired, purple-swathed cohorts, no doubt ready to quit.

The rest of the folks got out of there quickly, and then Jackson started to stroll in her direction.

"Oh Mr. Hawks, can we have a word with you?"

"Why sure, Dawson. I know you and the crew worked hard, but what can I say? Unit numbers don't lie." Jackson leaned against the conference table casually, next to the four horsemen of the apocalyptic creative team.

"We quit."

"What's that?"

"You heard us, we quit. We all feel that our creative differences are too vast to overcome. Pitman obviously has a limited growth potential in its toy development, and frankly we're tired of being the brunt of it all. Obviously if Marketing did its job, and if we'd outsource some production, we'd be able to expand into the more lucrative areas of action figures and fantasy realm items."

"Dawson, the top-selling toys from our 2004 line last holiday season were the Wiggles. Cute, heartwarming."

"With due respect, Mr. Hawks, the top-selling action figure for Dec. 04 overall was the Fusion Monster based on the Fi-Bu-Mo cartoon, and it sold triple what our heartwarming line did. And in case I didn't mention it, that was produced by Harcourt Toys, not Pitman."

"Dude, you've got to reach into your inner child, and get what Pitman is all about. Don't quit, think of it as a challenge." Jackson put his hand on Dawson's shoulder. "Besides, the job market out there sucks."

Dawson leaned in to his cohorts, and they buzzed together like deranged bees. He popped out of the hive and addressed Jackson. "Considering the job market, we will give you another month, but each of us officially gives notice. Is that right, Fletcher? Downs? Parson?" They each gave Jackson a dead-on nod.

Could this be happening? The creative team on the bread line in thirty days? Sounded like a pretty darn good idea to Jana Lee.

"I'm sorry to hear that, Dawson, but grateful for the extra month. Maybe you'll change your mind. But if you don't, to make sure you get unemployment, I'll lay you off instead." Jackson strode past the four stunned people and headed toward Jana Lee. The creative team made tracks out of the boardroom, leaving just Jana Lee, Oliver and Jackson.

Akk. Jana Lee shrunk down in her chair, fiddled with her scarf and tried to look invisible. Even though it sounded reasonable to realign a crew that wasn't in tune with the company, the reality of four people out of work was harsh when it was said flat out. She had the feeling people came and went from Pitman pretty easily. And here she was pretending to be her sister. Hopefully it wouldn't cost Jillian her job.

Jackson pulled a chair out next to her and sat very close.

"Miss Tompkins, I'm sorry to hear about your throat. I hope I didn't keep you out in the night air too late last night." Jackson smiled a very sexy smile.

It made her face feel hot looking at him. Parts of

her body that had been in an ice age state of dormancy came alive as he put his hand on top of hers. She pulled it away in an attempt to maintain sanity.

"Miss Tompkins's malady will no doubt lift by lunchtime. It's a purely temporary condition," Oliver presented.

"Oh, really?" Jackson looked straight in her eyes. "In that case, if you'd be so kind as to join me for lunch in my office, we'll have Chez Paris cater in. How does a chicken Caesar salad sound? Iced tea? Or perhaps a soothing soup?"

Jana Lee smiled and tried not to talk. She just nodded amiably in agreement. She had to make nice to the boss for Jillian's sake. She could tell him off later. If ever. Her sister's job was at stake here. She stared into his unblinking chocolate brown eyes and tried to remember what she was going to yell at him about.

No wonder women fell at his feet. Jackson Hawks was the most powerful, sexy, intelligent man she'd met in a long, long time.

7

Twin Streaks

Jillian had nervously waited a decent amount of time to call her sister back at Pitman to find out about the meeting, and the time had come. So even though she was in the middle of a giant home improvement store, she flipped her cell phone open and dialed her own direct office line.

"Hello?" She heard her sister's voice on the other end.

"I believe that's *'Jillian Tompkins here,'* sis."

"Oops. Hi, Jillian."

Jillian balanced the phone on her chin as she grabbed a box of nails off the shelf. "Hi, Jana, how's the Pit, as we like to call it? Get it? Pitman Toys?" she tried to sound casual.

"Oh, that's funny. The Pit is fine."

"I called to find out about the meeting." Jillian wanted to hear what solutions had been brought to the holiday lineup. She couldn't believe they'd been such idiots as to think the Byker Chikz line would fly in the first place, except to a very select and rather weird market.

"The meeting was very interesting. Jackson pretty much fired the creative department. Is that normal?"

"He *what?*" The cement block walls of Mega Home Base weren't conducive to cell phone signals. Jillian thought her sister just said Jackson fired the creative department.

"Well, really it was more like they quit. They gave a thirty-day notice."

Jillian heard that just fine. Her stomach twisted into a knot. An old, familiar knot. The work stress knot. *"Oh, my God,"* she blurted out. What was he thinking letting them go this time of year? And here their holiday lineup was short-numbered.

"Honestly, Jillian, I can see why. They're on a different planet. Remember all the cool stuff Pitman used to put out? We loved their toys as kids," Jana Lee said. "And he did suggest they try again, and maybe they'd consider it a challenge and not quit after all."

"You're defending Jackson Hawks? Yesterday you said he was an arrogant bastard. What's going on?" Jillian parked her big flatbed cart next to the MDF molding stacks.

"I didn't say bastard, just arrogant. He still is, but I sort of understand where he was coming from."

Jillian thought her sister sounded more lively than she had in years, and it made her smile to hear that. Maybe this deal was working after all. Maybe Jana Lee would be ready for a cute repair guy-sculptor when she got back.

As far as the work disaster, there wasn't much Jillian could do from here about the whole mess without tipping off everyone that she wasn't there. Besides, she'd call Oliver later and get the level-two dirt. She decided to change the subject before she let her mind unravel to the scream-out-loud point.

"There's a new Mega Home Base in Silverburgh. I'll have you know I'm actually rolling down the aisle right now with a big home improvement cart," Jillian bragged. "Carly and I are having so much fun."

"What the hell are you doing to my house?"

"Oh, it's all minor stuff. Just a tweak here and there. The place could use a few repairs, you know," Jillian lied.

They'd decided to gut the place in the remaining days before Jana Lee flew home. Dean had hired on a crew just today. He said he got lucky and found some old friends of his. They'd go into high gear as soon as the rugrats left for good. Thank God she'd only had three days with them.

She'd had such a great time with Carly last night, staying up late emptying the contents of two generations of stuff into boxes: her mom's stuff and Jana Lee's stuff. They'd found baby spoons, five corkscrews, and were left wondering why Jana Lee kept fourteen plastic lids for containers that no longer existed.

Gee, Jillian hoped her sister liked it. She was trying to stick to that country feeling Jana Lee seemed to like, but it had morphed into more like French country at this point.

Dean had great taste, it turned out. He also seemed to have an abundance of time on his hands. He said something about having avoided booking jobs this summer, so he was happy to give her a hand. He also looked great in a tool belt.

"Just don't get carried away. I don't want a big mess, okay?" Jana Lee sounded wary.

"Oh, it'll all be cleaned up when you get back." That wasn't a lie. Jillian had made Dean swear to it, although he hadn't understood why. She'd said relatives were coming to visit, which was true. Her new game was trying to tell fewer lies to Dean.

"You're supposed to be resting."

"I'm not very good at it. I'm having fun anyhow. Do you like that Martha Stewart bluish-greenish-chicken-egg-color thing? I'm going to paint the kitchen."

"Blue is fine," Jana Lee answered. "Just keep it sane. Muted, you know, like me."

"Dull?"

"Yeah."

"I'm just teasing. You are not dull."

"I love you too, sister dear, now get some rest. That's an order. That's the only reason I agreed to this, you know."

"Yes, dear, I'll curl up with a good book and a cup of tea after the kids leave this afternoon."

"Promise?"

"Yes, I do." Jillian made kissy noises in the phone and said good-bye.

Sure she would. She'd curl up with the manual for the nail gun she'd just bought and maybe a dozen decorating magazines for ideas. That would be keeping her promise.

Jillian resolved not to think about Pitman for the next hour just as an exercise. Besides, this place was fun.

The store was packed for a weekday morning, but it was the grand opening. There were free samples of tons of things, and she'd been careening her cart through rows of tiles, carpeting, bathroom fixtures and wallpaper borders. She'd amassed quite a collection of items and at this point was wishing she'd brought Dean just to push the cart.

Oh well, he was busy supervising the rewiring for lighting in Jana Lee's and Carly's bedrooms. The upstairs was fair game while the kids were still doing their afterschool thing. Carly's room was next on the pack-up list, although the girl had made a pretty good dent in it. It was amazing what a teenager could do when given a purpose.

Which reminded Jillian, she'd need some plastic bins for packing things up. How the hell was she going to get all this stuff in and out of the van? Maybe she'd have the molding delivered. She should have hit the gym more often than once a month.

Jillian turned the corner with her cart, doing a mini-wheelie trying to keep it in balance.

"Whoa there, you're top-heavy." It was Dean.

"Oh Dean, thank God you're here."

"I had to pick up some electrical. Pretty huge, isn't it?"

Jillian could only assume he was talking about Mega Home Base. "Yes, it sure as heck is. Can you take this cart off my hands?"

Dean grabbed the big deck cart and steadied her load.

"Let's just slow down—you've got plenty of time. The fine art of rcvamping a house is less complex than it seems. It's all in the planning. That, and the decisions. I see you picked some tile?"

"I thought this would make a great backsplash. What do you think?"

"Nice, very nice. Those insets are pretty pricy. Are you wedded to them?"

"I am wedded. Money is no object."

He watched her gaze at the tile sample board and touch the Celtic knot design on the tiny pewter-colored inset piece.

"It's a peach, isn't it?" she said.

Dean rubbed his thumb over the design, their fingers brushing. "It's beautiful." He was continually puzzled by the vast difference in the current space this lady was living in and the tasteful, almost professional-level design she'd been coming up with. Maybe she'd just never figured out what her taste was till lately.

"I thought we'd do a tumbled marble thing, maybe a niche over the stove, and place these in that area. You like?" she asked. Her face was close to his, and he caught himself liking more than the tile.

"I like." He was caught in her excitement. "And with two tile setters, we'll just be finished in time if we start tomorrow morning." He loved turning a sow's ear into a showcase. She was quick as liquid silver with ideas, and her vision was very clear to him. He looked over at her, with her cute work overalls on, with a tank T-shirt underneath, revealing her figure very nicely. Her dark hair was tied back with a blue bandana headband. The ends stuck up like a bow on top of her head. She had a smudge of dirt on her cheek.

"Here," he said as he took his clean white handkerchief from his back jeans pocket and brushed her cheek off.

"Oh, thanks," she murmured.

He felt heat rush through him. It had been a very long time since he'd had a lover. He better behave himself. This lady was a delicate package.

"Come on, I picked out grout." She barreled around the corner, went to the tile supply area with him hot on her heels, and proceeded to heft a large bag of grout off the floor. "Bisque. It matches the tile better."

Twenty pounds of grout. So much for the delicate package. "Nice. Did you look at sinks?" He took the bag out of her hands and packed it on the cart. Dean grabbed his clipboard off the top of a stack of tile and flipped to his supply list.

"Kitchen, bath and bath sinks, plus fixtures. That, and we should pick some lighting. I'm glad they opened this place, or we'd have five stores to go to. Plus it's all in stock, so no delays."

He was also grateful to spend the time with her. He watched her move through items and make decisions quickly and with amazing taste. She was good, very good.

After another hour they'd made significant progress with their checklist. She looked a little fatigued.

"Shall we go grab a cup of coffee at the Starbucks next door?" he suggested.

"There's free stuff in here somewhere." She held up an empty paper cup.

"That's fossil fuel. I'm thinking a cold iced latte and a chocolate chip brownie."

"You're on."

"We can take this through the contractor's line. I've got my ID card, and it's empty at the moment."

"Lead on, MacDuff."

Shakespeare. She had some book learnin', or she was quick with the phrases anyhow. He grinned and steered the large flatbed cart into the checkout line. The early crowd had thinned, but he heard some commotion outside as the next wave of people arrived—the ten o'clock folks. There was a clown outside the front of the store giving away free balloons.

After Dean flashed the clerk his contractor's ID, Jillian whipped out a credit card as he unloaded items. She seemed a little squirrelly about it, so he gave her some space.

Well heck, it wasn't his business. She'd said money was no object, and that's a phrase you don't hear every day. She'd also asked if he'd mind being paid in cash. As if. He'd had his eyes on a large piece of marble at the quarry in South Bend, and that guy liked to deal in cash. Everyone liked cash.

Damn it, here she was with her Jillian Tompkins Visa card and her Jana Lee Stivers driver's license, four feet away from Dean. They'd had to switch IDs for the purposes of plane tickets, and they'd forgotten all about any other use they might have.

She blocked his view in case the worst happened. Bless the clerk, she didn't ask for ID, just ran the credit card through. Hopefully that would hold true for all their visits. Jillian would just have to make a mammoth cash withdrawal for the rest of their needs. Or maybe transfer money into Jana Lee's checking account and forge some checks. What a mess they'd created. She'd just add bank fraud to her to-do list.

She turned and smiled at him in her best demure imitation of a helpless woman—which she'd rather forgotten to play at altogether. She was so grateful to see him muscle that big fat flat cart out the door that she made a mental note to be helpless more often. He'd surely brought his truck, so she was in luck. What had she been thinking anyway, that Jana Lee's minivan would hold all this?

As the wide doors swished open, she saw a seedy-looking clown in front of the store. Sheesh, you'd think they'd get a little nicer one for the grand opening.

She walked by slowly. She didn't like clowns. There was something about clowns and guys in big dragon suits. She felt her skin crawl. Oh, come on, she was an adult.

But this clown was staring at her. She knew it.

"Why don't you get us a table. I'll load this stuff

in the truck," Dean said over his shoulder, waiting for cars to pass.

"Can't I help?" She felt creepy. She didn't want to be alone.

"You look beat. I'll take care of this. I won't be a minute." Dean pushed off and headed into the parking lot, leaving her there.

She crossed her bare arms together and shivered in the morning chill. She should have grabbed her sister's sweatshirt off the cart. Dean would probably bring it back. She watched him in his jeans jacket and black jeans, until he turned behind his truck.

Jillian turned to glance at the clown. She should grow up already.

When she looked, she was startled to see him staring at her full out. She looked away quickly.

What? Was she that strange? She'd ditched her black Capri pants and high heels and dressed up in her sister's distressed denim overalls just to blend in with the locals. Had she screwed up? They used to wear these kinds of overalls when they were kids, usually in pastel girly colors. It seemed pretty rural and all. Maybe she reeked of San Francisco. They weren't too keen on Californians up here.

She could feel his stare. She turned his way again, this time facing him full out. Some kids came over, and he sort of shoved balloon strings their way. The girl whined about wanting a pink one. He paused long enough to extract her a pink one, then looked back at Jillian directly.

She had half a mind to ask him what his problem was. Him and his big red feet and rainbow wigged hair.

She decided not to cause a scene. Dean might think she was nuts, and Jana Lee sure wouldn't do stuff like that. She turned and headed toward the Starbucks. A big shot of caffeine would help. She'd obviously been focusing on little chips of paint color too long.

Inside Starbucks, Jillian slurped a big slurp of latte to snap herself out of it. She'd opted for hot since she'd taken on a chill. Or was she just shaken by the weird clown?

"You okay?" Dean asked as he joined her.

"I think so. I must have forgotten to eat this morning or something."

"Take another bite of that grilled ham and cheese thing," he commanded her with a finger pointed at the pastry-wrapped item on her napkin.

"Dean, have you ever had that sense someone stepped on your grave? You know, that strange chill up your spine thing?"

"I'm not much for being in touch with that side of myself. I have had the sense someone's spirit was still hanging around. I just pound metal when I get to feeling off-kilter. Why, what's going on?"

"I don't know, I just got the creeps from the clown."

Dean smirked. "Too many bad movies probably. I gave up television. It's improved my life quite a bit."

"You gave up television?"

"Sad but true. I read newspapers when I get a curiosity about the news. I listen to the radio sometimes. The media is extremely skewed these days. There's only a drop of truth, if that, in most things."

She wondered how he'd feel if he knew she'd helped orchestrate a national television ad campaign budget for Pitman toys in the millions-of-dollars-a-year range. He probably would not approve. But then again, he would fit right into Jana Lee's old-timey head-in-the-sand world. They were meant for each other. "Thanks for my sweatshirt." She zipped it up higher and pulled up the hood.

"No problem." Dean watched her bundle herself into an impenetrable pretzel. "You're still cold?"

"Must be a chick thing. I'd better be going. I've got to stop at the market and get chow for the little monsters. I'll meet you back at the house and help you unload this stuff." She got up abruptly and gathered her tote bag. "Thanks, Dean." She slipped out from behind the table and made a quick departure.

He picked up his iced latte cup and swiped the table clean with a napkin. Might as well get back to it. She wanted a whole lot done in just a short time: interior repainted, new lighting, redone kitchen floor, tile backsplash and bathroom improvements. Next to impossible, even with a reliable crew. He wondered why he'd taken this on. Summer was his time to kick back and work on large pieces that required outside space. He should begin a planning schedule on the commissioned work for the local library.

Maybe it was because he wanted to see this young widow's life lifted up. He shook his head at himself, always wanting to leave something better than he found it.

Who was he kidding? The truth was he found her fascinating and that hadn't happened in a long time. He'd agreed to this project so he could spend time with her. Mrs. S had gotten under his skin. He'd even dreamed about her last night, and it hadn't been about installing a hot spout in her kitchen sink.

8
Best-Laid Plans

Jana Lee felt a long, disturbing shudder run up her spine. She shivered and pulled her sister's black jacket closer around her, buttoning the front. They must have the air-conditioning cranked in here today.

She pushed her hair back behind her ear and resumed flipping through the page of the catalogue Oliver had given her to read. It was the history of Pitman Toys. She loved looking at the pictures of the old toys Pitman had produced since the early fifties and up through the eighties. She thought of Jillian and the things they used to play with in between taping Harvey the Dragon shows.

They'd been big fans of the Holly Dolly Dream House. She'd always played out little family scenes with babies and pretend meals with fake tiny food, while Jillian had always been racing around in Holly Dolly's sports car. Funny how real life had turned out so similar.

Jana Lee felt the hairs on the back of her neck prickle. She held her arms across her chest protectively for a moment. She had a bad feeling. She didn't like that. Impulsively she grabbed Jillian's fancy phone and clicked the headset on. She auto-dialed her own number at the house. It was nice to know she was on speed dial. Jillian answered. Jana Lee could hear kids laughing in the background.

"Jillian? Is everything okay?"

"What?" Her sister hollered into the receiver.

"I had a bad feeling."

"Oh good God, everything is fine. We're knee-deep in goldfish crackers, and your daughter is right here. Here, here's Carly." The phone was passed, and Jana Lee twisted the mouthpiece of the headset to be sure she could be heard well.

"Mom?"

"Carly, honey, is everything okay?"

"We talked yesterday, Mom. It's still fine. Aunt Jillian and I are having a blast."

"I was just having a feeling. I'm sure it was nothing." Jana Lee let out a breath she'd been holding without knowing it. Just then Oliver buzzed her on the intercom.

"Hawks alert," he hissed into the speaker.

"Okay, honey, well, I've got to run. I'm glad

you two are having fun. Give Aunt Jillian a hug for me."

"I will, Mom, bye!" Carly hung up.

It was probably the impending doom of knowing Jackson Hawks was expecting her for lunch that had given her the willies. She'd blown him off. It was twelve-thirty. She'd ignored Oliver's time updates for the last half hour. Before she could breathe again, Jackson swung open her door and stood framed in the light. He was amazing. Looks like a movie star, voice like a radio personality. He was a network blitz all unto himself.

"Your lunch is wilting," he smiled.

"Oh, I'm so sorry. I was absorbed," she said.

He knew she was lying. She was avoiding him. He stood straight and adjusted his tie. Not too many women avoided him. He couldn't figure it out. So far she'd slapped him, removed his hand, and refused all forms of outward affection.

He could tell he was getting to her, so she wasn't completely against male contact. He knew the signs—a parted lip, a quickening of breath, a heated blush, and the kiss he'd surprised her with had been well received—for a few minutes, anyway.

So what was it? Was he not her type? He was confused. "I'm here to escort you. Shall we?"

She'd gotten up from the desk, a good sign. She was carrying a book, not such a good sign.

"I'll come and have lunch, but I have some thoughts I'd like to toss out to you. I've been reading about the history of the company."

She moved from behind the desk and smoothed down her floral skirt. He didn't know if he'd ever seen Ms. Tompkins wear floral. It was pretty. It had a flounce on the hem. He checked out her legs. Very nice.

"I'm at your service," he bowed. Oh brother, was she going to talk statistics while they ate? He hated statistics. They were at best a necessary evil. She moved past him out the door, and he followed. Her perfume drifted by him. It was a familiar perfume. Something classic; maybe Chanel No. 5?

He had a shrewd nose for women's perfumes. He liked to surprise his more serious three-week relationships by presenting them with their perfume, at which they were usually properly amazed. Plus the girls behind the fragrance counters were always good for a date.

Most of the time by three weeks he was bored, gave them a large box of chocolates to console them, and broke it off.

Of course, there *was* Gabrielle, who'd entertained him for three entire months with her Italian accent, extremely smart manner and long, tan legs. But he'd never in his wildest dreams pictured himself married to her. Married. What a concept. He walked down the hall behind Ms. Tompkins, admiring the view.

Marriage. One woman, forever. Period. "Aughhh," he moaned.

She turned and glanced at him. "Did you say something?"

"No." He looked at the ceiling and whistled a tune.

She slowed down, letting him walk beside her. Nice of her. "Thank you for inviting me to lunch," she said.

"You're welcome." He steered them into his office. She must have forgotten it was this door. Kind of odd. She really was distracted today. His secretary smiled at her as they walked by.

Olga was the most discreet person he knew. She could keep four girls straight at a time. She'd told him once, with a straight face and tapping pencil, that four was her limit, so he'd kept to that. He'd chosen her for her extreme efficiency and age. He didn't want to get messed up with his own secretary. He knew when to separate work and play.

Maybe. Ms. Tompkins was sort of both. But so far not as much *play* as he'd like. How could he get her to loosen up?

"Would you like a glass of wine with your meal?" He held out a chair for her at a small café-sized table in the corner of his office. Very cozy table for two, and it had seen its share of intimate lunches.

"No, thank you, this iced tea is great. My, isn't

this lovely, right by the window, you can see the bay." She skirted herself into the chair and let him adjust her position. "Oh my gosh, I'm starving."

As if she'd never seen this office before. Weird.

She went right for her napkin, spread it over her lap, picked up a fork and dove in, spearing a hunk of chicken before he could get his own self to the table. He poured himself a glass of chilled chardonnay out of the ice bucket. He liked his wine cold, but not his women. Maybe it was him that needed to loosen up. Or give up.

"It occurs to me, Ms. Tompkins, that we've been out on a dinner date and I haven't really heard much of your life story. Would you care to fill me in? Where did you grow up?"

"That was just a business dinner."

He decided not to argue. "Nevertheless, your hometown?"

"I grew up partly in Hollywood, California, partly in a small town in western Washington."

"Hollywood?" He perked up. What an odd place to grow up.

"My sister and I were on a children's television show for about three years. Before that we did some advertising. Baby products, that sort of thing. Which reminds me, I was looking through the Pitman Toy history, as I mentioned—"

"Oh, yes." He was still stuck on thinking of her as a baby model and children's television show star. He recalled that from somewhere, just not the details.

"And I remembered playing with many of the toys from the seventies. Holly Dolly Dream House, and the old dress-up series with different career costumes for girls, like doctors and astronauts, those kinds of things. Why doesn't Pitman produce these items anymore?"

"I suppose we're trying to compete in this modern marketplace and don't see the value. Hey, I used to play with the Neil Armstrong rocket set. Did you see that one in there? It had an authentic moonscape and lunar module, and a little flag to stick on a blob of gray clay. I spent hours with Neil and Buzz reenacting the landing. It also had these funny little moon men. I'd watched a special documentary on the landing and gotten hooked."

"See? The whole video-obsessed generation is losing the ability to imagine."

"I have read some marketing reports about a movement by parents to get back to simpler items."

"And Pitman was really good at that at one time. Look at this page." She handed him the book she'd propped by her chair and pointed to a flagged sticky marker. "The yellow one." She went back to attacking her lunch.

Jackson flipped through the book and found her marker. "Oh yeah, that was a great ad campaign. *'You can be anything.'* Great slogan."

"What do you think about adding a retro sort of toy to the December lineup instead of, oh, vampires?"

"I think you might be on to something. After lunch I'll look into it further." Jackson put the book down beside his chair and stared at his lunch, not really in the mood for salad anymore. He stabbed at it aimlessly. He'd have to go for a nice steak after work. "Would you like to discuss this more over dinner?"

Without even a pause, she answered him. "No."

Jackson was actually startled. He searched for a comeback. "Hey, what happened to your sore throat?"

"I gargled with salt water."

"Oh, really? Sounds nasty." He looked at her across the table with disbelief undoubtedly written on his face. She stared right back. He felt himself swimming in her sea-blue eyes. Her eyebrow arched up at him; her pretty, dark, expressive eyebrow. It made him crazy. She was challenging him. He smiled and raised his wineglass to her. "Here's to salt water."

"Cheers," she said flatly and resumed eating her lunch.

After lunch Jana Lee all but ran back to her own office. She breezed past Oliver and closed the door behind her. She wanted to check on some things. This whole idea was exciting. Maybe she could just write up a suggestion and they could take it from there. It wouldn't be the first time an employee had come up with an idea, and it certainly wouldn't upset the balance of things, would it? She sat back down at Jillian's desk and buzzed Oliver.

"Ollie, can you come in here, please?"

He answered. "I only let you call me that because you are very nice, you know."

"I know. Bring your notepad, please." She flipped off the button and scrambled around for a blank piece of printer paper. She took one of Jillian's fancy black pencils and started sketching her ideas. She could hardly draw fast enough to catch the wave of her thought process. She didn't look up when Oliver came in. He leaned over the desk and looked at her sketches.

"My, you are a very good artist, Mrs. Stivers."

"Thank you, Ollie," she looked up and smiled at him. She was trying to remember the last time anyone had sincerely complimented her on anything. She and her daughter had fallen into a phase of taking each other for granted. Or worse, just existing together. The walking wounded.

"I wonder if you would mind looking some things up for me. I want to do a little research on the retro toy market and what kind of response that's getting. I'm not putting this very well, but I'd like to see some kind of charts on how toys that encourage imagination and creative play compare to interactive electronic-type toys. Also who else is producing reproduction-type toys? Retro toys, you know?" She made a few notes to herself on the side of the drawing. "And one more thing. Let's do a for-instance on, say, the *I Can Be Anything* dress-up box. What would a production run cost today? Am I making any sense? I don't know if these are the right words."

"You are explaining things very well, but I'm not sure I was signed up to actually work this week." Oliver peered at her over his leatherbound notepad.

"Oh my gosh, I'm so sorry."

"I'm *kidding*. I've been working my tail off doing your sister's reports. She called this morning after you spoke and promised me a new car or a yacht or whatever my heart desires if I'd help you out. There's a lull in the storm, so I'd be happy to do this. I love research and like your idea, too. Simple designs are the best in my book."

"Thanks, Ollie, you're a prince. How did my sister ever find you?"

"I found her," he smiled. "How was your lunch?"

"Oh, fine. Very delicious. I'm afraid I yammered on about toy ideas."

"Oh, dear."

"What, was that bad?"

"Well, let's just say your sister never ventured there. She had enough on her hands with recalls and unit pricing and sales data."

"I'm sure I didn't do much harm. I was mostly pointing out things from the Pitman history book."

"I'm sure." Oliver nodded kindly, excused himself and returned to his desk outside the huge eight-foot mahogany door that separated their spaces.

Oh brother, what had she done now? Jana Lee thought about her lunch with Jackson. Turning it over in her head, however, she didn't see anything unusual about their conversation. She shifted her focus back to her ideas and resumed sketching.

Jackson sat at his bistro table alone, picking at the lumps of chicken and wilted lettuce left on his plate. He was deep in thought. He thought of the lively conversation he'd had with Ms. Tompkins and how she'd made him remember things—things about his childhood.

The year he'd gotten that moon-landing toy had been the last Christmas his parents were together. He was hitting a pocket of painful memories remembering their announcement to him and his brother just after New Year's.

They'd tried to be civilized about the whole thing, but the truth was he'd heard them fighting in the middle of the night behind the closed doors of their bedroom. He'd heard his mother's voice raised in anger. He was very sure his father had been having an affair. To him it was like his father had abandoned his two sons as well as his wife.

He should call Marcus and see how things were going. At least his brother had his wife, Nan. She was a great gal, and their two boys were great. Maybe it was time for uncle Jackson to visit again. Their house in Mill Valley was pleasant and had a great backyard. They could have a barbeque. Perhaps he'd invite Ms. Tompkins to come along.

He washed that thought down with the rest of his chardonnay. What the hell was he thinking, inviting a girl over to meet his family? It must be the wine. He was getting sentimental and sappy. On the other hand, it was just the type of thing she might say yes to. Jackson noticed he was extremely compelled to get Ms. Tompkins back in the game. She couldn't turn him down every time, could she?

9
Identity Crisis

Dean Wakefield liked a woman who could take charge of things. He watched his boss, the cute lady with the red thong underwear, run around with her clipboard, checking things off her list. He was getting seriously hot for her. He wondered when he might make his move.

On the other hand she was extremely bossy and kept him so busy he hardly had time to make a move. It was obvious the way to her heart was to complete this project in record time, in a skillful manner.

It was always rewarding for him to see something dull and uninspiring shape itself into something bright and beautiful. He smiled to himself. He meant the house, not the woman, but he did remember that she had been rather invisible the first time he'd ever seen her. Now she was anything but.

They'd been blessed by a few breaks—wood floors in almost perfect condition under the ugly carpet, no inside dry rot so far, sound structural elements. The layout was completely whacked, but that would require a major remodel.

He had to say, she had excellent taste; she just didn't trust it. Her first instincts were often more modern and amazing, but every time it came to choosing a finish she would take it down a notch and go with something less risky, more . . . pedestrian.

It made him wonder two things: how the house had remained in its less tasteful format for so long, and why she didn't just *go for it* now that she'd gotten the nerve up.

"Mrs. S, last chance on the stone kitchen floor. I'd just need to reinforce the floor joists if we want to go there." He'd taken to calling her Mrs. S upon her request, although after having a great dinner with her, it was weird.

"No, Dean, let's stick with the beige tile. It's more mainstream."

He scratched his head. "Are you planning on selling this place? It's hard to find a piece this big next to the sound anymore. I'm sure I could set you up with a buyer if you really wanted to part with it."

"No, I'm just . . . tired of it the way it was."

"So why hold back? How about the black tile?"

"This is sort of a family house. I have to keep my sister and her tastes in mind." Mrs. S looked out the dining area window toward the sea. Her arms were crossed, and she looked thoughtful.

Dean chewed that over, but it didn't make sense. She lived here, so why shouldn't it be her own taste? Oh well, the lady with the checkbook knew her mind. Although right now she seemed confused. He put down his measuring tape and square carpenter's pencil and came up behind her very close. "Can I help?"

She could feel the heat from Dean's breath on her neck. Actually she could feel the heat from his entire body down every inch of *her* body. A feeling she hadn't felt for a very, very long time crept from the base of her spine slowly, slowly to the top of her head, and it made her dizzy. She closed her eyes and breathed it in.

Dean put his hands on her shoulders and gently massaged her tight muscles.

"Ahhhhhhh." A long, low sound escaped her. She could tell right away it sounded like way more than shoulder rub delight. More like *touch me more* delight.

Apparently Dean felt that way too. He gently turned her around and took her in his arms. She had never felt so enveloped with desire for a man as she did at that moment. She wanted to melt into him like a pat of butter into hot popcorn. It surprised her. She'd known she was attracted to him, but the lust factor was a real kick in the pants.

He tipped her chin up with his fingers and looked into her eyes long enough to erase her popcorn thoughts. Then he tilted his head and kissed her.

Having already lost her power of speech, her ability to think and her footing, Dean's kiss took away whatever was left of her resolve to keep that kiss from happening.

It was slow and sexy and hard and soft all at the same time. His kiss swelled with intensity, then slid into a lustful thing that intoxicated her more than any kiss she had ever had, or any vintage wine she'd indulged in. She forgot to breathe. Time spun on its elbow. More kisses. Or was it one, long, never-ending kiss?

Monty Python took this opportunity to bark at them. Or was he barking at someone else? She jolted out of his kiss.

"No kissing!" she said loudly. Now this was really meant to remind herself that she wasn't supposed to kiss the set-up guy she was leaving for her sister. But it sure made his eyebrows rise up.

He gently released his grasp on her and smiled a real bad-boy smile. Then he reached up and, with his thumb, wiped what must have been a smear of lipstick from below her lip. He turned and walked back into the kitchen. He picked up his yellow-and-black measuring tape as if nothing had happened, then resumed measuring the kitchen floor.

Jillian did a Carly and shot up the stairs, slamming the door to Jana Lee's room behind her. Her heart pounded as she caught her breath. She continued to Jana Lee's bed and threw herself face-first on top of the new duvet she'd bought today. The big fat European pillows in their blue floral chintz shams all fell over on her head. She didn't care.

In the darkness of her sister's bedcovers she tried to figure out what had just happened. She had to analyze it, turn it around, wrestle with it, and get control of it.

Dean Wakefield was not her *perfect*. Jackson Hawks was her perfect. The aloof, worldly, powerful Jackson Hawks, right? The man she'd been trying to convince to date her? Jackson was a man that could take it if she worked ten hours a day, because he wouldn't care.

Because . . . he wouldn't care.

She squealed into the duvet. She was screwing this all up, as usual. She screwed everything up. She screwed up their Little Princess jobs, she was screwing up her sister's house, she screwed up her sister's potential boyfriend. She could create production projections and PowerPoint presentations, but she always screwed up when it came to her personal life, which mostly involved her sister as well.

This had been a never-ending flaw with her. She'd stolen Elliot away from Jana Lee back in college without even thinking what kind of pain it would cause. She was always messing things up with men.

Of course Jana Lee had thanked her later, because she'd ended up dating Bill and they'd gotten together and lived happily ever after and had had Carly—until Bill had died suddenly and left her sister alone.

And *of course* she herself, Jillian the destroyer, had gotten what she'd deserved when Elliot had cheated on her after their marriage. But still. What kind of a sister was she? She was selfish, and Jana Lee was always forgiving her. Even during Jillian's years married to Elliot, Jana Lee had called and talked, although she'd never visited. And when Jillian had phoned Jana Lee, sobbing, when Elliot had left, Jana Lee had flown down to see her. It was her sister who'd made the effort to break their barriers down after all the painful years.

She'd never forget that horrible night at college when the deed had been done and she'd shown up with Elliot as her date to the end-of-the-year dance. Jana Lee had been so gracious, even though she'd hated Jillian at that moment and Jillian had known it. She and Jana Lee had gotten up on stage and sung the "Sisters" song from *White Christmas*, complete with blue dresses and huge feathered fans.

Jana Lee had looked at her hard when they'd sung about how the Lord better help the sister *who comes between me and my man!* and Jillian had seen Jana Lee's tears fall as soon as they'd finished the number. But had that kept her from marrying Elliot? No. She'd thought she'd been in *love* with him. She'd been blinded by her supposed love. She'd abandoned her sister for Elliot. Why had she taken her sister's fiancé away anyway? Just to be able to *win?*

And here she was doing it again in a weird, twisted-up kind of way. Even if Jana Lee hadn't even met Dean, Jillian had it in her mind to help her sister find some happiness with a new man. Instead she'd ended up kissing him herself. She was messing that up before it even had a chance to get started.

She was a complete bitch. A worm. A . . . hard-hearted, misguided woman. Jillian rolled over and stared at the ceiling.

And here she was, thirty-five, divorced, no kids. Her own marriage screwed up in five short years. Elliot. Even though there was no excuse for his behavior, in reality he'd hardly known what had hit him when he'd married her. She'd ignored him and spent all her time at the office. She'd taken him for granted. He wasn't a perfect guy, and she'd found his flaws irritating. Instead of trying to deal with that, she'd run away to work.

No wonder he'd cheated on her.

The day she'd returned home from a trip to Pitman's overseas marketing group to find all his belongings cleared out of their apartment had been a real eye-opener. She'd walked from room to room, where the absence of his clothing, his art, his music and books, had been like a wide-open mouth screaming at her. His note had been dead accurate and almost like a business letter. He'd carefully outlined the fact that he'd found someone else and was filing for divorce on such and such a date, and if she needed to contact him regarding this or that, blah blah it went on.

And the way their things had divided up so easily, as if she'd never really mingled herself with him. They'd hardly owned anything together besides a sofa. His stereo, her television, her appliances. He'd known so easily what had been his and what hadn't. He'd left the sofa, too, which at the time seemed like an insult to her.

That day she'd done the same thing she was doing right now. Thrown herself on the bed and what—cried? No. She'd tried to figure it all out. Analyze it. Make it into a pie chart.

She wasn't making much progress.

There was a knock on the bedroom door.

"Come in," she croaked.

It was Dean, of course. "Carly called and said she had a meeting after school and won't be back till dinner." All the while he was telling her this he was still moving toward the bed.

Jillian stared at him. Deep in her heart she wanted to fling her arms open and beckon him to join her in bed. She felt her face flush at the thoughts that were running through her mind. Dean, holding her in his arms. Dean without his jeans and flannel shirt. Dean, undoing the buttons of the funky blouse she was wearing. Her sister's blouse. *Gawd*, she was just wicked.

He was standing about two feet from the end of the bed, looking down on her like a wolf looks at a tasty free-range rabbit. No doubt about it, Dean was hungry for rabbit.

She bolted up like she had a spring behind her back and sat on the end of the bed, pointed at an angle from him. "Thanks," she said.

"I'm sorry about the kiss. It won't happen again." He was staring at her.

"I think that's for the best. We just met. We've got lots of work to do. You probably won't be thinking about kissing me after I yell at all your subcontractor friends and make them work like dogs."

"Are we square?" Dean extended his hand to her. She twisted over and met his grasp. His hand was warm, and that handshake was . . . very . . . seductive.

"We're square. Let's get back to work." Her voice didn't sound too convinced. It sounded like a sultry, sexy voice.

"Yes, ma'am." Dean saluted, smiled a very knowing smile, turned and left the room.

It was a good thing he left. She was in serious trouble here. She wrapped her arms around herself and tried to stop the sensations of lust from buzzing over her skin, over her breasts and . . . between her legs. Somebody should shut down her breaker box, because Dean Wakefield's touch just about blew her fuses.

With that thought, all the lights went out. Obviously Dean had heard her in his head. She stifled a giggle. Well, a man couldn't exactly work on the light fixtures without shutting off the power, now, could he?

After another half hour of painful self-analysis and pointless mind circles, Jillian gathered herself and got back downstairs to help paint the kitchen cupboards. But after a good hour, the scent of oil-based paint filled the room and made Jillian's head swim in circles.

"Whoa. I need air." She dropped her paintbrush into the tray and headed out to the front deck. A few deep breaths of salt-sea air would help stop the swirling effect.

Dean stuck his head out the open sliding glass door. "Okay?"

"I'm fine. Just dizzy." She dropped herself onto an aluminum chaise lounge with nylon strapping that was broken here and there. She had laid an old quilt over it earlier so it could be used without incident.

Jillian's butt poked through the bottom, but the quilt held enough so her butt didn't hit the deck.

"I'll grab you a glass of ice water and we'll take a break. It's been a long day." Dean went back in.

Time was getting away from her. Wednesday had just vanished, and here it was Thursday. Thursday! Where had the days gone? She felt her old panicky feeling start to creep into her thinking about the disaster area that was her sister's kitchen, living room and dining area. She closed her eyes and breathed slowly and deeply through her nose, the way the therapist at Serenity Spa had taught her.

Things weren't going very well. The tile setters hadn't shown up this morning, so she and Dean were giving the kitchen another coat of oil. The only blessing had been the weather. Sometimes June was just dreadful here. She'd seen it rain for the entire month. This week the sun had helped dry paint layers in short order, although working in the heat wasn't always easy.

Part of the *not easy* part was watching the sweat make Dean's T-shirt stick to him and show off all those muscles. She'd been having trouble concentrating. She'd mixed latex Flotrol into oil paint and ruined an entire gallon of Monroe Bisque watching Dean remove his T-shirt and walk through the sprinkler to cool off.

Jana Lee should have air-conditioning. But then again, it only got hot around here maybe two months out of the year. It seemed to her it was hotter in Seabridge now than when she was a kid.

Thursday. She had two more days before her Sunday flight. Before she'd be back to work at Pitman. She opened her eyes and looked out at the calm, lapping water. People were out in their sailboats enjoying the afternoon. Families.

She'd completely forgotten how to have fun. When was the last time she'd done *anything* fun? Jillian tried to remember. Well, she'd gone on vacation with Random Ron in January, but she'd mostly watched him gamble at the casino in the hotel they'd stayed at on Paradise Island. They'd quarreled; he'd been demanding and rude. She'd put up with him. What had she been thinking? The minute they'd gotten back he'd dumped her.

And she'd gone back to work with a vengeance to forget about her own stupidness with relationships.

She'd revamped the entire archival production database, she'd gone over the company's expense reports twice to try and add a few more items to the tax return in April. She'd worked Oliver to the snapping point as well.

Late hours, too much coffee and not enough

food—Oliver had warned her of the potential results if she kept up her unwise ways, and he'd put his foot down at skipping lunches. She'd let him go to lunch, but she'd worked through hers.

No wonder she'd gone over the edge. It hadn't been very far to drop.

Jillian tried to picture herself back at work, at her desk. She started to remember what was waiting for her; quarterly reports, possible recall of the Byker Chikz motorcycle with its defective muffler, the holiday trade shows in July and August.

She closed her eyes fast and tried to breathe it away, but a wave of panic hit her hard. Her heart started pounding. She gasped for air and clutched the arms of the lawn chair. Oh God, she hated these. Her mouth went dry, and her lungs burned. She'd left behind that medication the doctor in San Francisco had prescribed.

Her eyes flew open and met Dean's eyes. He was crouched down next to her chair. He set the water down and reached over to her. He placed his fingers gently on her forehead and rubbed softly between her brows. Then he used the palm of his hand to smooth her entire forehead, trailing his fingertips on her temples. He breathed deeply, and she found herself matching the rhythm of his breath.

In a few minutes she could feel her heart start to slow down. She felt the terrible grip of fear start to fade and heard only his breathing and the lapping of the waves against the rocky shore. It was a good sound. She realized he was holding her hand.

"Oh, Dean," she whispered.

"Shhhh." He laid his hand quietly over her eyes, and she closed them obediently. "You're going to rest for a while now." He got up from beside her, and she felt his absence sharply.

Jillian half-opened her eyes and watched him pick up a soft sofa throw pillow from the furniture they'd moved out here. He got her sweater off the deck bench, too. Dean came to her and helped slide the pillow under her head, then covered her bare arms with her sweater, like a blanket, tucking it around her. She sighed, and it came out ragged. A tear slid down one side of her face.

The sun dappled through the old red maple tree and danced across her, warming her bare legs. She let herself drift. She felt him beside her. Having a bad attack always wiped her out.

Dean sat beside her for another half an hour, watching to be sure she slept. He felt her pulse. It had slowed down. He also felt the grip she had on his one hand. She held two fingers of his hand as if she were afraid to let go.

He'd seen this before. Sometimes Trina would panic when she was facing a chemo treatment or before being put in an MRI tube for a scan.

But there was more than that. He'd felt it before. In the last few days, this woman had reminded him so much of himself from the old days, which didn't make any sense, really.

Those old days. Days when he'd been trapped in a self-made rat race pushing himself to build more houses, take on more remodels, make more money, work faster than a machine could operate. The pressure to produce, to be better than the contractor down the street, to push, push, push against those deadlines.

And what had it been for? To make more money? He'd pushed himself and everyone who had worked for him. He'd pushed so hard that he'd hit the top of the heap. His houses had been in magazines, his clients had become more elite, more demanding.

Part of him cringed, remembering his slick office and top team and how he'd become the driver of other people's lives. It was Trina who had changed all that for him. When he'd hired her for his office staff, she'd been just like him.

But through her illness she had shown him the meaninglessness of it all. He had never regretted for one day closing up Wakefield Construction, buying his property and taking care of Trina for the short years she had left. She had given him a belief in a different kind of life; a deeply creative, simple life.

When Jillian's grasp relaxed around his fingers, Dean slipped his hand away and picked up the glass of tea he'd brought outside. He sat there for a while, watching her. He wondered what it was that had triggered her attack. What had they been talking about before she'd come outside?

Dean rose quietly and went inside the house. He walked through the downstairs and looked around for a thin blanket or some kind of throw to put over her legs. He walked upstairs and looked in the linen closet but only found sheets and towels.

Her bedroom was freshly painted, and they'd packed up almost everything in boxes, but the bed was still intact, with the pretty new bedding she'd insisted on trying out. He lifted up the plastic sheeting and pulled out a light woven blanket he'd seen there earlier.

As he folded the blanket he glanced down at a box of books and framed photos shoved against the bed, covered with plastic. He saw one of Mrs. S and her daughter Carly, and what must be a sister. He pulled the picture out from under the plastic and dusted it off with the edge of the blanket.

That sister was . . . *identical*. Dean sat down on a nearby plastic-covered chair and stared at the photograph.

She'd talked about a sister. In the picture he could hardly tell them apart, except one had long hair, and one had short. He remembered the long hair from the first time he'd been here. Long, Earth Mother hair in a big braid down her back.

Earth Mother.

Like the way the house had been when he'd gotten here. Macramé plant hangers and fake brick vinyl flooring and the scalloped edging across the cupboard tops, ugly brown leather sofa, all the stuff they'd torn out or thrown out, or were having slip-covered in beige canvas to go with the artistic blue-green blended paint she'd chosen for the downstairs.

In the picture the Golden Gate Bridge was in the background. San Francisco.

Little tiny things started to creep into his mind. Little slips of the tongue. Tiny nuances. Her odd unfamiliarity with the area she'd supposedly been living in for most of her life. Things that made her jump. Comments about art museums in San Francisco. Time constraints.

A smile crept across his lips. Mrs. S wasn't Mrs. S at all. She was her sister. Could that be true?

He kept the picture, repositioned the plastic sheeting, and went downstairs with the blanket. Outside on the deck she was still asleep, and her bare legs looked a bit goose bumped from the breeze off the water. He covered her with one layer of blanket, then sat across from her on the deck bench.

Who was she? Why had she come here? He wondered what her story was. It was like seeing a completely different book where you'd set down another just a few minutes earlier. Alice Hoffman where you'd put down Tony Hillerman. A trick. And most of all he wondered why she was playing her sister. What in the world would make this woman take her sister's place? He shook his head. She must have a good reason. Right? Things that had confused him and disturbed him now made perfect sense.

Other things made him slightly mad. That came in a wave of realization with many sharp edges. It hadn't been very decent of her to pass herself off as a widow, making him think they shared a common thread of grief. But he supposed she'd found herself knee-deep in it and hadn't known how to get out. He remembered how she didn't really talk about being a widow. So the deceased husband would be her brother-in-law? Could that really be?

It would be if he was right, because hey, he could be wrong.

He shook his head again and rubbed the back of his neck. He looked at the picture, then looked at her.

He quietly watched her, comparing her to the image in his hand. Such a slight difference in the two women.

She was beautiful, lying here curled on her side, her exposed shoulder and neck soft and inviting in the sunlight. Her lips were slightly parted and drove him to distraction. She had such luscious, full lips.

Every day he'd been there he'd watched her put expensive red lipstick on. He still knew what expensive looked like from the old days with Trina. She'd had plenty of money till the medical bills had taken it all.

One thing was for sure; mystery woman was living on the edge. Dancing with her own shadow. He saw clearly that the woman sleeping on the deck was not Mrs. Stivers, the mother of Carly. She was the other sister in the picture.

Dean felt himself smiling. What a handful she was. He went back in the house and returned the picture to its upstairs box.

As he descended the stairs Dean considered the project at hand. There was no way it would all be done by Sunday. A few of his subs had no-showed, and the delays would snowball. Some chipped tiles had to be replaced and were on order.

He could jump in and do quite a bit of the work, but he liked to put quality into his work. Rush jobs weren't for him.

It looked like Ms. Whomever could use a little anxiety relief, and that would require some creativity in this case. Dean knew he would just have to break it to her and rearrange the schedule. He'd always felt that honesty cut down on unrealistic expectations and helped relieve stress.

The sound of a car coming down the driveway on the other side of the house broke his train of thought. Probably the electrician.

But it wasn't the electrician; it was a pack of teenagers. They burst through the door, laughing.

"Hi, Dean, where's my . . . *mom?*" Carly asked.

He raised his eyebrow at her. "She's sleeping on the deck. She got a little burned out."

"No kidding," Carly said. Her friends giggled.

Dean sensed a girlfriend conspiracy. "Last day of school?"

"Yes, YAY!" Carly answered.

"Your room is looking pretty good. We got the color just right."

One of the girls squealed, "Let's *see*, Carly." And they all pounded up the stairs. Carly waved at Dean with an odd backward glance. Somehow he caught a hint of understanding pass between them. Or the hint of something . . . like *I know what you know and now we all know?*

Except he wasn't sure what they knew. Dean picked up the paintbrush his no-name friend had dropped and placed it into a jar of paint thinner, then covered that with plastic wrap to cut down on the fumes. He retrieved his own brush and went back to methodically painting the trim edges for the kitchen. It was a nice classic crown molding for the top edges of the cabinets.

If there was one thing he was good at these

days, it was knowing when something had to take a new direction. He wasn't one for drama, but he was extremely curious about the woman asleep on the deck, who had captured his attention in so many ways.

10

Babe and Switch

Jana Lee stripped off her sister's panty-hose and wiggled out of a perfectly outlandish pair of bikini underwear. How did Jillian wear this stuff every day? She dipped her big toe in the bath water and pulled it back quickly. Hot, but do-able. Next she slid her whole foot in, then out again. It was coated with foaming bath oil. She reached over and turned the fancy water faucets off.

She'd been dying to slide into this tub of Jillian's since she'd been there, but she'd only had time for quick showers so far. This time she climbed in and slowly let her feet get used to the hot water. She wasn't a woman who threw herself into either hot water or a freezing cold bay easily. Not like Jillian.

As Jana Lee lowered herself into the delight of the hot steamy tub of water she remembered her sister on the rope swing in front of their house. The tide would rise very high against the bulkhead, and they would swing out and drop into the water.

Jillian would go right for it, getting as high and wide as possible, dropping into the cold water, coming up laughing, beckoning Jana Lee to *come on!* But it would take her a bunch of toe-testing and timid tries before she'd finally make the swing and drop. And it always turned out to be such a blast!

Jana Lee leaned her body back into the water and put Jillian's blow-up bath pillow under her head. Being on high heels for two days had like . . . rearranged her spine or something. She ached in places she hadn't ached before.

Jana Lee pulled a washcloth down from the niche in the beautifully tiled tub surround. She dropped it into the water and wrung it out. She closed her eyes and carefully draped it over her face, letting the heat soak into her pores. Her hair was tied back with a ribbon. Guess that ribbon was going to get wet.

The delicate scent of jasmine bath oil drifted around her. The whole apartment was so serene. The lack of clutter made her feel like there was nothing to fuss about. The colors were beiges and blacks and tans, but for some reason it came off rather warm and inviting. Jillian had acquired a few Asian pieces—vases, chests, a beautiful painting of Japanese peonies. Not too much, just enough to add a real San Francisco flair to the place. Those, and the Oriental carpets with their subtle olive greens and burnt golds, made Jillian's apartment feel like a luxury hotel.

Jana Lee took off the washcloth and looked around her in the dimmed evening light. She had a few of Jillian's beautiful, huge candles lit, and the room was glowing with serenity. They gave off a slight cinnamon and orange scent.

A sigh slipped through her lips. She'd been so numb for so long. It was good to escape the memories. It seemed like no matter what she did to her house—which wasn't much—she couldn't escape the shadow of Bill in the place where they had spent so many years together.

Even the fact that she'd spent many childhood years there didn't seem to matter. Until she'd come here to San Francisco, she hadn't really realized how much the house kept her in a state of emotional paralysis.

She closed her eyes and drifted. She drifted through the new ideas she'd come up with for Pitman Toys. Even if they didn't use them, it had been totally exhilarating to let her creativity loose. She wanted more. She'd stayed at the office till seven-thirty. Oliver had been so kind to order dinner in for her as his last favor of the day. She'd kept drawing and designing while she'd eaten the great ginger beef Chinese . . . with a fork, still. She'd have to get the hang of chopsticks if she was going to stay here much longer.

Much longer. For the first time Jana Lee realized she wasn't worried about home. She liked it here. More than that, other than missing her daughter, *she really didn't want to go home!*

She closed her eyes and sank under the water, submerging up over her ears. Her breath was laced with jasmine and spicy orange and steam, and she let the old pain drift out of her as she breathed and relaxed and let the water work its magic. She felt alive. She was still alive.

The dull, incessant tone of a doorbell made Jana Lee slide her eyes open. It must be a neighbor's. She glanced at her wristwatch beside the tub and saw she'd been half-conscious in her hot water for at least forty minutes. She stretched. The doorbell rang again. Couldn't that neighbor hear it?

Oh *crap*, it was not a neighbor's doorbell. It was hers . . . Jillian's . . . the door to *this* apartment.

Quickly she pulled herself up out of the tub and grabbed a large towel to wrap around herself. She could have just ignored the bell, but it scared her. She wanted to be sure the dead bolt was thrown. She didn't like being vulnerable in the tub when some stranger was at the door.

Jillian had warned her not to forget this was not

Seabridge, where they left their doors open all the time. This was a big, scary city with nuts running around. Hey, there were plenty of nuts in Seabridge, too. She'd figured that out reading the local police blotter over the last ten years. Things weren't as genteel as they used to be.

Dripping her way across Jillian's bamboo floors, she made it to the large black-and-gold-lacquered front door. She snuck up on the peephole and glanced quickly to see who the idiot was ringing the doorbell this late in the evening.

She couldn't believe her eyes.

Jackson Hawks looked like a nervous schoolboy. He had flowers and what looked like a box of chocolates tucked under his arm. He was doing a little jig between punching the doorbell repeatedly.

Jana Lee turned back to the wall and put her hand over her mouth to keep the laugh from coming out too loud.

Then she got mad. What the hell right did Jackson Hawks have to show up unannounced at a girl's apartment? Who did he think he was?

The doorbell chimed again, rendering her practically deaf in one ear.

She turned to the door, twisted the top lock, and flung it open. "What the *hell* do you think you're doing here, Mr. Hawks? Did I miss something? Do we have a meeting scheduled? Did I invite you over?"

* * *

Ms. Tompkins was standing holding the door dressed only in a large towel. Her dark brown hair was tied back in a black velvet ribbon, and water streamed down from each tendril. Her skin was pink from what must have been the hot bath Jackson had pulled her out of. She looked delicious. He ached to touch those smooth, creamy shoulders and run his mouth down her . . . "I'm *very* sorry. I called, but there was no answer. I-I just had to see you."

"Did Pitman burn down? Did hell freeze over?" She crossed her arms and tapped her foot, which made a slapping noise in the water puddle she'd created.

"Yes, hell froze over." For him, that was almost true. It must have, because that was the only thing that could make him be such an idiot.

She smiled just a touch. His heart skipped a beat.

"You can have five minutes, because you are my *boss*." She took the candy out of his hands—somewhat awkwardly, considering the towel. "I'm going to put a robe on. Make yourself useful and mop up this mess I made before it ruins the floors."

"Kitchen through there?" He took one step inside and pointed to a logical direction.

"Yup." She slammed the door behind him and stalked off. The towel dipped down in back like a low-cut dress. He could see the curve of her rear end taunting him.

Jackson marched himself into the kitchen and

laid down the flowers. He was in. The sleek black granite countertops were practically bare, but he found a kitchen towel neatly folded next to the sink.

The next thing he knew he was down on his hands and knees in his best Caraceni suit, blotting water spots off the bamboo slat floors. Nice floors. He'd always wondered what an installation of bamboo would look like. He had dark cherry hardwood at his place. It went better with that old traditional Frisco Victorian row house, the kind he'd inherited from his family when he'd been given the Bayview house.

Boy, he must like this woman a whole lot.

Jana Lee peeked around the corner to see the handsome Jackson on his hands and knees blotting water off her sister's floor. She smiled to herself and zipped up the fleece sweatshirt she'd dug out of Jillian's drawers. They were a little snug, but sweatpants, a warm-up jacket and a T-shirt didn't send the wrong message, and that's what she wanted.

Even so, she had to be a little nicer to the vice president than asking him if hell had frozen over. She walked over and stood above him, trying not to laugh.

"Thank you, Mr. Hawks. Can I fix you a cup of coffee to go with these chocolates?"

He got off the floor and handed her the damp kitchen towel. "That would be nice. Can you put a shot of bourbon in it?"

"Are you driving?" She headed for the kitchen. He followed her.

"No. I took a cab. I don't drive in the city much. Parking is nuts."

"Do you think it's right for you to show up unannounced at a female employee's house at night?"

Jackson leaned up against the counter and crossed his arms. "Technically, you are my equal at work. You're the CFO of the most important department. I'm only the vice president. That's like CEO of nothing, you know. Vice presidents are dinosaurs. No one really needs them."

"Oh, please. You're one away from being the head of the company. Was there a financial report you wanted to discuss and thought it might go better with flowers and chocolates on the side?" Jana Lee was opening cupboards trying to find a vase and coffee filters for Jillian's coffeemaker, thinking how *she* was CEO of nothing in real life. She located all of the items and remembered the coffee was kept in the fridge.

Jackson threw his hands in the air. "I confess; this isn't business related. Well, not completely. I've been thinking about what you said in regards to the retro toy concept. I've been thinking about it so much I can't think about anything else lately. It brought up a whole lot of memories and . . . things, looking at that book."

"Really?" Why he'd had to come over here in

the evening to discuss this eluded her, but the fact that he liked her idea was exciting. Jana Lee poured water into the vase and plopped in the extremely beautiful flowers—day lilies, orchids and all sorts of stuff she couldn't identify. Then she filled the coffeemaker and flipped the On switch. Jillian had a very pretty art deco bar in the living room, and Jana Lee was sure there'd be something drinkable to be had in there. Her sister had good taste in most things.

"Really. Then I thought if I had that kind of reaction, maybe other people would too—parents who are my age, parents with little kids."

"Right, that's what I was thinking."

"I guess you and I missed out on the kid thing so far."

Jana Lee didn't answer that one. "I think there's whiskey in the bar. I'll take you up on the Irish coffee. Maybe there's whipped cream around here somewhere."

That must have given Jackson all kinds of ideas, because he followed her to the living room and watched her open the mirrored bar. "Is this okay?" She held up a bottle of Jack Daniel's.

"Tennessee, not Ireland, but it will do nicely. A bit of sugar, and we'll scour your fridge for whipped cream."

"I will," she said. She'd glanced in Jillian's fridge once when she'd first gotten here and found a really strange assortment of nothing in there. Jillian must eat almost all her meals out. She'd have to talk to her about that. No wonder she'd had an *episode*. Her diet probably stunk.

Of course she wasn't one to talk—she'd been living out of the freezer section of Central Market for a few years now. Anyhow, she didn't think Jillian would appreciate Jackson looking through her bare fridge and cupboard.

When the coffees were made and squirted with whipped cream from an aerosol can that amazingly hadn't gone sour, Jackson carried them and the chocolates out to the living room. He perched on an odd orange modern sofa directly across from her, feeling somewhat uncomfortable but very interested in what she was saying. It was an unusual moment in his life for some reason.

"Anyway," she went on, "I think the whole thing will work with the right marketing. If kids get that magic combination of educational and fun, we'll be doing a good thing at the same time. Like Lincoln logs, you know? The moon-landing toy teaches about history. The dress-up box will have more career possibilities than just being a princess, because as we know, we're not all Grace Kelly."

"Which reminds me, weren't you on some kids' show when you were young?" Jackson asked.

"Yes, *Harvey the Big Blue Dragon*," she answered.

"You and your sister," Jackson added. She

looked really uncomfortable. Maybe she didn't
like to be reminded.

"Yup. Ancient history."

"But it has possibilities, all that medieval stuff,
and that was a popular show at the time. Knights,
princesses, that's history too. Somewhat glamor-
ized history, but still history."

"We could have a little sword-wielding cru-
sader out to crush the Huns," she said dryly.

"Oh, you *do* have a sense of humor under that
sweat suit." Jackson stirred his coffee and took a
big slurp. "You know, Jillian, I never noticed this
creative streak of yours. As a matter of fact, there
are a whole lot of things I never noticed about you."

"And there I was, right under your nose." She
poked around in the open Ghirardelli chocolates,
picked one, and nibbled on it. Jackson watched
her with interest.

"You seem different than before. I mean, I heard
about your little—"

"Crackup? It was minor. I just needed a rest."
She looked away.

From what he'd heard it had been anything but
minor, but he could see he had embarrassed her.
He better segue out of this subject. "Obviously
the R&R did you good. Work can eat you up if
you let it."

"How do you keep from letting that happen
yourself, Jackson?"

"I'm fairly self-indulgent. I get a massage once a

week, I dine out with beautiful women, even on Mondays, and I have an odd group of friends that keep me from getting too serious. They drag me to basketball games and make sure I don't get too full of myself." Jackson didn't mention that in his crowd he was the last remaining single man. Even Scott and Scott had paired up and were domestically content, writing gay romance novels together.

"Sounds like you're doing well."

She seemed to be dancing around getting too personal, and she sure didn't want to talk about herself. This evening wasn't going the way he'd thought it might. She'd been sipping her Irish coffee, keeping to polite conversation. There wasn't much of an in for him to get closer. He finished his coffee and stood up.

"Well, I guess I should let you get back to whatever you were doing. Work tomorrow, and all that. If we're going to add any of the products we've talked about, it will take some real magic to get them into production." He headed for the kitchen to put his cup in the sink. She followed him.

"I'm glad you like the ideas. I'm sorry I snapped at you. I should learn to be more spontaneous, I guess. And thank you for the beautiful flowers and chocolates."

"I should have called."

"You did, remember? I just didn't hear the phone."

"Would you like to have dinner with me Friday?" he asked, going for a traditional approach.

"I think that would be fine," she answered.

Well, that was progress; she didn't slap him or spit in his eye. "Maybe a movie or something?"

"Maybe."

Don't press your luck, buddy. He headed for the front door. "Goodnight then, I'll see you tomorrow."

"I'll be there." She walked him to the door and opened it for him.

He stepped into the hallway and nodded one last time as the door closed in his face. He heard the locks click from the inside.

Jackson stuck his hands in his pockets and guitar-walked himself down the hall to the elevator to the imaginary rhythm of *American Idiot*, his favorite Green Day album.

He had a date with the reserved Ms. Tompkins. Boy, would he like to see what she was like loosened up. Maybe he'd take her dancing. Somewhere sort of Starlight Room-ish where the music was slow and you held each other close. Maybe a little body heat would warm up the cool and controlled Ms. Tompkins.

He was sure about one thing; she had been known to go a little crazy.

He whistled his way down the street and let himself feel . . . hopeful.

* * *

Jana Lee stuffed a pillow over her face and screamed. Why had she agreed to go to dinner with him? She was so confused. Impersonating your sister was so confusing. *Jillian* had a crush on this guy. This was just crazy.

For once in her life Jana Lee understood why Jillian had allowed Elliot to seduce her. He had been an extremely charming man. Jana Lee had always suspected that in the back of his mind he'd been fantasizing about having sex with both sisters at once.

She shuddered.

And Elliot: He'd just known what to say to make a girl fall in love with him—if she was twenty and ready to fall in love.

But the whole deal where your brain just departs for parts below, *that* she was starting to understand.

She and Jillian had been so close most of their lives that she hadn't been very good at making new friends. Jillian had taken up that space where a best friend usually goes. Jillian was who she'd learned to share with. No one knew her like Jillian did. They were made of the same stuff—literally. The years they had lost because of the Elliot incident were just tragic. She could never let that happen again.

She rolled over on Jillian's serene, pale olive green and deep gold duvet cover and stared at the ceiling. She had to honor her sister's interest in Jackson.

She stripped off all her clothes and threw them on the floor. Then she slid her naked, bathed, scented body in between the silky, expensive sheets of Jillian's bed. The whiskey had spun a warm cocoon around her.

She smoothed her hands over her body. She ached to be held again; to be made love to. She'd wanted to let Jackson have his way with her tonight, but she just hadn't been sure how, or if she should, because she would be hurting her sister's feelings. Just like Jillian had done to her. Was she that much like Jillian?

All the while they'd been talking about toys and memories and his friends she'd been watching his mouth, his hands, and the way his body moved when he walked. He was so tall, so lean and muscular. She could just imagine him taking her in his arms. She could just taste him, taste his kiss, and feel the pleasure he would give her. The more she'd had to drink, the less she'd been able to focus on his conversation.

She only had a few more days here.

She looked over at the flowers he'd brought her and breathed in their scent.

What the hell was she going to do now?

11

Swap and Go

The sound of a pounding hammer worked into Jillian's deep, dreamless sleep until she stirred to a slightly more conscious level. Then the buzz of a power saw, the rustle of plastic sheets and the giggling of girls seeped in. She pulled her sweater over her head. How long had she been asleep? The old quilt and squishy pillow had formed a warm pocket beneath her. She breathed in the comfort and slowly opened her eyes. Sun filtered through the fabric of the sweater, tinting everything blue.

Her legs felt heavy and somewhat cramped from being in one position so long. She wiggled her toes and made them come alive, stretching and squirming like an inchworm.

She thought about coffee, then remembered she drank too much coffee. They'd told her at Serenity Spa that cutting back on caffeine would help her attacks.

The memory of her panic attack rolled over her quickly, like the realization you've just backed into someone else's car in the parking lot. Oh God, Dean had just watched that, hadn't he? She curled back up in a ball and wished that away. She wished she could stay here on this lumpy, warm, makeshift bed forever.

Her mouth was dry, which was typical of her post-nutcase symptoms. Once she started thinking about how dry her mouth was, getting water became a more pressing need than staying curled in a ball and hiding from everyone.

Jillian sighed and gathered herself. She pulled on Jana Lee's comfy old sweater to ward off her chill. The sun was still above the mountains, orange and patient, but she felt shaky and cold.

Easing herself into a standing position, she pushed her feet into her slip-on Keds, which Dean must have slipped off. They were spackled with paint splatters: lavender blue from Carly's room, pale cottage yellow from Jana Lee's room, and the robin's egg Wyeth Blue from the kitchen and living room. Her sneakers had turned into art.

Shuffling through the open sliding glass door she surveyed what had become of her sister's kitchen. Her mother's kitchen. The family kitchen. She wondered what Mom would say about it.

Suddenly Jillian missed her mother and the way she used to smooth down her hair and tickle her under the chin to make her less cranky. It was strange to think of her now and how Mom had slowly evolved from this hippie existence, living on the beach in Seabridge, to being a stylish Scottsdale woman surrounded with Southwestern art.

Why Mom and Dad had had to go live in Arizona beat her. They'd dumped this house on Jana Lee and Bill, ranted about rain and dampness, and split to their Scottsdale stucco condo. Dad did have allergies, and Jillian guessed that was about as good an excuse as any, but they hardly saw them except on the holidays. They'd sure looked all tan and Southwest at Christmas. Her mother had looked slim and pretty in her designer clothes, and her dad had looked very . . . golfy.

Sometimes Jillian felt like she'd only had her sister to talk to while they were growing up. Her parents had been so busy with their own lives. Dad had been such a workaholic. Mom too, for many years, with her broadcasting job. Why they hadn't just settled in Seattle instead of out here in the sticks, she'd never understood. They had always said something about giving their girls a better childhood and how much they loved the water.

Well, if they'd asked her at the time, she'd rather have lived in the city and had them commute less.

But now was a different story. She did see how her parents had fallen in love with this little cottage next to the beach, with the vast Cascade mountain range framing the bay. There was such peace here. And really, she and Jana Lee had had a great childhood, playing on the beach, walking down into the village to the old drugstore for root beer floats, all those special memories.

She'd never forget the night they'd discovered that their rope swing could catapult them out past the deck into the water on a good high tide. After that it had been their favorite summer game. Well, it had been hers right off the bat, and Jana Lee had finally gotten brave enough to try it, then it was tops for both of them. Had Carly ever tried it? she wondered.

Dean came out of the old storage room lugging a huge orange extension cord. He looked at her and smiled an odd smile.

"Damned electrical outlets are few and far between in this little gem," he mumbled.

"Thirsty," she rasped.

"Oh, sorry, I took your drink. There's a pitcher of iced tea in the fridge, too," Dean said.

"Water," she said. She'd lost herself in thought, standing in the doorway. Her brain was still fuzzy. She walked carefully over the rubble, grabbed a glass out of a packing box, and poured herself water from the tap.

"Careful, it's an obstacle course in here."

"So I see."

"We need to have a meeting about the project."

"I see that, too." She chugged her drink and didn't stop until she felt results.

Dean moved slowly in her direction and was now close and intimate beside her. He'd approached her like a skittish cat. She wasn't sure how she felt about that.

"Sometimes when it's all laid out on paper, it helps decrease the stress. Facing facts is always good."

"Or standing on them." She looked down at the chipped fake brick vinyl and glanced at the pile of plywood underlayment stacked in the living room, which Dean was having installed over the old kitchen floor. That, and the boxes of bisque-colored tiles to be installed once the floor was prepped. It was all about timing.

"Yup. Are you up for a meeting?" he asked.

"You've already seen me freak out; I don't picture anything worse than that occurring."

He reached over to her and touched her cheek. "It's okay. I've seen worse."

She actually put her hand over his on her cheek. It felt so good.

Her cell phone rang to the tune of the *1812 Overture*.

Where the hell was that phone? She looked frantically around. Dean started looking too. He followed the sound and found her purse on top of the refrigerator. Jillian grabbed it from him and dumped the contents on the floor, located the phone and flipped it open. The caller ID said Pitman Toys. It made her stomach twist.

"Hello?"

"Jillian?"

"Hi, sis." Jillian glanced up at Dean, who stood there smiling, not moving. Apparently he was going to eavesdrop on her entire conversation.

Jana Lee's voice sounded different on the phone today. "Hi, Jilly, how's my daughter?"

"She's fine. I've given her a project, and that's keeping her out of trouble," Jillian answered. This was really hard with Dean next to her. She walked back toward the open sliding door to the deck and her cozy deck-bed. "It involves doing her own laundry," she continued.

"Ah, a lost art," Jana Lee laughed.

"How's Pit Bull Toys?"

"I'm actually having a great time. I had no idea how fun working at a toy company could be."

"Are we talking about the same toy company I just deserted? Tar Pit Toys? You are in the right building, aren't you?" Jillian sat down on the rickety lawn chair. It felt as unstable as she did.

"Yes, you goose, I am in your shiny clean office. Although it's not as shiny clean as when I got here.

I'm not doing your boring job though, I've been messing around with other things and leaving the hard work to Ollie."

"Well, your house isn't exactly as clean as you left it either." *What an understatement,* Jillian thought.

That part about Oliver made her feel slightly better. He knew exactly what to do with the details of Jillian's job. But Jana Lee messing around didn't sound good. "Messing around as in what?" she asked sharply.

"Never mind, it's no big deal. But I have a little proposition for you. How would you like to stay another week? I'm having too much fun."

Jillian couldn't believe her ears. After her little episode earlier, it sounded like a miracle. She obviously needed more rest time than she thought. Not to mention the fact that it gave her the extra time to tackle the house repairs. She wasn't even going to think about all the side issues. "Yes," she blurted out before her mind started picking apart the details.

"That was quick. Are you doing okay?" Jana Lee sounded surprised.

"Not really. I could definitely use the extra time. I seem to be a little more fried than I thought. I will have to talk to Oliver and see if he feels okay about it. Maybe a bonus would help," Jillian said.

"He definitely deserves a bonus," Jana Lee said. "And I'll need to talk to Carly. Have her call later and I'll see how she's doing. Can we agree she's got a ten o'clock curfew for these summer nights?" Jana Lee said.

"No problem. I really do have her on a project, so most of the time she's around here. I met the crazy girlfriends, and I think I can handle it. No boys so far."

"Speaking of boys, how's the repair guy?" Jana Lee asked.

Jillian didn't know what to say. All of a sudden she was very confused about her whole involvement with Dean. "He's . . . handy. How's Jackson?"

"Warming up to you." Jana Lee snickered.

"W-weird. I-I'm not sure what to say," Jillian stuttered. Handy? Dean was handy? Jackson was warming up to which one of them? She put her hand to her forehead.

"Me neither, so let's not. I've got to run. I have a drawing to finish," Jana Lee said.

A *drawing?* Jillian didn't even want to know. The less she heard about what was happening at Pitman Toys, the better she felt.

"I . . . love you, sis." Jillian stumbled over her words.

"I love you too, Jillian. Have Carly call soon."

They ended their conversation, and Jillian wondered how long it had been since she'd told Jana Lee she loved her.

She leaned back and closed her eyes. Another week. That would be heaven.

The breeze off the bay ruffled her hair against her neck. A long, slow breath gave her the scents of the garden and the beach mingled together. This place was very peaceful. She needed peaceful.

Dean couldn't stop smiling to himself. He shook his head in disbelief. The strange deception on the part of Carly's aunt whozzits was really a puzzle. He also wished he knew her real name.

He balanced the newly painted trim pieces on the sawhorses he'd set up in the living room area. They'd dry quickly with the sun streaming through the house. He couldn't really do anything more with the kitchen until those were done. Time for that meeting. Maybe it would go down better with food.

He cleaned off his hands with a rag, then went to the utility room to use the sink in there for a scrub with Goof Off paint remover. He stripped off his T-shirt and washed up to his elbows.

The window was open, and he saw her stretched out on the chaise lounge again. The evening sun had moved slightly under the tree, and she looked like she was soaking up the heat. That was probably good therapy.

When he finished he went to his duffle bag, took out a clean white T-shirt and pulled it over his head. Then he looked up and saw her standing in the doorway, framed with light, staring at him. She'd gotten up from her warm spot.

"Hey, Mrs. S, are you game for a pizza? I'm buying."

"I'm game. The girls would no doubt be game too. I'll chip in and we'll get a couple of them."

"Are you a ham and pineapple girl?"

"Akk, no fruit on the masterpiece. Meat. Lots of meat: pepperoni, sausage, Canadian bacon, whatever. Maybe some cheese, too," she smiled.

"Okay, meat it is. And what does your *daughter* like?" He phrased it that way just to see the little tweak of her mouth, and he wasn't disappointed. It tweaked.

"She's the veggie girl. Pile them on. On second thought, I'm not sure about her friends. Maybe you should ask. Or I will."

Before she had a chance, he bounded toward the stairs. "You look up Central Market Pizza, I'll take orders," he called over his shoulder.

Jillian snapped her fingers and flinched at his preemptive pizza strike as he ran up those stairs before she got a chance. Let's hope Carly really did like veggies.

She hated this whole deception. Maybe she should give it up and tell Dean the truth. He sure deserved it. She liked Dean. She liked him a whole lot. If she'd met him at a different time in her life, she might have gone for him.

But here she was, impersonating her sister, teetering on a crack-up, and only in town for another week, if it was okay with Carly, which she was sure it would be.

She'd really boxed herself into a corner where Dean was concerned. Maybe she could still salvage him for her sister to start up with when she got back.

How strange would that be? Impersonating her sister on a one-night date was one thing. But a full two weeks would leave her and Dean with some background. She'd have to try and keep track of it to tell her sister about. Jillian started to get a headache again, trying to sort it all out. But one thing she knew: She felt happy. That was weird. She was happy that she'd have an extra week here at the house, and . . . with Dean.

She heard girl giggles from upstairs. Probably Carly blowing her cover.

"So let me get this straight. You, Carly, hate all vegetables on pizza and love pepperoni. You, Ashley, hate mushrooms and are fine with pepperoni, Brianna and Emily hate everything and only want cheese? Did I get that right?" Dean crossed his arms and watched the three girls sitting cross-legged on the bed, devoid of its plastic covering.

"Yup, that covers it," Carly answered.

"Okay, half pepperoni, half cheese, coming up. I assume any soda will do?"

"Pretty much." Brianna and Ashley did simulcast answers.

Funny how they all said the same phrases. Dean smiled. This visit to the land of teenagers had been very enlightening.

"So, Dean, what's next for my room?" Carly asked.

"I think it all falls under the realm of decorating at this point. The paint is dry, the molding's replaced. It's in your *mom's* hands now."

They all fell apart laughing. Carly kicked Brianna in the foot and made a face.

"Thanks, Dean, we'll fold up the plastic stuff. Yell when it's pizza time, okay?"

"I can hang that curtain rod for you after I order the pizza."

"Okay, thanks." Carly got up off the bed. "Come on, you promised to help, you bums." She pulled Emily's leg toward the side of the bed. The two buddies continued to squeal.

Dean figured he'd learned enough. He gave Carly a little salute and walked out of the room, closing the door behind him. But he paused for a minute.

"You bozos, I told you to play it cool. Have you *no* self-control?" Carly's voice carried through the door.

"Absolutely none," one of the girls replied, then all he heard was more teenage hysterics, so he headed back down the stairs.

His lady in paint-spattered tenny runners abruptly finished her second phone call. As soon as he came into view, she snapped her cell shut quickly.

"Find that phone number?" he asked.

"Yes, here." She handed him a sticky note with the phone number on it. Her handwriting was very neat: *Central Market Pizza*, then the phone number.

"Thanks." He went to the old-style harvest gold wall phone and rang up the order desk. "Yes, two large, one meat-lover's special, one half pepperoni and half cheese." He glanced Jillian's way and saw her sigh. She headed back out to the water-side deck.

Dean finished his call and started to clean up. As he stacked paint equipment next to the big laundry sink in the utility room he looked up and found an old plastic tablecloth on an upper shelf. He'd make a nice picnic outside for the girls and . . . let's see, what should he call her? Aunt somebody. She'd be the aunt. This should be interesting.

He went outside with the tablecloth and proceeded to cover up the old wooden picnic table with the two attached side benches. "We'll dine alfresco. Is beer okay?"

"We probably shouldn't in front of a bunch of impressionable teenagers. Let's drink soda, and later we'll have one." She shielded her eyes and looked at him from her reclining position. "Thanks for doing this. I'm not much of a cook."

He kept any comments he had to himself. He'd noticed a clear absence of dinner magic happening this week, but during a remodel, things were like that, so he'd figured he wasn't one to judge. Although he remembered that when it had come time to make chicken nuggets during the little kids' last hour, she'd had a momentary pause over how the oven worked. Strange little things were beginning to make sense, now.

"Soda it is. Now you promised we'd have a straight-up talk about the house. Can you handle it?"

"I think I can shorten that talk up. Let's add another week and see what we can get done. I'm not expecting miracles anymore."

Dean was surprised. And after all that crazy time-crunch talk she'd done? "Change of plans?"

"Yes, thank God. We'll sit down tomorrow morning with a cup of coffee and revamp our to-do list, okay?"

"I'm going to hang a curtain rod in Carly's room. It will only take me a few minutes. Just relax."

"Thanks, Dean, I appreciate that."

He watched her lean back on the lounger and close her eyes again. If it weren't for the fact that there were people in the house, he would lean over and kiss her right now, just to see what Sleeping Beauty might do.

There was a purely male animal part of him that

was imagining having her at this moment. He was glad to feel that that part of him was still alive and well.

The pizza tasted so good that she actually relaxed. Obviously she needed to eat more. The whole picnic pizza dinner thing had been a great idea, and she was surprised how well Dean handled teenagers. Which just went to show how much of a favor she'd be doing her sister by leaving Dean ready to date.

She was exhausted from trying to keep her lies straight and feeling extra guilty the nicer Dean got. It was a great relief when the girls decided to walk down to the Alamo Theater for a movie. At least she didn't have to pretend to be Carly's mom for the rest of the evening.

She and Dean couldn't seem to tear themselves away from each other. They'd talked about art for at least an hour. They'd talked about his former girlfriend, which was very sad.

Jillian had skillfully avoided her own life story or even her sister Jana Lee's and instead talked about her thoughts regarding the house. They'd drawn up lists on yellow legal pads, and he'd sketched out a few ideas. He was good at that.

She found it very interesting that Dean seemed to have an uncanny ability to understand what she was getting at in regards to concepts and thoughts.

Except when she'd decided to strip the popcorn off the upstairs bedroom ceilings and he'd yelled at her and said she should have decided that first, not after they painted, and it was an ugly job, but *could* be done. And *would* look better. She'd laughed as he'd come around to agreeing with her.

They were still nibbling on the leftover pizza slices and talking when the girls came home. The teenagers went straight for Carly's room, where they were all spending the night. Jillian wasn't sure how they'd manage to make room for themselves, but fifteen-year-olds were resourceful.

"You've got pizza sauce on your chin." Dean reached over and wiped her face with a paper napkin, which made her jump with surprise. "I didn't mean to scare you. You're kind of high-strung, aren't you?" He took another bite of pizza and raised an eyebrow at her simultaneously.

"Thank you for that brilliant analysis, Dr. Freud. What are you now, a repair guy-slash-contractor-slash-sculptor-slash-shrink?" she snapped.

"Sorry, I guess that wasn't the best thing to say in light of your rough afternoon," he said.

"I'll say," she replied. Gosh, did she need to be so horrid? Her sister sure wouldn't be. "I'm sorry, Dean. I'm stressed out about everything."

"Remodels are stressful. Don't sweat it. I'm a big boy. I can take it."

"Thanks for the pizza party. It was the highlight

of the week." She stopped talking and took a big swig of her beer.

Beer and pizza. Here she was straight from the apple martinis, seared scallops with lemongrass, watercress salad set, and something about this stuff tasted and felt *so* much better than any of that precious food she ate in San Francisco.

It reminded her of her mom's dash-and-serve cooking. Jillian smiled thinking of how hard her mom had tried to get it together for dinner. Her dad had actually been the better cook.

They'd really had some good times here. She looked out over the deck at the dark blue water that gently washed against the bulkhead below the house. The moon was almost full and reflected in a swath of light that seemed to lead right to this house. It also highlighted the worn-out paint and the rotting deck railing.

"Geez, this deck has seen better days," she said.

"I noticed. Most of the time a good sanding and refinish will do the job, but I'm worried about the pilings. I'm going to check them tomorrow."

"I see I've taken on more than I expected. A face-lift might have been a little premature when some of the more basic things need repair."

"Yes and no. If the structure is sound, the finish work is all you need."

"If the structure is sound," she echoed.

"Gotta have a good foundation."

"And a good roof. Is the roof okay?"

"The roof is good. Can't be more than ten years old."

She drifted off again, lost in her thoughts, he assumed. Dean swigged his beer and wondered what made her tick. He'd like to unravel that old blue sweater and find out what *her* foundation was like. But she seemed to be coming to grips with some basic facts tonight, and the timing was just off. That, and an upstairs full of teenage girls made his possibilities impossible.

"Why don't you go to bed? Things always seem better in the morning. I'll clean up down here."

"Would you mind? I feel bad."

"Not at all. You've hit the wall. You worked hard today. You're a great little stripper."

"Ha-ha, I guess I'm sandpapered out. I think my fingerprints have been sanded off."

"Take a nice shower. I'll stay and work if it's okay with you."

"Okay. You're not going to do a Norman Bates thing while I'm in the shower, are you?"

"Hacking you to pieces is the last thing on my mind in regards to you in the shower. It would be a waste of hot water."

She smiled. "You're funny." She moved slowly, and he saw how tired she really was.

"Goodnight," he called to her. He watched her go back in the house. His Mystery Date.

12
Sibling Rivalry

Jackson's head was two inches away from hers as they leaned over the light board in his office and studied the animated illustration media that advertising had sent down. She could smell the subtle scent of his cologne and how it mingled with the heat from his skin. She breathed him in.

He was intoxicating: his dark hair, his striking brown eyes, and his angular good looks. He had his shirtsleeves rolled up, and his muscular arms were outlined against the finely pressed cotton. No wonder Jillian had a crush on him.

He pointed to the drawing of a dragon. Harvey the Big Blue Dragon, to be exact. "He looks mean," Jackson said.

"He was mean, actually." Jana Lee gave Jackson a quirky smile. She felt a little embarrassed for lusting after him instead of focusing on the project.

"We'll have to happy him up. Your drawing was better. Can you find that sketch you did and we'll give the design department something to compare?"

"I'll take it down there." She'd actually love to see what the design department was like. Jana Lee wondered why she hadn't wandered down there already, but she'd been busy.

"Olga can do that," Jackson said.

"No, no, I'd like to see what they're working on." As if she even knew where they were. She'd have to consult her company map.

"Sure." He straightened up and looked at her. "We're moving ahead on this one, you know. I like it."

"You mean after you do a comparison of all the production numbers and time elements compared with the other two ideas?" Wow, she sounded official.

"Just the comment I'd expect from you, Ms. Tompkins, and I read those reports already, I promise."

She glanced up quickly and hoped Jackson didn't notice her lack of knowledge. She realized Oliver had done all Jillian's work and covered for her like a champ. Ollie was amazing.

"By the way, it's Friday, you know."

"It's been a long week, hasn't it?" She smiled slyly, knowing he was fishing for her to acknowledge their dinner date.

He rolled his eyes and slumped against the desk dramatically, hand against his heart. "You have no mercy, do you."

"Just a little. Where are we going?"

"Somewhere special. How does Top of the Mark sound?"

"Like I should change my clothes?" Jana Lee looked down at the black casual clothes she'd found in the back of her sister's closet. Plain Jane.

"You look great now, but if you want to go home first and throw on some pearls, I'd be happy to pick you up there."

"Since you know the way."

"Yes, I do, don't I?" he smiled.

"That would be great. I'm going back to my office to hunt up that sketch." She unhooked the drawing off the light board and rolled it carefully into a tube. "I'll see you about what time?"

"Six-thirty?"

"Seven?" she suggested. She felt the need for more prep. Or just more delay. Or something.

"That's fine. Our reservations are for seven-thirty."

"This time I'll be expecting you."

"Does that mean you'll have on more than a wet towel?"

She didn't answer that, just moved out of his grasp. On her way out she glanced behind her to see him watching her every move. Funny guy.

Jackson waited till the door clicked closed and tried to find something to smack himself in the brain with to stop the streaming video of his upcoming date with Jillian. He was going crazy. He settled for his own hands and decided to hold his head in a viselike grip until his thoughts of Ms. Tompkins became more orderly and less carnal.

It didn't work. She was completely naked in his mind. Actually she still had on a pair of pink bikini underwear—and pink high heels.

He'd hardly been able to keep himself from going in for a kiss a few moments ago. She was so round and luscious. Her lips were a soft rose and her eyes were so sexy blue. And he liked the way she thought. It was all rambly and disorderly, and ideas came tumbling out of her like clowns out of a VW bug.

Which really made no sense at all, when he thought about it. She was the numbers lady. Her reports were always impeccable. Sometimes she flipped back to being that, and other times she was just the most out-there girl he'd ever met.

She confused him and delighted him, and he didn't know his ass from his elbow anymore.

He only knew that he needed her. When she

was in the room, he felt alive. He liked that feeling. He worried about that feeling. He was a lovesick idiot.

The design department made her stop and stare like a kid. There was chaos and color and walls filled with illustrations and photographs of Pitman's various toys.

Pencils and markers, and oh, my, she resumed breathing and slowly took in as much as she could. Light boards held transparencies being sketched in pencil. Storyboards showed frames of television commercials, a few of which she recognized from last holiday season. There were parts of toys and strange creations in every corner and on every shelf.

What a wonderful job these people had. She'd taken an art major in college. How she wished she had finished. As it stood now, she had no training. She gulped back a lump of emotion.

Better get out of here. She had no idea who to hand this to, but Jana Lee figured that Jillian probably didn't get down this way too often. There was a path worn in the floor between her office and accounts receivable as far as she could tell.

"Hi, is that for the Little Princess preliminaries?"

A striking, very petite girl in black capris and a paint-stained T-shirt came up beside her and took the drawing out of her hand. "Very, very nice, you're good. Aren't you from accounting or something? Where have they been hiding you?"

In a cave, Jana Lee thought to herself. "Jackson—Mr. Hawks—wanted me to bring this to you. Something about the dragon looking too mean?"

"I getcha. Did I hear right about you and your sister being the little princesses on the original show in the seventies? The copyright people told me when they purchased the franchise rights your names were in the legal forms. And Pam over there says her kids used to watch the show. I'm Petra, by the way, nice to meet you."

"Nice to meet you, too." Jana Lee stuck out her free hand and shook Petra's. "It's true, we were the princess twins, but as you can see, we didn't make any shrewd business deals in that respect."

"That's not what I heard from legal. I heard you need to sign a release form and if we go ahead with the dolls, you'll be paid royalties."

Jana Lee stared at her blankly. Could Uncle Cyril have done something right for a change? Her mom would always say that using her mother's brother for their attorney had saved them lots of money and that's all they'd thought about at the time. Then Mom would make the *tsk-tsk* sound. Bad investments, along with Uncle Cyril's taste in plaid golf pants, expensive women and yellow Cadillacs, had pretty much emptied the pot of their princess money before her parents had known what had hit them.

They'd managed to buy the house in Washington, which had served at least Jana Lee well, as she and Bill had had a place to set up house when he'd just been starting out as a Boeing engineer. It had been a commute, but free rent had been a big break and had made up the cost of traveling.

"Anyhow, you'll have to check with legal about all that stuff, but look at these sketches. They were taken from publicity photos of you and your sister. We sort of jumped the gun on these, but legal always takes too long and we figured what the hell, we'll get started." Petra took Jana Lee's arm and led her over to a section of the department. There, pinned on the cork walls, were their old princess photos, pink frothy dresses and all. They'd both had long dark hair at the time, all curls and ringlets.

Jana Lee stared at the photos, then to where Petra was pointing. The sketch was of two dolls that had her face. Well, both their faces—hers and Jillian's. Their seven-year-old faces anyhow. It was a little spooky. As if it weren't strange enough having a sister who was identical in every way, now they were going to be cloned.

"I'm speechless. The drawings are very nice."

"Okay, you hate them?"

"No, no, it's just strange to see your face on a doll, you know?"

"I guess I see your point. We'll try and do you

justice, anyway. And in the final package I think we'll have different colored sashes and bows just like you two did on the show, so the audience could tell you apart."

"I'll be sure and visit more often as things progress."

"We're toying with having them sing the song. You know, this one:

> *We are happy little princesses*
> *in the land of make-believe,*
> *we have a big blue dragon,*
> *and he will never leave—*
> *because he loves us, he loves us,*
> *and yes he loves you too.*

Did I get it right? We had a video running yesterday."

"That's it all right, but wouldn't you have to pay more for the music rights?"

"Good point. That's your area anyhow. Let us know about that, will you? I think it's cool they picked this product to replace Byker Chikz. I thought the retro ideas from the Pitman archives would have been easier, but it turns out the whole process is just as crazy, so it was Jackson Hawks's final word we go with the Dragon thing. Production says we're using the Cindi Lou Who body from our Grinch movie series. Terrific body. Great seller. It's just a matter of new heads and dresses, and a great dragon." Petra pointed to her drawing of the princess outfit. "I've sewn up a few mock-ups of the dress. Would you like to have a sort of working lunch and give me a hand with that?"

"You sew too?"

"Jack-of-all-trades," Petra laughed. "Art is more than a sketch pad, as you know."

"Yes. Well, I'd love to have lunch with you. I'll have some food sent over and we can look at what you've come up with," Jana Lee answered.

"That's cool. I brought my own, so just order for yourself. Don't forget to sign those pesky papers. The sooner you get that done, the faster this project can proceed."

"Thanks, Petra, I guess I'll go to legal and take a look at the paperwork."

Petra looked at her funny. "You get all that stuff in your office, sometimes before they do."

"Oh, right, I'll go check my office." Jana Lee made a quick exit and all but ran down the halls of Pitman Toys. Round turquoise metal beams and expanses of glass whizzed by her, almost making her dizzy. She felt like she was in an aquarium.

Jana Lee was dumbfounded. She had to talk to her sister. The whole issue of signing permission releases should be interesting. Little did Jackson know what a twist he was putting on things.

She was out of breath when she swung into

Oliver's end of Jillian's office. "Ollie, what's this whole princess deal?"

Oliver smiled and gestured to her to sit down. He got up and closed the door. "The papers came over earlier. What have you been up to all morning, anyhow?"

"Going over ideas with Jackson. You must have been away from your desk when I came in for my dragon sketch."

"So, sit, sit, catch your breath. Can I get you a cold drink? It's warm today, isn't it?"

"Oliver, are you stalling?" Jana Lee held out her hand for the papers. Oliver handed them to her.

"Maybe a little. I've had to think things through regarding signatures. Fortunately they left it to you to obtain your sister's signature on these, so we might be able to pull this off with some finesse."

"Haven't I been signing my sister's name all week? I think I'm getting pretty good at it." Jana Lee slid into the black leather upholstered chair across from Oliver.

"An initial here and there, nothing vital or . . . legal." Oliver tapped his black pen on the blotter that covered most of his desk. "You should really consult an attorney before you sign these."

"Oh heck, we had our uncle back when we were kids, and he did so well we ended up with barely enough to buy our parents a beach shack in Washington. Why start now?"

"It could get pretty sticky. Jillian and I read legal

documents all the time and it looks very good to me, but your sister is going to want to read this very carefully. Is there somewhere we can fax it to her?"

"Maybe the Kinko's in Silverburgh. She's in no-fax land. I do have a computer, if that would help."

"If you have a computer hooked up to the Internet we can fax it through your phone line. I'll try and reach her and we'll set it up. I assume there is a printer attached to that computer?" Oliver asked.

"Why, certainly." Jana Lee made a face at him, then skimmed through the papers in her hands. She didn't know much legal jargon, but she was no dummy. She saw that they'd be getting royalties off the toys Pitman produced. That was a very interesting turn of events for her, an *income* of some sort.

"Ollie, what do you think the royalties off the toys might be like?" she asked.

"Well, at two percent per unit with a production run of . . ."

"Never mind, there's math involved. Maybe you could make some sort of projected thingy for me if you have time."

"Projected thingy in the queue," Oliver smiled. "How goes your Pitman adventure, anyway? Seems like you've found something to occupy your time—or should I say *someone?*"

"What, Jackson?" Jana Lee felt a rush of heat flood her face.

"Did I say that? You're blushing, you know."

"He's just the vice president. I have to be nice to him."

"Uh-huh."

Jana Lee put the papers back on Oliver's desk and looked down at her empty hands in her lap. "Jillian's expecting to come back to him all warmed up to her, you know."

"It seems to me Jackson has warmed up to you more than any woman I've ever seen. Just because you and your sister are twins doesn't mean you're the same woman. It won't do to deny what's going on between you." Oliver laced his fingers together and stared at her.

"My sister's love means more to me than a slight infatuation with some guy," Jana Lee replied. She held her head up and felt a hardness in herself she was surprised at.

"Surely there is a compromise here somewhere?"

"Don't forget I'm going to be leaving in another week."

"So I hear. You seem to fit in here very well. It must be fun to play with the creative teams and see what it's all about."

Jana Lee was still feeling a little huffy about Oliver's direct hit on her feelings for Jackson, but she accepted the change of subject. "I have to say, it's been wonderful."

"Your spirits seem considerably brighter since the first day you arrived."

"I've noticed that myself. I *feel* brighter." Jana Lee got up from the chair. "I've got to try and reach Jillian on the phone. As soon as I've talked to her, you can do that computer stuff together. Oh, and I'm having lunch down in the design department. Can I have one of those pasta salads sent over there? And maybe an iced tea?" City food. She loved it.

"No problem. Buzz me when Jillian is on the line."

"Thank you, Ollie, you've been wonderful."

"It's been a very interesting adventure so far."

Jana Lee went into Jillian's office and looked around. In one week she'd managed to stack papers all over the credenza, create an entire land of Pitman toys on the window ledges, and make a messy little tea corner on the side table, where Ollie had set up a morning station for her. There were three easels with different product sketches on them, a stack of old retro ads from the space landing, the dress-up box and a very seventies organic farm set she'd found in the archives.

The cleaners came in every night and tidied up, but there was no denying Jana Lee had a completely different way of working in a space. She and Jillian were truly opposites in some respects.

But when it came to Jackson Hawks, it looked like she and Jillian were more similar than Jana Lee could have imagined.

Her own comment came back to her about how her sister's love was more important than an infatuation with a man. Her insides twisted something fierce. For some reason she almost wanted to cry. She had forgiven her sister for running off with Elliot a long time ago. So what was bothering her? She wiped away a hot tear.

Maybe, just maybe, it was the thought of giving up Jackson.

Jana Lee sat down to call Jillian about the contracts. She auto-dialed her house in Washington. The phone rang and rang until the answering service picked up. After the beep she left a message.

"Hi, Jillian, it's me. Ollie needs to fax you something. You won't believe what they're going to make—a toy you and me. Anyhow, there's more to this story, so call when you can. Where the heck are you guys?"

Jana Lee hung up and leaned back in the black leather office chair, contemplating her date with Jackson. She'd found a black T-shirt in her sister's closet, and even if it was fancy Ann Taylor, it felt better than all those button-up office blouses. She'd also located a pair of black slacks, but they were a squeeze. She hadn't even thought of Jackson taking her anywhere too fancy.

Jillian's wardrobe was hardly lacking, but maybe Jana Lee needed something of her own this time. Maybe after lunch she'd take a little personal afternoon and go get herself a dress. After all, this was San Francisco, shopping mecca of the West Coast.

She touched the intercom button. "Ollie, pop in here for a minute, will you please?" She sounded so bossy and *executive* that she was embarrassed. She re-pressed the button. "If you have time, I mean."

Oliver opened the office doors, closed them, and came over to her desk, ready with his usual leather-covered notepad. "I'm here when you need me, madam. Don't worry about it." He smiled his Oliver smile, which was very patient and wry, then sat down across from her. "What can I do for you?"

"I'm sorry, it will just take me so much longer to figure this out than if I ask you. I need a . . . uh . . . dress. A dress of my own. For tonight. Jackson said something about the Top of the Mark, and I don't fit into Jillian's clothes that well. I'm rounder."

"Jillian is too thin. There's a Nordstrom on Market Street, which will have a good selection. It's downtown and fun. There's quite the elevator in that building."

Jana Lee listened to Oliver talk about a few other shops. "I know this is crazy," she said, "but is there any way we can both take a few hours off after lunch? I need a . . . guide."

"I'm sure we can arrange that, besides, I live to shop. I'll be the 'Fab One,' and you can be my makeover of the day. This will be very fun. I'd love to help. There's also a champagne bar on the same floor as all the lovely coats."

"A champagne bar? That sounds a little odd with dress shopping."

"Darling, where have you been living, the outback?"

Hours later she was giddy from Oliver's recommended champagne cocktail—something with Drambuie and bubbles that made her head light. "My goodness, how will I ever get back down the spiral escalator?"

"That dress is stunning. You have the perfect figure for vintage looks. Black Chantilly lace. Ahhh. And those little bow-tipped shoes— Jackson will be putty in your hands."

"I didn't think putty was the desired effect."

"I suppose not," Oliver snickered.

"Oh gosh, that's not what I meant."

"I know. *Silly* Putty." Oliver couldn't stop his laugh, which was a pretty funny sound altogether.

"I'm *silly* with bubbles." She tried to stop giggling like a twelve-year-old.

"So you are. What would it be like if Jackson fell madly in love with you and asked you to marry him?"

Jana Lee choked on her sip of champagne and laughed out loud. She looked around, suddenly self-conscious. The bartender gave her an eyebrow but smiled after that. "Jackson Hawks, as we all know, is not the marrying kind. So the odds of that happening are just . . . not even slightly possible."

"That wasn't the question—the odds. The question was, what would it be like?"

"Don't be a goose. I have a house and a daughter back in Washington."

Oliver tipped back in his chair and sipped from his champagne flute. "Love happens."

She glared at him, then moved her gaze out the high glass windows to take in the city of San Francisco. It was a great city, with old hotels like the St. Francis and a history that made her feel excited and mysterious, as if she were unraveling a good story.

She loved the parts she'd seen—Chinatown, the wharf area—and she wanted to see so much more. She loved the diversity, the open and accepting attitudes of the people she'd met, and basically everything about the town.

"Where do you live, Ollie?"

"My partner and I have a row house on Sacramento Street. We've lived there for ten years now. It is very old, but we refurbished the entire thing. He's very handy, and I can strip ugly wallpaper like a champ. Oh, and faux finish so fine you'd think it was real marble."

"Do you like antiques?"

"Addicted. I can go into a full swoon over an eighteenth-century American highboy. How about you?"

"I'm not sure. To tell you the truth, I haven't really explored the whole interior design realm much. I covered the seat of my ugly couch with an old terry-cloth table cover after the dog wore through the leather."

"Oh, my."

"Yeah. See what I mean?"

"Well, you are teachable. There is a dormant diva in there, I can tell. That orange jacket, and the Pucci scarf? So retro, and to *die*, really. I'm glad you bought something new to wear to the office. You've really got a lovely figure."

"Thanks, Ollie. I think my lovely figure could use a few Pilate moves."

"I think Jackson likes your figure just the way it is. Let's get you back to Jillian's apartment and I'll go back to work and make up for this lovely afternoon of playing hooky. You've got primping to do, and it will take you a good half hour to master those undergarments."

"No kidding."

Oliver left money on the table and swigged down the remaining champagne, and she followed suit. He looked very dapper in his summer linen jacket, pale yellow shirt, gray tie and gray trousers. Oliver had style.

She had zip. But she also had four shopping bags full of goodies to make a dent in it.

13

Twice as Nice

Jillian bolted awake. What the hell was everyone thinking, letting her sleep this late? She fell out of bed, stumbled around, tripped over boxes of packed books and her sister's personal things, and made it out Jana Lee's door to the upstairs bathroom she and Carly shared. She heard the sounds of work coming from downstairs. Good God, it was Friday.

In the streaky medicine cabinet mirror she saw a ghost. Oh, now wait, it was *her*. Here she was supposed to be resting, and all she saw was a twisted-up, tired woman reflected back. The lines on her forehead seemed deeper. Her eyes had dark circles under them. Guess her mother had been right when she'd said, "Don't frown like that, Jilly, your face will stick that way."

She splashed cold water on her face and felt around for a towel, blotted the moisture off and looked again. Same basic face.

Jillian realized she really had no skills when it came to taking care of herself. She was thirty-five, and the signs of her unhealthy lifestyle were catching up with her. Maybe she should slap on some of that expensive cream she'd purchased at the Serenity Spa.

She brushed her teeth quickly, dragged a brush through her hair, and went back into Jana Lee's room. Her head still felt fuzzy and disoriented. Where the hell had she put that stack of clothing she'd left out?

Plastic sheeting still covered most of the room so they could work on the ceilings. She dug around and found the dresser with the one drawer that was now her own. It was full of neatly folded undies, cotton bras, socks, T-shirts and shorts. At least she was neat. She, Jillian, was neat. That was a positive trait, right?

She grabbed one of each item and slapped the drawer closed, wiggled out of her oversized sleep shirt and pulled all the appropriate items of clothing onto her body.

It was already warm in this room. This was turning out to be such a hot June. She put a bandana over her head to keep the paint flecks off and started downstairs. Coffee. She smelled coffee.

The coffee turned out to be pretty skanky, having sat in the coffeemaker for probably seven hours, but she poured herself a cup anyway and cut it with a little milk. Scissors would have probably worked too.

Through the small window over the sink she could see Dean, sawing boards on the skill saw out on the deck. A spray of sawdust fluttered around him. His white tank T-shirt was tight on his muscled body. Man, Dean was the best-built guy she had ever been around. Certainly the best-built guy she'd ever been kissed by. She felt her lips, remembering that kiss, then she sipped the horrid coffee, which burned her lips with acidity and heat. Yak. Coffee was definitely something she should give up.

But great-looking guys, well, that was something she should take up. There was something about a guy in a white tank T-shirt and jeans and the way you could hold onto his bulging bicep and have him lift you off the ground that turned her on more than she'd ever been turned on before.

Who would have known she was a secret voyeur of buff guys? She smiled to herself. She had definitely missed the boat dating those soft city boys.

Hunger of a different sort made her start scrounging around the completely trashed kitchen for food. When she opened the fridge she saw a plate with plastic wrap and a sticky note that read *Mrs. S—nuke this.* Dean must have saved her some breakfast.

She took off the sticky note and put the plate full of scrambled eggs, fried potatoes and thick slabs of bacon in the microwave for one minute. Then she grabbed a fork and found the roll of paper towels for napkins. Might as well ditch the coffee for a glass of orange juice. There, she was trying anyhow.

Over on the counter she cleared herself a space and perched on the high bar chair. She'd over-nuked the eggs a bit, but the potatoes were perfect. It didn't matter, because she was starving.

Wow, this stuff was great. There was a touch of basil in the eggs, and the potatoes had sweet onions, fresh pepper and cheddar cheese mixed in. The bacon was a major indulgence, but it tasted divine.

Dean came in carrying a board. "Hey, you're up."

"I must have been tired. I'm sorry. I'll make up for it."

"You needed it. Don't apologize."

"Thanks for breakfast. Did you make this?"

"Yep. I brought some groceries. Your fridge was kind of . . . naked."

Interesting word choice he'd made. Dean looked her over in a very hungry way, although she couldn't imagine what there was to see. She looked like crap. No makeup, scruffy as hell, just crap. She stuffed another bite of eggs and bacon into her mouth.

"Where is everybody?" she asked.

"Lunch break, and Stan is picking up the French doors. They'll all be back in twenty minutes. Enjoy the peace."

"Yikes."

"Your cell phone rang a few times. I figured they'd leave you a message."

"Oh, thanks." She popped off the chair and rushed to check the voice mail on her cell phone. Why did she run to check the phone, as if it were on fire? It was a habit more than anything, and as she dialed the exchange she wondered why she'd done it. She had a perfectly good hot breakfast sitting there getting cold. She sat back down while she listened to the phone go through its thing, then punched in her codes.

Immediately she wished she hadn't. She didn't like the sound of Oliver's message about faxing her something, or Jana Lee's garbled nonsense about Pitman producing a set of Little Princess dolls. She just couldn't deal with any of that till she'd finished her breakfast and had some decent caffeine, whatever form it took.

Shutting the phone off, she picked up her fork again. But now she had a twist in her guts. Nothing went down right, and she gave up after two more bites. Well, three. Those potatoes were delicious. But now she had to know what was going on, and it made her extremely tense.

Dean was positioning his board on the kitchen floor, and once it was set, he looked up at her. "I've got to make some noise. Shall I wait?"

"No, go ahead. I need to make a call. I'll go outside."

She found paper and a pen and walked out to sit on the old picnic table where they'd had their pizza party last night. Jillian auto-dialed her office, and Oliver picked up quickly. He sounded odd.

"Oliver, what's up?"

"Oh hello, Miss Tompkins, nothing very burning, we've just got a little pile of legalese for you to go through and sign. It's a bit sticky with you being not actually here and them thinking you are, but I'm sure I can ruffle or shuffle or rearrange the papers well enough to hide the fact that your sister is neither here nor there."

Jillian could have sworn she heard a hiccup. "Oliver, are you . . . *drunk?*"

"What could possibly give you that idea? Two champagne cocktails does not affect me in the least, and that nice bartender put extra Drambuie in just for us, and your sister is going to look like a million dollars on that date."

"What date?" Jillian felt a real strange twisted-up feeling come over her.

"Her date with Jackson Hawks. Oops, I probably shouldn't have mentioned that," Oliver blathered. He did that when he'd had a little too much wine. She'd actually never seen him do that at work, though. Things were going nuts at Pitman without her.

As to Jackson, Jillian felt herself have a rather interesting reaction: She had a knee-jerk jealous response. What was Jana Lee doing dating Jackson?

"And where is Jana Lee?"

"She's taken the rest of the day off to primp."

"Sounds serious."

"Jillian Tompkins, you need to let your sister know she can have Jackson."

Jana Lee with Jackson? Jillian couldn't even wrap her head around it. "Are you joking? They are all wrong for each other. Listen, Oliver, how can you fax me the papers?" She reverted to her business persona.

"J.L. informed me you've got a computer setup on that end. If you'll go set up a fax program, and e-mail me the number, I can make it happen. Got it? Paper should start spitting out of your printer before you know it. I'll be ready the minute you give me the signal, Captain."

"I can do that. So what's this about the Little Princess dolls?"

"Apparently if you remove Cindi Lou Who's head and replace it with yours, then add a little pink princess dress, you're ready to go. The dragon has been a little harder. But we need to get your permission on that face as quickly as possible."

"What about Harvey?"

"Since he was in a suit, his licensing rights revolved around the creator of the series, which we obtained gleefully, from what I hear. Although I think they might get Mr. Dragon's permission anyway, just to cover all their legal asses."

"Are there royalties involved?"

"Yes, there are."

Jillian heard Oliver take a big slurp of something, and assumed it was coffee, because he started to talk more clearly. Royalties—that was great, but Jillian was nervous about not being there for a new product conception.

"Did you go over any recall data for Cindi Lou and see if there were any complaints? Are they using snaps on the dress? Or can we do Velcro? We've had so much less trouble with Velcro. And what about the unit packaging costs, have they considered all those damn wires they like to hold these things in with?"

"All of these details are in order. I learned from the best, you know." Oliver sounded huffy.

"Shit. Should I fly back?"

"I'd be offended if you did."

Jillian rubbed her forehead hard to make the pain go away. She felt that horrible pounding panic come creeping through her body. "I'm going to go set up the fax now, Oliver. Thank you for all this."

"Consider it a gift. And think about what I said about your sister. This thing with Jackson has potential."

"Potential for what, disaster?"

"If so, it's a natural disaster."

"I'm going now. Watch for my e-mail."

Jillian hung up the phone, which she now wanted to throw off the deck into the harbor waves. Why did she have this reaction every time she had to deal with work? And why did she care whether her sister went out with Jackson Hawks? After all, her sister was entitled. Her sister could probably win over Jackson easily. Not like her. He'd run screaming away from her—again.

She took deep breaths and closed her eyes. But instead of calming down, she did the oddest thing; she started to cry. She cried because Jackson hadn't fallen for her, and because her sister was a better person than she was, and because she just hated her job. She hated it. She'd be happy if she never had to go back there.

Jillian sobbed. She put her head on her arms, and the pain inside her just spilled out. Oh *God*, she just couldn't stop. The tears seemed to flood down her face as she tried to wipe them away with the edge of her T-shirt. She didn't know where the girls had gone to, but she sure didn't want Dean to see her like this. She got up and edged through the giant hole in the wall where the French doors would go, stifling her sobs with a clean rag she'd picked up. Relatively clean. The sawdust made her sneeze and cry at the same time.

Just as she tried to scoot quickly from the doorway to the stairs, he came around the corner, out of the utility room, and she ran smack into his chest. She looked up at him, startled. He grabbed her arms to keep her from falling.

She looked up and tried to smile, hoping it didn't show. He looked in her eyes and in one small moment took in everything. He dropped what he was carrying, pulled her into his arms and leaned them both against the wall.

The warmth of his body moved her emotion to a different place: a place that made it even harder to stop crying. She let out a huge sob, then put her hand over her mouth to keep the rest in. She lay her head on his chest, melting against him. It felt so, so good.

He stroked her hair and talked softly to her. "Whatever it is, it's better to let it out. Keeping it bottled up makes bad things happen."

"I can't."

"Can't let it out?"

"It will swallow me up."

"I'll be here to pull you out."

"I'm sorry, Dean." She stepped back and wiped her eyes on her T-shirt again. "I shouldn't even be doing this to you. I don't know what's wrong with me. I'm just all screwed up."

He touched her arms again. "Remember how I told you I used to have a construction business?"

"Yes," she answered.

"I had a first-class burnout. I know what it feels like. If you want to talk about it, I'm a good listener," he replied.

His touch was so soothing. She pulled a big breath in through her nose and closed her eyes for a minute. "I'm okay. I just need to get back to work. Give me a job to do."

He sighed and let go of her. She just couldn't surrender to whatever was eating her. He'd given her a big opening to just tell him the truth, too. Like why she was pretending to be her sister. He took another breath and refocused. "How about more painting? The living area needs another coat. I'm almost done with the underlayment for the kitchen, and we'll be having that French door installed today. We can focus on the living room while the kitchen floor tile goes in." He handed her his handkerchief. She wiped her eyes on it and handed it back.

He stuffed it in his pocket. "Also we need to move everything out of the upstairs bedrooms to strip and paint the ceilings. There are too many boxes in there to move around well. The garage is dry; we could keep stacking them in there. Pick a job. Prep the living room, or move boxes. I'm going to finish in here." He motioned to the kitchen.

"Move boxes it is." She saluted him and marched upstairs, then stopped and called back. "Oh, I have to work on the computer upstairs for a few minutes—e-mail, that sort of thing."

He nodded. When she was out of sight he shook his head and wished he could ease her pain. There was something going on. Whatever it was, it was probably the reason she'd come here to her sister's house. Her job in San Francisco, whatever that was, must be a major source of stress.

Of course it could be a man. That would explain a whole lot. A big fat nasty breakup could make a basket case out of anyone. But more likely it was work. He knew the signs too well. He felt like she was at a crossroads he had been at once himself.

He pulled out his framing hammer and started pounding nails into the floor underlayment that was now covering the old vinyl. They seemed to have connected last night in a way that was rare between people. Their ideas had meshed, their ability to visualize what the other person was saying had been nothing short of amazing. He'd hoped she'd seen that and decided to trust him. Whatever it was, she'd have to eventually tell him or go back and face it alone.

Aside from all that, she was a special woman. Sometimes special women needed a careful approach.

*   *   *

"Shit!" Jana Lee had a dial-up modem. Who even *had* those anymore? Jillian had gotten the damn fax program set up, e-mailed Oliver and was receiving her pages, but everything was moving in slow motion. She squirmed in the chair. *Gawd*, she hated waiting for things. She flipped open her cell phone and pressed the office line hard.

"Did it go through?" Oliver said right away.

"Hey, it could be someone else."

"Caller ID, welcome to the twenty-first century, Miss Tompkins."

"Jana Lee has a dial-up. The file is uploading, but it's like molasses in January. I wish I had a tele-transporter. I'd just get the papers and reassemble myself back here."

"Beam me up, Scottie. Just relax. It will get there. Is there anything else, Princess Leia?"

"Yes, I'll sign these here and overnight them to you. Let's not make *J.L.* forge my name on something this touchy. Here it comes. Gotta go, *Darth*," she said. Oliver was just hilarious today. And he was mixing metaphors, too.

She snapped the phone shut and stuffed it in the pocket of the shorts she'd put on. The file finished, and she printed it off. She took some time to read through the papers and was surprised and pleased by what she saw.

It was also interesting to learn that Harvey the Dragon, aka Harvey Higgins, had to be contacted but wouldn't have the same sort of royalty structure because he'd appeared in a big blue dragon suit. She snickered. He was such a jerk.

She signed the papers, called FedEx and requested a pickup. Oliver would need these back fast. Jillian picked up a box on her way down just to be efficient. She saw a picture of her and Jana Lee on the top. Geez, right out there for Dean to see. Better deep-six that.

She took careful steps down the stairs and headed out to the garage. As she passed, Dean was talking with the tile guy, who had already started setting the countertop backsplash into place.

Boxes, boxes—the garage was full of boxes already. They'd removed most of the contents of the kitchen, the living room and the spare room to make way for Jillian's crazy idea of a gift for her sister. She'd put the new box in a fairly clean spot and moved a book on top of the picture.

What the hell was wrong with her? Probably Jana Lee would have liked nothing better than to come back to her same old house and relax. But no, *she* had to make a huge mess, and it probably wouldn't even be done by the time Jana Lee got back.

Jillian would just have to throw herself into this project and quit thinking about what was happening back at Pitman. And about Jackson. And about Dean.

* * *

Dean watched his boss-lady hustle up and down the stairs a dozen times, clearing the contents of the upstairs bedrooms. She was tackling her tasks like a woman driven by some demon, that was for sure. And Carly was being put to work too. She and her two friends had returned from a girls' day downtown and late lunch at the local Dairy Queen all rosy and relaxed, only to find the demon aunt on the warpath. He felt pity for them.

Carly had gotten help from the two friends for an hour, but they'd split when she'd tried to get them to paint the second coat on the living room walls. Carly was stuck with that one while her aunt was upstairs stripping popcorn off the ceiling. Not an easy job.

Dean felt pretty good about today's progress. It was nearing six, and the backsplash was looking very good. The French door was shimmed into place, and the floor was ready to be laid. He had retrofit new lighting into the kitchen and living room area, and all that was left was a trip into the attic crawl space by the electrician. But that was a morning thing, before the day's heat oven-baked that area.

Break time. Dean wiped off his brow with his handkerchief. The handkerchief she'd mopped away her tears with.

She seemed to have redirected all her emotion into working on the house. It had been a strange day. A FedEx guy had shown up about four. She'd given him a pile of papers. He'd come up with an appropriate envelope, and she'd filled out and signed the shipping slip.

Dean would have liked to have gotten a look at that packing slip and found out where his shady lady was from, but she'd stuffed it in the pocket of her shorts. It was obviously all part of her other life. The life that was driving her crazy.

He walked up the stairs and turned back to look at the space below. A very fine backsplash was set and only needed grouting. The kitchen cabinets were much improved by their coat of paint, and the floor looked better already—even just with overlayment, before the tile went down.

The sea blue-green color she'd picked looked great as Carly put on another coat.

"Looks great from here, Carly. That extra coat makes a big difference. Maybe we'll put a glaze on it later."

"Thanks, Dean, but I'll pass on the glaze. Let nutso woman do it." Carly motioned with her paint roller to the upstairs.

Nutso Woman. They all needed to come clean so he'd have a name for her.

In the meantime, though, he could see where the mysterious sister's vision had taken downstairs. Beige linen slip-covered sofas, seashells, light colors. Nice. Too bad the layout of the place was so crazy. If it was him he'd knock some walls out and turn this into a really usable space.

Good God, he better not share *that* vision, or she'd have a sledgehammer in his hands in a New York minute, knocking down some load-bearing wall. He chuckled to himself, knowing how true that was.

He continued up the stairs and stuck his head in Carly's bedroom. There she was, his Nutso Woman, up on a ladder in the far corner of the room, wedged against the wall. Her face was covered with a mask, and she had on eye protection goggles. The *rest* of her—her great figure, her bare legs, her short shorts—was covered with speckles of ceiling junk. Like, *covered*.

She had a spray bottle of water in one hand and a wide putty knife in the other. Dean could see it was going rather slowly, despite the fact that she was attacking it like a demented beekeeper.

"Did I mention this was a hard job?" he said as he strolled into the room.

"Yes."

"Be careful not to gouge the drywall. Gently is the only way. Also we might try the hose method. We'll drag in the garden hose through the upstairs window and use a spray nozzle to wet down a larger area. Much faster than the spray bottle method."

"Now you tell me." She picked up a large blob of ceiling texture and threw it at him. He ducked but got it in the hair anyhow.

She laughed. That was a good sign.

"I won't stoop to your level and return fire," he said.

"I'm not on your level, I'm on a ladder. You're already stooped." She swiped her hand along a rung of the ladder and fired another blob at him. This time it hit him in the forehead.

He shook it off like a dog and bent down to create a large ball of junk from the wet texture material. "I'm a better aim than you, so cease fire!"

"Better aim? That was a direct hit to your bean." She laughed a fake evil laugh.

He aimed and fired his blob ball. She cowered, which left her ass as target, which was exactly what he'd figured.

"Ow! Okay, I surrender."

"So easy." He climbed up the ladder behind her and dusted off her rear.

"I am *not*." She squirmed under him and started down, which was quite a feat. They both took a few fast steps to the floor, where she turned and faced him. "I'm not easy, I'm *difficult*," she yelled.

"Who says so?"

"Everyone."

He carefully moved her face mask down on her neck, then put her goggles up on her head.

"Not everyone." He pushed her back against the ladder and kissed her hard. He let his tongue glide into her mouth and play. He held her neck and slid his fingers up the back of her head, cradling her against him. He put his knee on the ladder rung and pressed his body to hers.

First she was limp with surprise. Then she dropped her spray bottle and putty knife. Then slowly her hands reached around him and he felt her smooth touch on his back. What a hot, hot kiss. He groaned. He could feel his arousal jump to life between them, and so did she. Their mouths duplicated the rhythmic motion of lovemaking, and she let him explore her openly.

"He-l-l-o-o."

They both shot upright and stared at the doorway.

"How's that ceiling coming?" Carly stood with her arms crossed, grinning from ear to ear. "I'm hungry. Can you two like . . . hose down and think about food?"

Jillian reached down and grabbed her spray bottle off the floor and headed directly toward Carly, twisting the nozzle to stream so she could get off a good zap across the room. She kept coming while Carly shrieked and ran down the stairs.

"I'm telling!" she laughed and screamed.

"So am I," Jillian returned. "We'll order in something. Find a phone book."

She turned back to Dean, still holding the spray bottle. He put his hands in the air. "I give up," he said. He walked toward her. He was covered with ceiling texture from pressing up against her.

"Stay where you are, mister, hands up."

"No way." He grabbed her before she got one squirt out. They rolled against a wall, and he gave her one more kiss. "Don't think this is over," he mumbled into her mouth.

"I hope not," she whispered back. Their eyes met, and she saw a pure lustful look dancing in Dean Wakefield's light brown eyes. There was no doubt in her mind he was seeing the same look in her hungry blue eyes.

14
Double Image

Jana Lee stood in front of the full-length mirror of her sister's walk-in closet. The black dress was pretty, even without the shoes. If she threw in a swing coat and a pillbox hat, she'd be very Jackie O.

When did she start looking so much like her mother? Over this week she'd thought about her mom and the passion she'd had for her career. But somehow Mom had been able to balance her children into the mix. Sure, she and her sister had run a little wild and free, but there had been an underlying sense of her parents being there, as well as a fine line between youthful adventure and misbehaving, which would have made their parents disappointed in them.

At least for her there had been. Her sister had been another matter. Jillian had always run a little wilder and a little freer. But the odd part was that Jillian had ended up being the sister who worked too hard. Jillian just did everything a little too over the top.

Jana Lee made a mental note not to let work overtake her life when she settled into some career path. Balance. That was the key.

She sat on a small bench and slipped into her new shoes. They had a shorter heel and felt so much more like *her* shoes, but the little bows on the front and the pointed toe were very hip—for a woman who had just recently and most temporarily given up being a Keds devotee.

There. She was kind of pretty. At least as pretty as her sister. Why did she always think Jillian was so much prettier? Hello, they were identical twins. When she thought of it, it was kind of surprising that Jackson hadn't gone for Jillian. Maybe they weren't a good match. Maybe it would be okay for her to get involved with Jackson.

And lie to him. And leave town. And leave a mess. Jana Lee leaned into the mirror, frowned and examined her face. Her eyebrows looked uneven. She rubbed her eyebrow with her fingertip. She'd have to draw that one over again. And at this rate she could just draw herself some really evil eyebrows to suit her terrible thoughts.

She loved her project with Pitman toys. She loved her sister's apartment. This wasn't turning out the way she thought it would.

Most of all she really liked Jackson. She wanted him. She wanted to be made love to and have that feeling of a man seducing her. Jana Lee closed her eyes and drifted into the thought of Jackson making love to her.

The doorbell rang right in the middle of Jackson unzipping the back of her dress and running his hands all over her silky new underwear. This time she knew it was her door.

There was Jackson with red roses and another box of Ghirardelli chocolates. The way to a woman's heart was truly chocolate, and Jackson obviously knew that.

"Hey, you look fabulous," he said as she let him in the door.

Jana Lee looked into Jackson's handsome face and felt the strangest mixture of fear and excitement. He was devastatingly good-looking—more so tonight than she'd noticed before. He had on a suit and tie, and something else—his eyes ate her up. Under those fine clothes dwelled a wolf.

"You look amazing," he growled.

"So do you. Ain't we a pair?" she joked.

"I think so," he murmured as he leaned in and gave her a soft kiss on the cheek.

She touched her own cheek with surprise.

"Shall we go straight off?"

"I have to draw in my other eyebrow," she blurted out. Oh, smooth.

Jackson grinned at her. "Well now, just go right ahead. I'll wait for your eyebrow. I'll just put your flowers in water and put the chocolates on the counter. I know the way to the kitchen."

Jana Lee streaked to the bathroom and finished up her eyebrow, muttering to herself about stupid things to say and why she couldn't be more . . . together. She refreshed her new orange lipstick and went to grab the rest of her date gear.

"Ta-da." She posed against the door frame.

"I'd say that eyebrow is looking good."

He moved close to her, and she thought he might kiss her little orange lips for a moment. Then he removed her sister's black-and-gold cashmere shawl from her hand.

She shivered—*not from being cold*—as he wrapped it around her bare arms. Jana Lee held the shawl close to her, clutching her small beaded evening purse in front of her.

"Don't worry, I'll warm you up."

She was afraid of that.

Sitting across from Ms. Tompkins at the restaurant, Jackson tried to brush away the overwhelming feelings that kept creeping up on him. Things like— m-m-*marriage*. Like . . . honeymoons. Like . . . waking up every morning to see this woman sleeping next to him. Reading the Sunday papers and having coffee together. Getting a dog. This was quite insane; they hadn't even had sex yet. And hello, he'd only been dating her a week. And he hadn't had a dog since he was a kid. His dad had gotten the dog in the divorce.

Sure, he'd heard of a few couples that had met and just never stopped being together after that first date. Rhonda and Pete in shipping.

But not him. He was a man of the world. He ordered champagne and gulped down a large portion of the glass to dull his thoughts, but she only sipped at hers, saying something about a previous headache and how she was going to be practical this time. She was so wise.

All during their meal he watched her full, soft lips as she talked. He looked into her beautiful blue eyes. They were large and surrounded with the most amazing fringe of lashes. She could have been a model; she was so lovely. But she didn't have that edgy model thing going on. He knew; he'd dated his share. She was more like someone's very lively, very graceful wife. Wife.

Oh my *God*, what was he saying? He took a big gulp of ice water.

"Shall we dance?" he asked.

"I'd love to," she answered. She placed her white linen napkin on the table and waited as he pulled her chair out for her. She rose and held out her hand for him.

He led her onto the dance floor and smoothly

moved them into a slow waltz to match the sixties "Sinatra Night" music. The song was "The Nearness of You." The singer, who sounded a whole lot like Sinatra, made it count, and so did Jackson. He whispered to her about how good she felt in his arms. He felt her melt against him. He closed his eyes and hummed along about the nearness of *her*.

When the song was done they went back to the table. He felt like she was so close, yet so far away. He wanted to catch her and hold her. Did she have the same feelings about him?

"Shall we indulge in dessert?" He wanted to indulge her. She didn't answer; she had a faraway look. "Jillian?"

"Oh, I'm sorry, I was thinking about something else."

Jackson reached across the table toward her. "Family or work related?"

"Both, I guess."

"I know about that family thing. My father is a formidable character. Of course you've met him, you know what I mean. I guess it's pure nepotism for him to put me in the vice president position."

"It only makes sense though; he'd want you watching after his concerns. He must trust you."

"He must. But that is very kind of you to say." Jackson signaled the waiter as he walked near. "Dessert?" he asked her.

"Love some," she answered.

* * *

Jana Lee took another spoonful of chocolate mousse and tried to put the huge wave of guilt out of her mind, but it nagged at her like a mosquito on a summer night, buzzing in her ear while she was trying to sleep. It buzzed *"Liar, liar,"* at her.

And for once, it wasn't guilt about chocolate. It was guilt about Jackson. He wasn't the way she'd figured him, and it was scaring her. Either he was supremely good at making a woman feel like she was the only one he was interested in, or he was actually interested in her.

Jackson had depth. His stories were great. He'd had a rich, interesting life, and she could picture it so clearly when he talked about his brother and the mischief they'd gotten into as a child. She loved talking with him.

But most of all she felt herself wanting to do more than just talk with Jackson.

When he'd held her in his arms on the dance floor, he'd been like a prince in a fairy tale, and for once, she'd been a real princess—the mysterious princess who wasn't what she seemed. Jackson Hawks was pretty close to sweeping her off her feet.

When was the last time she'd felt this alive? Her whole life had changed in one week. She felt like she was tingling all over with aliveness. She was falling for Jackson, that was obvious.

If it weren't for two big fat elephant-sized things bothering her, she'd be in date heaven. One was her concern for her sister's feelings, and two was the fact that she was leaving in one week. Oh, three, the little detail that she was lying her head off to Jackson. Three elephants.

Jackson talked, and she leaned on her elbow, savoring the chocolate mousse, listening carefully and imagining his lips on hers.

"I guess my father trusts me, but he does have his watchdogs keeping an eye on things."

"Watchdogs?" she asked dreamily.

"Hey, here we are talking about work and we're supposed to be unwinding. Let's not think about work." Jackson sat back and looked at her until she felt a blush creep up her neck and cheeks. "Let's just think about how pretty you look tonight."

Jana Lee felt the heat work its way up her face and trickle back down over her entire body. He was so, so sexy. He was like the boy in high school everyone wanted, who went steady with the head cheerleader for three years, then finally broke up with her, and every girl in school threw herself in his path but none succeeded. The coveted boy they all wanted who vanished to a college back East like a dream that hadn't been real. Unattainable perfection.

She tried to think about something else besides his kiss. "Work is such a big part of our life, though, and I'm so excited about the ideas we've come up with."

"I am too, but there's a time to work and a time to play. So let's play. Come out and dance with me again. I like having you in my arms."

She took a sip of water to cool herself off. "Jackson Hawks, you are a sweet-talker. I'll be a notch on your bedpost and forgotten within another week." She couldn't believe she'd said that. A notch on his bedpost. Her fantasies were creeping out.

He stood up and came over to her side of the table. "You, my dear, are not a woman to be forgotten easily. At any rate, since the night is young, and so are we, and since Sinatra himself is inviting us "Dancing in the Dark," we should go with it, don't you think?" He pulled her up and she let him take her.

Here she was with a handsome, interesting man, dancing to the smooth, soft rhythm of the song, loving every minute of it. Should she feel guilty? Probably. She closed her eyes and let it go.

"And you in my bed would be more than a notch," he whispered in her ear. "It would be heaven."

She melted.

Finally, he thought, *finally she's giving in a little*. Jackson lost himself in her, sliding a gentle kiss up her neck to her earlobe. He felt that old familiar feeling of having seduced a woman over the edge. He liked that feeling.

But weirdly enough, he felt guilty. He removed his mouth from her neck and put his cheek next to hers. She smelled like violets.

He remembered that smell from a patch of special flowers his grandmother had grown in a shady spot under a cherry tree in her backyard. He remembered her falling to her knees in the soft moss and having him do the same, burying their noses in the newly emerged flowers. She was quite a woman, his grandmother. She was as constant as spring. As a holiday. She was always there for them.

God help him, he was thinking about his grandmother's garden instead of some of the more exotic ideas he could be having.

And how can you seduce a woman who reminds you of your grandmother? He rolled his head back and groaned a quiet groan.

"Are you tired?" she asked him.

"No, I'm confused. You make me feel things I've never felt before."

The music ended, but she was like a soft breeze in his arms. She slid her lips over his cheek and whispered, "Shall we finish up here?"

Despite her warmth, he figured she was now going to dump him and crawl into bed with a good book. "Whatever you'd like," he said absently. He felt like he'd revealed too much of himself. The thought of the evening ending stabbed him, and he wanted to figure out why it hurt so much.

He escorted her back to the table and signaled the waiter for a check. He had bought her a single yellow rose to be waiting at the table. She picked it up and took it with them, wrapped in a bit of plastic she'd had the waiter bring. Such a practical girl.

She'd kissed him in the limo. She'd let him get very hot and bothered, and she'd even let him run his fingers lightly over the tip of her very excited nipple. She'd let him walk her to the door, wanting more, expecting more. Then she'd dumped him.

She was a first-class idiot, no doubt about it. She dropped her rose on the sofa, plucked one of her fancy shoes off and threw it across the room. It hit a square column that held some arty vase. She watched it teeter, then sprinted over and caught it.

Once it was steadied, she limped into the kitchen and flung open the bottom freezer unit of Jillian's fancy fridge. Thank God her sister had the sense to stock ice cream. And good ice cream at that. Ben and Jerry's Phish Food—chocolate ice cream with gooey marshmallow, a caramel swirl and fudge fish. Bring it on.

She found a big spoon, sat down at the kitchen island and popped open the carton. She was going to turn into a chunky monkey if she kept eating stuff like this. But she didn't care at the moment. She was completely bothered and bewildered. She had no idea how to fix the mess she'd gotten into, let alone the mess she'd gotten Jillian into.

She shoved a big spoonful of ice cream in her mouth. When Jackson had gotten her in the back of that limo and kissed her until her toes had curled and her shoes had fallen off, there hadn't been a doubt in her mind that her sister would have been in bed with him by now.

But she wasn't her sister. She had guilt. She had that stupid angel on her shoulder that was way louder than that little devil on the other shoulder.

Her lips were still burning from his kiss. He'd kissed her in the backseat, he'd kissed her in the elevator, he'd kissed her as she'd unlocked the apartment door, and she'd literally put her hand on his chest and closed the door in his face with a polite "Thanks, Jackson, I had a wonderful time."

And every one of those kisses she'd eaten up like she was eating Phish Food now. With a spoon, with passion, with the promise of what their love-making could be like.

Then, just as she'd been about to let him in, she'd remembered her lies, her other life, her sister, her daughter, and her mission, not necessarily in that order.

Augh. Ice cream was *not* as good as sex. She thwacked her head with her spoon hand, and bits of ice cream flew around her. One bit landed on her dress. She jumped up and blotted the spot, then found club soda in the fridge to finish the cleanup. She stripped off the dress and blotted with the club soda–soaked towel. Then she tossed the dress across one of the bar stools.

Here she was in her underwear, a very sexy black slip, a very sexy bra, and stupid pantyhose. She took off her remaining shoe, which she'd forgotten to remove, stripped the pantyhose, climbed back on her chair and pried another lump of ice cream out of the carton.

Poor me.

Poor miserable me. She sniffled.

Up to my eyebrows in principles and morals and . . . ice cream. She shoved another mouthful in and licked the spoon. She needed to talk to her sister.

Jackson paced the hallway six times. Then he went back downstairs and told Pops to take him home. Pops winked at him and said better luck next time. Jackson shook his head. Everyone was so used to him being a ladies' man. It would ruin his reputation when it got around that he'd been rejected by Ms. Tompkins.

And did he care about that anymore? In a matter of days he'd been reduced to pacing a hallway. She'd bewitched him, that was it.

What did he really know about her? She'd worked at Pitman for quite a while, but she was a master at avoiding his questions regarding her past. She was elusive to the point of ridiculousness.

Jackson thanked Pops and climbed the stairs to his front door. He took out his keys, unlocked the door, stepped inside and took a deep breath. His sanctuary. He stood in the black-and-white-marble-tiled entry for a moment, taking in his world. The sitting room to the left, the office to the right. He slid open the pocket doors and stepped into his dark cherry-paneled den. The scent of his books, fine leather and warm wood gave him some comfort. He sat down behind the old desk, turned on the small brass lamp and swiveled in his large leather chair.

He felt so lost—like he had when his parents had split up. Like he wasn't sure where his feet should stand because the earth might shift underneath him. A sensation a San Francisco native knew well.

He reached over to a nearby shelf and grabbed the very fine decanted port and the accompanying glasses. He could be having this glass of port with her. He so rarely took his women here to his house, but she was different.

He sat stunned for a moment, then poured himself a glass and took a rather large swallow. His eyes watered.

What would his father do? Probably take a mistress and forget about it. Jackson felt a chill go through his bones. That's basically what he'd been doing, just without the marriage bit. Maybe he should forget about her.

But he just didn't want to forget her. The taste of her lingered on his lips, just as unforgettable as every other kiss he'd stolen from her.

He stared at the ceiling with its coffered square patterned beams. He needed to know more about this woman who was driving him to distraction. He should read her personnel file. He should get a little background information on her. Was that a bad thing? Probably.

Was he going to do it anyway? Without a doubt.

15

Tipped Tiaras and the Wet Dog Blues

Why couldn't Jillian just say the words? *Go ahead, Jana Lee, take Jackson for yourself. He obviously wants you. Have some fun. Have a romp with him. He'll dump you anyway.* Maybe that was it. Maybe she was protecting her sister. Sure.

Dean had dragged the old barbeque out from the garage and cleaned it up good. He'd cooked up a whole batch of burgers for the crew, the girls, and her, complete with corn on the cob, grilled onions, potato salad that he'd scored from the supermarket, and a huge watermelon. A classic combination.

Dean was a very talented fellow, she'd noticed. A tall, good-looking, talented fellow that all the other guys seemed to respect, as if they'd been working for him for years.

The crew had gone home, promising to work through the weekend, and the girls had gone off to spend the night at Ashley's house. Musical sleepovers. At least Jana Lee had given her thumbs-up approval to all of Carly's friends. Jillian felt like a responsible aunt for asking. Jana Lee had even expressed surprise that Carly had been hanging out with girls her age. It seemed Miss Carly was a bit of a loner and liked to hole up and paint more than socialize, according to her mom.

Of course Jillian was no dummy. She'd partied her way through her junior and senior years in high school and knew all the signs. Fortunately Carly seemed to be having a safe and sane summer so far, although talk of a drive-in movie theater in Gorst scared Jillian speechless. Boys, cars, drive-ins. She'd been lucky to make it through high school alive and not pregnant. She'd have to impart some of her wisdom on Carly before departing Seabridge.

Jillian picked up paper plates and dumped them in the large plastic garbage can they'd dragged up on the deck. It had been nice of the girls to help with dinner, but too bad she was on clean-up detail. At least Dean was there to help her. She felt slightly self-conscious about the fact they were obviously alone.

She'd watched Dean with Carly and the other girls, and she'd noticed how patient he'd been with them, teaching them some crazy thing about getting the big pot of water boiling, then putting the fresh corn in fast so it wouldn't lose its flavor.

She'd had a completely weird moment of remembering her parents and her and her sister sitting on this deck, having a family moment. It had been a warm, loving moment. Things hadn't been perfect, but they'd been good.

She'd really blown it. She'd let all that pass her by. Children, a marriage, a real home. Well, her apartment was certainly artistic and functional. But Jana Lee had made a real home here. Jillian sat down and opened another beer. She gazed out on the moonlit bay and remembered that day so long ago with her family.

"Good memory?" Dean looked at her.

"Yes, Mom's bad cooking, Dad's burgers on the barbeque, and a day a million years ago a whole lot like this. I guess we had quite a few barbeques, but this one, I remember, was special. My sister and I figured out how to swing off this deck when the tide was high—at night, just like this. There was a rope swing my dad hung up . . ." Jillian looked up at the old fir tree next to the deck. "Up there, see?"

Dean looked to where she was pointing, turning his head to the side. "Oh yeah, I see, hey, we should get it down!"

Before she could even think about what he was saying, Dean stood on the picnic table and hoisted himself up on the lowest branch.

"Dean, you'll break your neck!"

"I've been climbing trees since I was a kid," he called down to her.

"You're not a kid now, you're an old dude."

"Boy, you sure know how to flatter a guy." He was higher now and could almost reach the rope, wrapped over two high branches.

"You're crazier than me."

"Probably." Dean pulled on the rope and looped it over the branch. "Watch out below!"

The rope swing dropped between the fir branches, and Jillian caught it. "So what's up there, Columbus?"

Dean was examining the rope at the tie spot. "Looks secure." He turned and scanned the horizon. "Red sky at night, sailor's delight."

"Come down from there, you nutcase." Jillian stared up at him.

"Here I come!" Dean climbed down and hung like a monkey, then swung and jumped on the deck, a perfect landing.

"Ta da, ten points from the judges," Jillian laughed, watching his antics. He certainly was fit. And extremely cute in that boyish way some men have. She forgot about everything else for a brief moment except how close he was standing to her now.

He looked into her eyes. "You go change into some swim thing. I have a pair of cutoffs in the truck." Dean stuck his hands in his pockets, turned, and whistled down the stairs of the deck, walking toward the back of the house, where his truck was parked.

Jillian ran into the house and up the stairs. God knows where Jana Lee had a swimsuit. She got to the bedroom and peeled back plastic to get to the dressers. Except for the one drawer she'd made her own, her sister's drawers were a hodgepodge of weirdness: underwear, photographs, decks of cards, art pencils, business cards, a worm-pile of mismatched socks, all jumbled together.

Underneath a scrunched-up pile of old T-shirts she found a swimsuit. Whoa, it was old lady blue with a skirt, even. Did Jana Lee think she was that ancient? Good grief, they both still had good figures.

Oh well, it was better than going naked. Jillian shimmied out of the shorts and T-shirt she'd changed into after their ceiling texture fight and pulled the ugly swimsuit on.

She looked at herself in the mirror and laughed at the floppy hanging fabric of the suit. Boy, she was going to buy her sister some new clothes. New clothes, new kitchen floor, new house décor, new boyfriend. What was it with her and her extreme need to remake her sister's life?

The reflection in the mirror made her feel uneasy. She touched her face in the glass. Who was she? Was she just a clone of her sister? Was it her own life she kept trying to remake? She'd read stuff about how similar identical twins were, but it didn't seem like she and Jana Lee had the same taste or desires or thoughts at all. They were one cell split into two people. Two very different people.

But Jana Lee must have gotten the larger share of the goodness genes. Jillian had done some rotten things to her sister. And then to have watched Jana Lee suffer so much grief when her husband had died so young—it just wasn't fair.

"Hey Jane, Tarzan wants to go for a swing," Dean called up the stairs.

Jillian broke out of her thoughts. "Coming, Tarzan."

"Grab towels out of the hall closet, okay?"

"Will do."

Dean now knew where everything was kept in this house. He'd made himself right at home. He was such an easygoing guy. She should try to be more like that.

She pulled up the straps and reshifted herself. It was hopeless. She slipped into her sister's flip-flops and flip-flapped down the stairs.

"Oooo, wow. Jane looks um . . . is that your mom's suit?"

"Shuddup, it's the only thing I could find. Are you ready to freeze your ass off?"

Dean climbed on top of the picnic table bench and readied himself, one foot on the big knot of the marine-sized rope, one on the table. "Aye aye ayyyyyyaaaaaaaa eya eya . . ." He did a pretty good Tarzan yell and went for it. The swing went a decent distance out across the deck, but not quite far enough to jump in. He landed back on the table.

"Hmm. Logistical difficulties. Let's get higher."

"It was easier when we were twelve."

"Everything is." He let go and hooked the swing on the deck railing. "I'll get the ladder."

"I'll help."

They went around the side of the house and retrieved the tall ladder together. Dean set it up while she steadied it. He climbed up halfway, and she handed him the rope.

"Wait, I have to turn the lights off. It's cool, trust me." She ran in and flicked the downstairs lights off. She'd already turned off the upstairs, so now it was pitch dark except for the moon and the glittering harbor lights across the water.

"Okay, this is it! No giant boulders out there, right?"

"Just barnacles and crabs. Go for it!"

She watched him, his strong, muscular legs flexing, his bare chest with more muscles than the original black-and-white Tarzan movie for sure. He swung out wide and dropped right into the bay with a big huge yelping cannonball.

He came up sputtering. "It's great! Water's warm. Hurry up!"

Monty the dog took this opportunity to prove that he was a Golden Retriever and leaped into the water after Dean. He yelped and swam and yelped again, probably surprised by his own boldness.

"Monty! You insane mutt!" Jillian called and clapped her hands. "Come on *back* here."

Dean caught Monty and gave him a big dog hug, then sent him back after a piece of kelp. It looked like a tennis ball and smelled like seaweed, but Monty went for it. Jillian caught the dog on the return and made him sit. Monty shook all over her, then lay down very nicely like he hadn't just jumped in the sea. "Akkkk," she yelled. She was soaked. She might as well jump in now.

She took the rope with her and climbed up the ladder, positioned herself, and swung out. It was a perfect hit, and she knew just when to let go, as if by instinct. She'd done this so many times as a kid. She hit the water, which was just deep enough, resurfaced and gasped. "Wow, it's just as good! It's warmer than I thought, too." They swam to where they were chest high and stood for a moment. Monty barked a few times but didn't join them.

"Look, you're glowing." Dean came close to her.

"That's why I turned the lights off. Watch." She took his hands and ruffled the surface of the water. A strange greenish sparkle shimmered around them.

"Beautiful," he whispered.

"Phosphorous." She submerged slowly, then rose out of the water. She could see the flicker of tiny light molecules all around her.

He was there when she surfaced, very close. Her hands touched his arms. He moved back one step and held her hands at first, then slowly drew her back into him. The feel of his touch encircling her sent a shock wave of realization through her. She looked into his eyes.

He was smiling a very friendly come-over-here-and-play smile, then his whole look changed as she sank into the pleasure of his warmth. She knew that look. Her head went dizzy. Her body felt like the phosphorous was on the inside.

She parted her lips and did what she'd wanted to do a thousand times in the last week, and at least twenty times today. She kissed him. Rivulets of water danced between them. He took her kiss and sent it deeper. So deep she forgot about everything in the world, and went shimmering away into the perfection that was his mouth. He hungrily devoured her in the tenderest way she had ever experienced.

She ran her hands across the muscles of his back and sighed inside that kiss, pressing into him. His first touches were slow and easy, as if he was being sure—asking for permission. She slid her hands across his waist and down to his low, wet cutoffs. She wanted to feel every part of his tan, strong, gorgeous body.

He held her away from him for a moment, which made her gasp for air—or sanity. She watched as he moved his hands toward her under the water, flickering with phosphorous every move he made. He started with her belly, smoothing the loose fabric of the swimsuit. He used his two thumbs to stroke across her hipbones and make tiny circles.

Between her legs she felt the most monstrous ache; it made her moan out loud. Then his circles moved slowly up her waist and reached her breasts. When he slid his thumbs faintly over her nipples, she wound her arms around his neck. He kissed her, all wet and dripping hot, his tongue dancing across her lips lightly. She let her aching body tell him everything.

Tell him *everything*. Oh, God.

"Dean."

"You are the most beautiful mermaid I have ever found." His voice was husky with desire. He kissed her again and ran his mouth down her neck. She felt heat like underwater lava against her, his cutoffs straining with what must surely be the most amazing underwater erection ever, as far as she could think. Tarzan had a hard-on.

It took every ounce of her self-control not to go deep-sea exploring and find that treasure, just there, under the frayed, wet opening of a pair of very old cutoffs. But she needed to tell him everything. It just wouldn't be right.

Oh *God*, why did she have to develop a conscience *now?* Maybe she was more like her sister than she thought.

"Dean, stop."

He held her back from him an inch and ran his hand across her forehead, smoothing back her wet hair. "Too fast?"

"I have to tell you something. I'm not who you think I am."

Dean looked into her eyes without reaction for a moment. Then a slow, knowing smile spread over his face. "I know."

"You know? You know what?" She pushed herself away from him. Unfortunately she also lost her footing on the slick rocks and splashed backward into the water.

Dean laughed as her head disappeared and her two hands stuck out of the water like periscopes. He dove under the water and scooped her up like a fish, his arms a net.

She sputtered as they surfaced. "Let me go!" She flailed her arms and almost smacked him.

"Okay." He dropped her back in the water, then went to retrieve her again. This time she put her arms around his neck and let him bring her up without fighting. "Now will you please behave?" he said.

She was laughing this time. "Yes, yes. Don't let me go."

"I have no intention of letting you go, Miss whoever you are."

"Jillian. My name is Jillian Tompkins."

He carried her out of the water and up the deck

steps, depositing her on the handy old deck chaise still covered in blankets. It was anything but cold tonight, but he sat next to her and dried off her legs with the corner of the blanket.

The chaise collapsed. They ended up flat on the deck, and he pulled her into his arms protectively, while they both laughed again. Monty, still very wet and now rather stinky, came to join them on the chaise.

"Monty, you are something else." Dean gently removed Monty and gave him a nice towel to lie on. Monty sighed. Dean brought Jillian close to him again.

"We're a pair, aren't we?" he whispered in her ear. "You, pretending to be your sister, me pretending to be a repair guy."

"You're not a repair guy?" She felt a small shock go through her.

"I used to have my own contracting business, remember? I haven't done a regular repair job in years, except for a volunteer group, but mostly I gave it up for art."

"I guess we are a pair." She kissed him softly, and he deepened that kiss and took it to a more interesting level. When she could talk again, she blurt out more of her confession, which he'd been expecting to erupt eventually. "I was supposed to be saving you for my sister Jana Lee, to cheer her up when she came home."

He stopped kissing her after she told him this

little tidbit. "Oh, like a cat with a mouse, you just tease me and she comes in for the kill later?" He tickled her chin.

"Something like that," she answered with a breathy voice that reeked of desire. Her lips pressed against his neck, just below his ear. She was wrapped around him as tight as a starfish. He buried his face in her hair. He made a bold move and slid her underneath him. He gently moved against her until she moaned. He felt her body become extremely aroused. His was pretty far along, too.

Their wet bodies actually steamed as the air cooled around them and the heat they were creating hit the night breeze. He kissed her again and swam in the feeling of holding her in his arms, their bodies pressed together.

"Carly is gone for the night?" he whispered.

"She's my niece, by the way, and yes," she breathed heavily as he slowly moved his hands down her wet, swimsuited body.

He wanted to give her a taste of the pleasure to come. He looked around them at the secluded, lush yard that created a private screen from her neighbors. The maple tree was full and green and shadowed them where they lay on the deck, on the broken chaise, which had so conveniently collapsed into a bed for them. It was enough for a few minutes of wildness.

He ran his fingers down the strap of her swimsuit and pulled it away from her breast. His mouth followed. She tasted of salt water and something so sweet it left him aching for her. He let his tongue tease her and circle to her nipple. It was hard and hot, and he took it into his mouth. She had ceased to talk, and only a deep, throaty sound emerged from her as he slid the strap of her suit all the way down and cupped her breast into his mouth.

Dean moved and kept his mouth on her so he could brush his hand between her legs and feel the flash-heat mounting in her. He had to touch her. He ran his thumb under the loose fabric of the suit and found the hottest spot.

She bent her knee up slightly and let him in, arching against his touch. He was a very good locater of things that drove her insane, and not in the bad way—in the good way. He had her panting and clutching him in seconds. He tried to slow it down, but he couldn't help it, he wanted to watch her have an orgasm on the deck. She obliged him, digging her fingers into his shoulder as he pulled at her nipple with his mouth, making her come harder beneath his gentle fingers.

She tried to be quiet, but she finally had to press her mouth into his other shoulder and whimper with pleasure. This wasn't working, because he just wanted to make her do that again and again, with his mouth, with his hands, with . . . him. He felt his own erection throbbing between them. If she touched him he wouldn't be able to think.

She touched him.

"We've got to get somewhere . . . more sheltered." That was all he could say as her fingers smoothed over the sensitive skin of the head of his erection, which had escaped the bounds of his wet cutoffs.

He moved off of her and gently removed her hand, which returned immediately and very disobediently and followed him up, that devil woman. She had a look in her eye that made him almost forget they had to get out of there. He pulled her up to her feet and wrapped the blanket around her.

"Yum," she said.

He brought her close to him. "Yeah, me too." He kissed her, then he thought about more practical matters. "Don't move, I have to go to my truck for a minute." He ran barefoot, which probably wasn't the best idea in this construction zone, back behind the house to his truck. He had condoms in the glove box, like every self-respecting guy who had the hots for a woman he was working for.

He moved back to her like a man pursued by lions. He pulled her against him and kissed her again, hard.

She came up for air. "Get me to a bedroom,

Dean. Right now." Not behaving again, she stroked up his leg toward his really ready-to-go little Dean. Well, more like *big* Dean now.

He grabbed her and her blanket and carried her inside. She was like a hot tamale in that blanket. He pounded up the stairs to the bedroom. She nibbled on his neck.

"Stop that, I'll drop you."

"You would not."

He dropped her on the bed. She looked slightly shocked, then grinned at him. "You next."

"We should have that talk responsible people have," he said.

"Screw it," she said. "We're in our thirties."

"I'm clean, I assume you are, whoever the hell you are, and I know how to use a condom. Does that about cover it?"

"Works for me. Now shut up and kiss me." He was standing next to the bed trying to get off his wet cutoffs. She crawled over to him and sat where she could reach him. Her hands explored his bare chest and anything that wasn't covered by the cutoffs, and a few things that were barely covered.

Then she removed the cutoffs herself. Then she put her mouth on him. Just a flicker, a quick, teasing tongue. He could handle this. Then she took him . . . deeper. He thought he would have to maybe stop her. He grabbed for the bedpost to balance himself. He thought how he didn't want to stop her, but he did. Then he stopped thinking.

"*Augh*, you are so . . . naughty!"

"I see how much that's bothering you," she whispered against him, taking pause.

He needed to take control here, or he wouldn't last ten minutes. He pushed her backward onto the bed, leaving her legs dangling over the side, then just dove between her legs, burying his mouth against the fabric of her suit. He breathed his hot breath on her and she moaned his name. He pushed the fabric aside and slid his thumb into her, then covered her with his mouth. She moaned again, and he felt her hard, throbbing reaction against his tongue. Her body convulsed against his thumb repeatedly.

"Oh oh *ohhhhhhhhhhh*," she moaned.

He didn't stop but moved so slightly and gently that she rose back up to the top and exploded again. My God, she was quick and responsive and wildly wet beneath his hands and mouth. He moved up her body with his mouth sliding against the fabric, then just rested his insane erection next to the hot fire that burned between her legs, without entering her. This took quite a bit of maneuvering. She squirmed against him like a wildcat and pressed him into her until he knew he couldn't play this game anymore. She was too hot to handle. He'd definitely ignited a spark in Miss Jillian Tompkins, and now he had a full-blown fire on his hands.

He got up and grabbed the condom he'd managed to bring with him just on the off chance she needed more than her cupboards painted. There was one small lamp beside the bed, and he turned it on. The light was soft, and he could look at her.

He started by unpeeling her swimsuit off her. She lay naked in the lamplight with only one thing on her mind. You just had to love a woman like that. She groaned waiting the two seconds for him, and she made strange animal noises.

He couldn't manage to get the damn thing on before she flipped the whole game again and there she was, torturing him, with her mouth traveling everywhere. She was just so, so ready.

He ran his hand over her dark, silky hair, gently, lovingly, letting his eyes close and her mouth make him lose his mind. He wasn't long for this world. He was in the outer limits already.

When she sort of figured that out, she stood up slowly, kissed him with that mouth, and felt every inch of him with her smooth hands.

"You are so, so delicious. Please have me now, please," she teased her mouth over his ear and begged him. He put his arms around her and lowered her to the bed.

He felt the warmth of her desire beneath him. He barely had time to slip on the condom before she guided him down into her deep and slippery heaven. Her legs arched against his hips, and he moved so deliberately into her that she climaxed.

He felt so primal with her—so completely in

tune. He slowed everything down and moved his gaze over her face, kissing each corner of her lips, her eyes, and her forehead. She twisted under him with tiny, little twists of movement that drove him completely wild and made the buildup of heat between them become more than he could stand.

Or could he? He tried. He moved her, flipped her, so he was leaning against the headboard, with a pillow behind him. She had positioned herself around him and straddled his lap. Oh my God, she felt so good, and he could reach his mouth to her breasts, and she could move in that crazy way, and he just couldn't take any more and she knew that too, so she got very jungle animal on him and drowned him in hard, deep movements that made her nipple hard as a rock in his mouth.

Then the juicy sweetness of her just spilled all over him like hot coffee, and he just . . . exploded—yelled—screamed out her name—"Oh, oh, *Jillian*."

And so did she. She screamed *"Dean,"* then started laughing, and she fell against him and the throbbing between them was so amazing that he couldn't tell which one of them was throbbing.

It took him a minute to recover, and then, being a guy, he wondered why she had laughed and hoped it wasn't anything he'd done, but it made him laugh, too, because it was infectious.

"What the hell is so funny?"

"I don't know. I guess I just feel so *good*," she giggled.

"I'm glad you feel good. Damn, woman, you are one amazing lover." He talked softly in her ear. He moved her to a more comfortable reclining position on the blanket beneath them. He pulled her close to him and lay on his side, facing her, balanced on his elbow.

"When you came, that was the first time you said my name." She teased his hair and ran her fingers over his lips. "My, my, you are good, Dean. You are . . . so *damn* good."

"Thank you, *Jillian*—is it Jill sometimes?"

"It is Jillian and sometimes Jilly to people who want to remind me I was once a kid."

"Dean Wakefield, nice to have you." He shook her hand.

"Sounds like a famous artist."

"Would you like to see my sculptures?"

"Great line. Someone should do *you*, your body is a masterpiece."

"Geez, Miss Jilly, you're going to make me get a big head."

"I think that could happen in another hour or so." She skimmed over his resting man goodies, and they made a little jump of recognition. Sometimes they seem to have a mind of their own, those parts.

The moonlight from outside came through the bedroom window and danced over their bodies. She watched him with her blue eyes that just a few minutes ago had been filled with that look—

that vacant, pleasured look that he loved seeing on her now.

They lay like that for the better part of an hour, talking, and he learned the twist of fate that had brought her to his little town in the Northwest. Very interesting. Very strange, he thought. But obviously he wasn't going to be courted and prepped for the twin sister. He had found his partner in this chess game. Now he'd just have to see how it played out.

16

Double Trouble

Gloria Kissinger was enough of a politician to know that her moment was close at hand. When her pal Virginia in human resources had given her the heads up about Jackson requesting Jillian Tompkins's personnel file first thing in the morning, she'd known this was it. Showtime. Pay dirt. Revenge was hers.

Dear Virgi was another Jackson cast-off, and she was more than willing to rattle his chains. As a matter of fact, Gloria had quite an underground alliance in the former dates and playmates of Jackson Hawks, in and out of Pitman Inc.

Just goes to show that old saying was true: Don't date where you eat. Well, her cleaned-up version anyhow. A lady doesn't talk trash talk. And she was a lady.

Gloria felt quite sure and extremely excited to know that her moment was at hand. One thing, among many, that she knew about Jackson was that he detested dishonesty and lying. He'd fired someone flat-out at a meeting for trying to lie their way out of a mistake. His motto was that a person should stand up and take the consequences of his or her mistakes like a man—or a woman, for that matter. Anything else was a fatal character flaw in his opinion. He'd said as much in meetings. He didn't care about mistakes, just owning up to them. Gloria thought that was one of Jackson's most honorable traits, among many he possessed.

She sat back in her cubicle in the accounting area, which they shared with some of the data entry girls. There were a few girls here that Jackson had toyed with and left brokenhearted. One-date girls. Girls who wouldn't mind seeing Jackson get a shock. Maybe he'd stop being so arrogant if he knew he was being fooled but good by Jillian Tompkins's twin sister, Jana Lee Stivers.

An MBA from UCLA, an undergrad degree in accounting from University of Washington and UCLA, Jillian Tompkins certainly had credentials. No wonder his father had hired her to be the comptroller for Pitman Toys. Jackson sat back in his office chair and had another gulp of coffee.

Something was nagging at him.

Everything he read about Jillian said that she was a whiz with numbers. He'd known women like that; there were lots working right here. As a matter of fact, he could divide up all the women he'd ever dated or met into two categories: left-brain math whizzes and right-brain creative types. If there was one thing Jackson knew, it was women.

So how come Miss UCLA accounting degree was so good with new toy ideas and suddenly could create amazing drawings and brainstorm costume design with the design department?

He'd thought about her all weekend, and even discussed her with his brother, Marcus. They'd had a great dinner Saturday night and played soccer with the boys until they'd all dropped from exhaustion. He'd actually invited her along, but she'd declined. She was good at that.

Marcus said she sounded delightful and mentioned that she was the first woman Jackson had actually *talked* about.

Jackson knew she was special. Even their not-so-perfect dinner date had been above average. She listened to him, and they had fun, but he still couldn't break through to her heart. It was like she was holding a part of herself back from him.

And what woman shouldn't? She probably knew his reputation well. It would take some time to win her heart. It was up to him to admit his mistakes and prove to her he was sincere. Was he sincere? What was it about Jillian Tompkins that had him so tied up in knots?

Jackson stuck Ms. Tompkins's personnel file in a drawer and tried to focus on other things besides the way her hair flipped up around her ear in a smooth, sexy line.

Jana Lee shut herself up in her office and told Oliver to hold all her calls. She'd only glanced at the beautiful summer bouquet of flowers Jackson had sent over this morning. She'd admire them later. This whole Jackson thing was driving her nuts, and the fact that she hadn't been able to reach Jillian on the phone all weekend had her completely freaked out.

She hurried behind the desk and auto-dialed her house in Washington. Surely whatever Jillian had been up to all weekend, she'd be back in the house today. It was early too; she'd probably be asleep. Jana Lee drummed the desk with her newly painted fingernails while the phone rang and rang. Oliver had made her sit still and have a mini-manicure before her date. She stopped drumming and gazed at the warm orange-tangerine color.

"Hello?" Jillian's voice was on the other end of the phone. Thank God.

"Jillian, it's Jana Lee. Where the *hell* have you been?" Like they didn't know each other's voices.

"Why, is something wrong? I FedExed those papers back to you. They should be there already."

"No, no, it's not the papers," Jana Lee sighed. "Sorry. I just. I don't know. I had something to talk to you about. And I was worried."

"Take a deep breath. I'm in good hands."

Then Jana Lee heard it—a *most* amazing sound. Her sister, Jillian Tompkins, giggled. Jillian did *not* giggle. "What's going on?" Jana Lee asked.

"Oh, nothing, Carly's helping me paint stuff, and I've sort of taken up with the handyman." There it was again, the sound of Jillian giggling. This time a groan went with it, and Jana Lee heard a slap.

"You *what?*" Jana Lee demanded. "Is he like . . . in bed with you?"

"Sort of."

"Where is my impressionable fifteen-year-old daughter?"

"She spent the weekend with Ashley and Brianna. Apparently Ashley's folks have a boat and they're motoring around the sound having a great old time. She'll be back at noon today."

"Carly on a boat?" Jana Lee felt her mothering instincts kick in. Danger: boats, water, boys, summer, beer, sex—that sort of thing.

"She's *fine*, loosen up, sis. Carly is a great kid. I'd know if she was trying to pull the wool over your eyes. I wasn't exactly an angel in high school, you know," Jillian kidded.

"I know, I just worry. It's my job."

"Not this week, this week your job is to be me. Tell me that job is going well. Don't tell me anything else. I don't want to think about anything else today."

"I'm holding my own." Jana Lee fidgeted with a letter opener. "And I've been avoiding Jackson."

"Why?" Jillian sounded surprised.

"Well, I can't just lie to the man—it's cruel. The less I see of him the better. I've painted myself in a corner, that's for sure."

"Listen, sis, I don't know why I haven't said this before, I guess I'm just selfish. Once I'm back, maybe we could somehow get you out of this mess with him and you and he could start over. Like . . . when Barbara Stanwyck comes back and marries the guy she conned in the first place in *The Lady Eve*, you know?" Jillian said.

"I don't remember that movie, and this is real life." Jana Lee felt herself choke up as she was talking. Not until this very moment had she realized what she'd done. Any chance she might have imagined with Jackson was absolutely out of the question. She could never tell him what she'd done; he'd never understand. Ever. The whole thing was insane anyway. And she was going home in five days, and that was that. "I have to go, Jilly, tell Carly to call me."

"Okay, hon. And don't worry about Jackson, he's a hound dog anyway, he'd have dumped you before the week was out."

"Thanks," Jana Lee said.

"You *know* what I mean, he's a cad!"

"He's a cad. Okay, Jill, I've got work to do. We'll talk soon." Jana Lee said good-bye and hung up the phone. There was only one good thing about the conversation she'd just had, and that was that her sister had turned out to be better than fine, so her worry over Jillian's mental health was relieved for now. And the fact that Jilly had taken up with this guy Dean actually sounded good.

Jana Lee picked up the letter opener and stabbed the blotter a few times, making dents in the paper portion till they looked like chicken tracks. She'd been such an idiot. Why was she so foolish about love? She was just a mom from Washington, not some smart city girl who knew her way around a man like Jackson.

She'd gotten lucky with Bill, and despite the fact that he'd probably been her rebound guy from Elliot, it had worked out between them. She teared up thinking of the loss she'd suffered when Bill had died. Not just the loss of her husband but the loss of her ideas about life as well. She was completely adrift. The tidy package that had come with Bill had been destroyed.

She put her head on her arms. What would she do when she got back home—slip into the same fog she'd been living in for two years? Was Jackson going to ride up to her house on Seabridge

Bay in his limo and whisk her away? Then there was the little matter of a teenage daughter.

What a fool she'd been, getting dressed up for Jackson, dancing with him, kissing him, letting him get to her. All that had to stop. She'd throw herself into the Little Princess project for the rest of this week and stay out of his way.

From what she'd heard there'd be another girl to take her place by the end of the week anyhow.

After lunch Jackson put his signature to a dozen items and read reports from each department before Olga slid another manila envelope under his nose.

"Interoffice mail."

"Thanks," he said. What now? Another report? He scanned through his pile of folders; he'd thought he'd seen one from everyone. He undid the string twist and let the contents fall on his desk. There were phone records with highlighted calls and an assortment of odd papers. He picked through them carefully. What was all this; didn't it belong in accounting? He must have gotten it by mistake. He looked for the sender notation on the outside of the envelope, but there was none.

One page caught his eye. Paper-clipped to the top of a stack of memos was a photocopy of six signatures, each the same, but different. Jillian Tompkins, six ways, six times. There were arrows connecting a set of three, and someone had written the dates down under each signature and numbered them.

He stared at the paper. He didn't get it. Under that sheet were six memos Jillian had written. They had numbers matching the signature photocopy.

He put that aside and looked at the phone records. They were all from Jillian's office to a 360 area code, long distance. These were the things Jillian herself usually did—examined the phone records for repeat long-distance calls that weren't company business, then busted the caller with a bill and a warning. The listing said Seabridge, Washington, and they were all dated last week. Whoever had put together this report must have accessed the account records online.

Another group of papers clipped together had the press photos of Jillian and her sister when they were just kids. He smiled at their frilly dresses and slightly tipped tiaras. Gosh, they were *so* identical. Except for the different sashes and trim colors on their dresses, he didn't know how anyone could tell them apart. There were three of those photos, and so? He'd seen them before when they were looking at the concepts for the toys. Boy, that blue dragon dude was grumpy looking.

If he'd gotten all this by mistake, someone was going to an awful lot of trouble to examine Jillian's habits very closely.

He smiled to himself. It was no secret around

the office that he'd been dating her. Hell, it was *never* a secret around the office who he dated. Jackson was surprised it wasn't announced on the lunchroom bulletin board. *This week our VP will be dating Susan Sweeney. Please leave your applications in human resources if you'd like to apply for next week.*

Someone must be trying to throw a little dirt on Jillian. His father always told him not to date within the company, but who was he to talk, a man who'd had an affair with his secretary while he'd been married to a terrific person like Mom?

Jackson bristled. Old pain rolled around his temples. He really resented what his father had done to them. And he hated the fact that he'd taken on some of his father's traits. Why was he constantly unable to make a commitment to one woman? He was thirty-six now, and this was all wearing extremely thin.

His reputation had caught up with him, and now, when he was actually interested in a woman, she was backing away from him.

Jackson decided to bury himself in work. He put aside the folder that had mysteriously arrived on his desk and picked up a pile of advertisements to approve. What did he care what a bunch of meddling women thought about him dating Jillian?

It *was* kind of strange she'd been calling her sister from work. She could use her cell phone for that. But of all people, she'd be the first one to audit her own phone records and pay her long-distance overage.

He stared at the advertisement for a pack of ice-skating Snotz dolls and sighed.

There was something about Jillian Tompkins that was making him nuts. He didn't need a memo to figure that out. He needed *her.*

"You've got a three-thirty meeting with Jackson and the design department." Oliver had come in and given her the bad news personally, rather than delivering it over the intercom. He'd also brought in the blousy, pink and peach summer bouquet Jackson had sent over. He plunked it on the desk. "It's making me sneeze," Oliver said.

"Say it isn't so."

"What, the sneezing? Or the meeting?"

"The meeting, of course. I mean, I care if you have allergies, but the meeting can't be cured with Kleenex and a Benadryl."

"I see your point." Oliver blew his nose. "Excuse me."

"You're excused. What am I supposed to be doing at this meeting? Numbers?"

"Actually, no. Since you got yourself into this whole mess with the Little Princess promotion, it's all about approving the preliminary samples and other non-math-related things, although you should throw in a few stock phrases about unit pricing and packaging, which are Jillian's pet peeves."

Jana Lee, who had spent the entire day reading magazines, eating her lunch, drinking tea and trying to forget about this whole fiasco, felt panic creep up on her. "Why does Jackson have to be there?"

"Apparently he specifically requested the meeting. Don't take it all personally—producing a new product for holiday lineup at this late date is a minor nightmare, and he truly has to keep an eye on the details. He's taking a risk, and he wants to be sure things are done right."

"Oh, really. So you don't think it's an excuse to see me?"

"Of course it is. I've never seen Jackson Hawks so befuddled in my entire time here. He's no doubt having to confront all kinds of personal demons."

"He *is* a personal demon."

"At any rate, gather yourself up and off you go. I didn't give you much lead time so you wouldn't get all worked up about it. They're expecting you shortly. And by the way, the orange jacket looks divine. Throw that scarf over your shoulder and just muster up some attitude. You'll be fine." Oliver left the room.

Jana Lee hung back and tried to clear her head. Maybe she should just shrug Jackson off and let Jillian reignite him when she got back. Now *that* was not a bad idea.

She'd put on her new clothes today—stretchy black tank dress with her new orange linen jacket and the Pucci scarf. She loved the high-styling lines of this jacket with the asymmetrical shape. She knew it made her look good. Did she want to look good?

Her new little bow shoes looked great, with their pointy toes. Jana Lee retied her scarf around her neck the way Ollie had suggested, then Tangerine Summer went on her lips.

Jana Lee had never felt so conflicted in her entire life. She was sprucing up for a man she was supposed to be avoiding. Her sister's words kept haunting her. *"You and Jackson could start over."*

They could not. She'd gone too far. She needed to be Jillian for the next few days and end this madness as soon as possible.

When she finally emerged from the office, Ollie gasped, then grinned.

"You go, girl," he said. He handed her a binder—to look the part more, he said.

A swaggering walk wasn't her style, but she tried to access her inner Jillian as she entered the design department space. Jackson just about fell off the swivel stool he'd parked himself on next to Petra's presentation table.

"Miss Tompkins, you're looking . . . well," he sort of fumbled.

Jana Lee thought Mr. Hawks looked like he hadn't slept in days. Poor fellow.

"Let's get right to work, I don't want to run late." Jana Lee positioned herself carefully on a chair and let Petra, who was looking at her like she'd seen a ghost, do her bit. Probably she had seen a ghost, the ghost of Jillian Tompkins come to life. Jana Lee had been much too *herself* last time she and Petra had talked.

"Ahem, well, here's our princesses, and the dragon in a rough form, six ways, six fabrics, and we burned the midnight oil on these, if I do say so myself, sir." Petra held up two dragons and danced them around while she talked.

"I appreciate that very much, Petra. Which one do you like?"

Petra danced the one in her left hand. "This guy. He came out very well with the vinyl scalloped contrast in purple. Soft Goods found a brushed velour that works nicely."

"What's the cost breakdown on fabric?" Jana Lee knew an opening when she saw it, although she looked around to see if anyone was staring at her funny.

"Number two is the least expensive, see the number under their tails?" Petra picked up a sample and flipped it upside down. "But I'm not sure if we'd be looking at some seam stress. We don't want to produce a carnival booth toy, here, folks."

"What's his pose-ability due to—wires?" Jana Lee asked. Hey, she was a mom, she knew about toys and their problems.

"Plastic coated, and we're using top grade there. We didn't have any issues with the Titans of Terror characters."

"Isn't this for a lower age range?" Jana Lee asked.

"Yes, true."

"Good point, Jillian, let's go with a stuffing and axe his pose-ability. He's supposed to be a pal, anyway. Let's add the music box and he'll be singing instead of having the ability to hold a martini glass." Jackson crossed his arms.

Everyone laughed and they started in on construction and fabric content and left the dress selection till the end. Since Jana Lee was out of her league here, she nodded and smiled a lot. This was most definitely a meeting Jillian would have ruled court over, but the lofty silent approach was working as far as Jana Lee knew.

When she'd picked a couple of very cute dresses and they'd rearranged the age-appropriate level to include the tiny little tiaras, she got up.

"Thanks, Petra, and please send a report over to me. I'll run up the hard figures based on your new selections." Jana Lee hoped that sounded official and somewhat accurate.

"Sure," Petra said. "Thanks for coming."

"I'll walk you back to your office, Miss Tompkins."

Petra made a brief eye-rolling face that only Jana Lee could see. It made her smile.

"Let's go then," she said as she headed for the doorway. Jana Lee could feel Jackson directly behind her. She slowed down so he was beside her. They walked down the halls of Pitman together, with many eyes following. An audible ripple of whispers followed in their wake.

"I tried to reach you this weekend. Did you get my messages?" He sounded pretty casual.

This was her moment to decide. She decided she was doomed anyway, so she might as well cut her losses.

"Mr. Hawks, as much as I've enjoyed your company, I think we should cool it. Office dating is difficult."

"Are you kidding? I think we're way beyond that. And Friday, well hey, call me crazy, but we both felt the earth move, didn't we?"

Jackson looked around and noticed people were staring. Here he was running after this very beautiful woman, who was really making tracks down the hallway. He liked her better when she wasn't all orange and black and harsh all over, even though that jacket was amazingly cool.

What the hell had happened to her, anyhow?

He'd seen her act like a kid over toy ideas and brainstorm advertising ideas like a champ. He'd seen this magic spark in her that had attracted him like a moth. As a matter of fact, here he was, chasing that spark down the hallway, beating his wings against the glass, waiting to be burned up in her flame. She was going to scorch him for sure.

He stopped in his tracks. She didn't. She kept on going. Damn her, she was as stubborn as any female he'd ever met. He gathered his pride and headed down a side hallway, the back way to his office. It might be an early cocktail hour for him tonight. *Damn* her.

Jana Lee made it into her office without closing the door, then started to cry. She didn't mean to—it just burst out of her. She made an odd sound and felt the tears flow down her cheeks. Oliver followed her in, and she motioned wordlessly for a tissue. He grabbed a full box out of a drawer and started handing her a stream of them, shutting the door behind them.

"Bad meeting?" he asked carefully.

"I told Jackson to cool it. I brushed him off." She threw herself into her office chair, sniffling and sobbing.

"That sounds reasonable, and very wise, considering."

"It does, doesn't it? But the truth is, the earth

did move." She knew this didn't make much sense, but Oliver seemed to understand.

"Oh, dear, don't get yourself all worked up about this, I'm sure things will work out." Oliver looked distressed. He sat down in the chair across from her and handed her more tissues.

"How can it work out?" Jana Lee blubbered. "I'm not Jillian, and when Jackson finds out I've been lying to him, he won't ever want to see me again. Not that I *care*, I mean, I hardly know him. It's just that what I have seen, I actually *li-i-i-ke*." Her "like" came out in little hiccupping sobs.

"Oh, not that you care," Oliver kidded her.

"And if he doesn't find out, then who am I? He thinks I'm Jillia-a-a-an." The same sobbing hiccup divided "Jillian" into seven syllables.

"Wow, I see your point. You're screwed."

"Thanks," she sobbed harder. "Not only that, I certainly haven't left much for Jillian to work with when she gets back."

"Isn't she all cozy with the carpenter man at your place?"

"Oh, that's just a summer fling. She has it bad for Jackson. She told me."

"My, my, things are certainly a mess. On the other hand . . ."

Jana Lee lifted her head up slightly, hoping Ollie had some words of comfort.

"No, I was going to say that sometimes love has an amazing way of overcoming all odds, but in this case, I'd say you're screwed no matter which way the wind blows."

"Geez, Ollie."

"Might as well face facts. Now wash your face and quit that caterwauling. There are other men out there. Buck up, honey. You'll be out of here by Friday, and from what I hear from Jillian, there's a large selection of cute manly builder types running around your house. Oops, I shouldn't have said that."

"What is she up to now?" Jana Lee sucked in a breath and stopped crying. There were tissues piled five inches high on the desk.

"Minor repairs. A little painting. Nothing to worry about." Oliver got up.

"When it comes to Jillian, nothing is minor."

"See? You can think about what she might be doing to your house instead of your hopeless situation with Jackson. Jillian has great taste, even if she is a little over the top," Oliver reminded her.

"So clever, changing the subject. She does have good taste, though, there is at least that." A deep sigh escaped Jana Lee's lips, and she flopped back in the chair.

"Her apartment *is* marvelous," Ollie said.

"I have enjoyed the peacefulness of the place. It's been a great break from my mess of a house." She took in a few ragged breaths and held out her hand to Oliver. "Thanks, Ollie, I don't have too many friends to talk to. Jillian took up a whole lot of space when we were young, and I guess it's a notorious trait of twins to have problems opening up to others."

"You're welcome," he said, patting her hand. "And I consider you very easy to talk to." Oliver smiled at her. "Now, I'll tidy up the last-minute things and you get ready to leave early today. You're in a state. There's no reason you have to stay late." He let go of her hand, nodded and slipped out the door.

"Easy to talk to, but not so easy to love," she said to herself, very quietly.

Suddenly she missed her daughter terribly. She thought how nice it would be to at least spend some time with Carly here in San Francisco. They might mend some mom-daughter fences and take in the galleries.

She poured a glass of water from the pitcher she kept on the shelf and sipped till she felt calmer, then she acted on her impulse. She dialed her house in Washington.

17

A Pair of Hearts

Jillian had forgotten how much she liked sex. Sex was good. Sex with Dean was *really* good. They'd taken every opportunity over the weekend to explore just how good. It was how good in the kitchen, how good in the bathtub, how good in the shimmering Seabridge Bay water at night, and quite a few how good in the bedroom.

They'd made it two steps into the house after a quick hamburger dinner run Saturday night and stripped each other down for a frantic, crazy, hot session on the new area rug. Monty Python was not amused and huffed off through the plastic sheeting into the utility room to eat. Jillian had rug burns, but she didn't care.

Dean Wakefield had scratches, but he didn't care either. He also had the hands of an artist; a very, very creative artist. His strength was a constant turn-on to her, and she could hardly keep her mouth to herself.

As if that wasn't enough, Dean could cook.

He sent the crew home at noon on Saturday and Sunday, much to their delight, and much to her pleasure. Carly came home right on time after her boat trip, and boy, that kid knew exactly what was going on. After an afternoon of cleanup and preparation for the finishing details, she cornered Jillian.

"You, my aunt, are *doing it* with the Dean man. Look at the way he's looking at you. It's like . . . close to disgusting. And look at you, you're all glowing and . . . I don't even know how to put it."

"Well, there's hardly any point in denying it. I am an adult, you know, and long overdue for a torrid affair."

Carly poured herself a glass of lemonade that Dean had made and left to chill in the fridge. "Is that all he is, Aunt Jillian? A torrid affair? Aren't you supposed to be leaving on Friday?"

Dean, fortunately, had stepped outside to hammer on something. He was busy building a new storage cupboard for the corner of the living room. They'd picked out a cool prefab unit to hold the TV and stereo stuff. Dean was fun to shop with. Jillian loved this whole shopping-painting-sex-food thing they were doing. The shopping had really been fun, with Dean showing her all kinds of antique stores around the county so they could shabby chic up Jana Lee's house.

Jillian didn't say anything to Carly. She just stared out the window at Dean in his T-shirt and jeans. He had on a backward Mariners baseball cap.

"So?" Carly pressed.

"Maybe we'll find a way to see each other."

"Ya, right, with you back working your butt off at Pitman Toys?"

"Maybe you're too young to be talking about this, young lady."

"Nice try. I'm wise beyond my years. I have friends whose parents have been married several times. We've seen stuff."

"And where are you on the boyfriend scene?"

"I'm not seeing anyone special. We go to the movies in groups, you know, maybe there's three boys and four girls, or whatever, and there is one boy I like, but I've got other things to do besides moon at some boy. I'm serious about my art."

"I love that. Just remember to have fun too when you get older. God forbid I should encourage you to loosen up, your mother would kill me, but there's more to life than work. I should know. I've completely screwed up, and here I am thirty-five and alone."

"No kidding." Carly drank more lemonade and made a face at Jillian.

Jillian made a face back at her. "So what about the boy?"

"He's an exchange student. He's going back to France at the end of the summer. His name is Averil. So what's the point?"

"Wow. Those French exchange students with that accent and all. Very hot."

"He's very sexy," Carly said.

"Okay. Your mom has had the big talk about birth control and safe sex and all that jazz, right?"

"Mostly we had to sit through that in sex ed, but she did a pretty good job. I thought she'd faint, really," Carly laughed.

"I bet. So my big advice is before Averil goes home, kiss him. That's all, just give him a big, juicy, American-girl kiss. No extra stuff. He's European. You never know what he's been up to."

Carly snorted a laugh into her lemonade. "So, so funny. By the way, my mom doesn't sound so good. Are you sure she's okay?"

"Why, did she say something?"

"Not really, just the sound of her voice. She sounds sad. I know that sound in her, she's worn a hole in sad."

"I didn't notice. She told me everything was fine."

"Aren't you supposed to have some psychic tie with your identical twin?"

"I think she's better at that than I am."

"Whatever. You should call her."

"I will. What's up for today?"

"I'm working on a canvas outside. I'm trying a landscape."

"Need help hauling stuff out there?"

"Sure. Is this okay, or should I be painting walls instead of boats and seagulls?"

"Na, go paint seagulls. We've got things under control here. We're almost done. Dean's going to clean the floors in here so we'll all have to be outside."

Jillian followed her niece to the spare room, where all her art supplies were neatly housed in a rolling tray unit. They decided to set up a mobile studio and hauled it all through the back door down toward the water's edge.

Carly set up her easel and a card table and ordered Jillian around as if she were an executive. That girl definitely took after her aunt. Really, she was an interesting combination of Jillian and Jana Lee. Artistic, but business minded. Of course that organizational streak had ended with the art supplies, as evidenced by the original state Jillian had found Carly's bedroom in.

As Jillian left her niece on the sloped lawn and

flat, stone-covered landing that made up Jana Lee's side yard, she heard her cell phone ringing. She ran for it and felt an interesting strength in her legs, like maybe all this fresh air, hard work and lovemaking had finally paid off. She felt *wonderful*.

And she noticed that when Carly had mentioned going back to Pitman, she hadn't felt quite as panicked. Somewhat, but not the full-out heart-pounding deal.

The caller ID said Pitman Toys. Jillian was stupid not to have left Jana Lee a new cell phone, but she would just settle up the long-distance charges when she got back and tell them her cell had fritzed out on her or something. She was getting good at making stuff up, sadly.

At least she was being honest with Dean now.

"Hey, Jana, what's up?" Jillian said. After a few minutes of her sister talking about their contract, the weather, the office, nothing really, she had to agree with Carly; Jana Lee sounded down. Maybe Pitman did that to everyone. Maybe this whole thing had been too much for her sister.

"God, Jana, you sound stressed. I feel terrible for putting you in this position." She did, too. But at the same time she also felt better than she had in years, so there was a selfish part of her that was really glad she'd asked her sister to do this, and a caring part that was sorry she had put her sister through it. She was nothing if not a woman with two sides.

"I'm okay. I just miss my daughter. I know this is asking a lot, but do you think we could arrange to have her flown here? We could see the city, and it could just look like she was visiting you, you know?"

Jillian was taken by surprise. She fell silent and thought about the logistics of that, but really, it was obvious that Jana Lee was having a hard time. "Would you like me to come back early?" she asked. She felt a knot in her stomach when she said that, but it wasn't so much about going back to Pitman this time: It was about leaving here. Leaving Dean.

"No, no, I really don't want you to come back yet, I have something I'm finishing up. I just wonder if Carly would be up for a trip."

"Did you ask her yourself?" Jillian asked.

"No, I didn't get this wild idea until just now. You can go ahead and ask her."

Jillian could feel the importance of this thing in her sister's voice. And after all, she'd gotten her into this; it was the least she could do. "I'll talk to her and get back to you."

"I might leave. I had a late meeting and I'm tired."

"Should I know about this?"

"No, it's all about the Little Princess project, and believe it or not, I was actually quite capable of approving doll dresses and fabric for a blue dragon toy."

Jillian laughed. "I always thought there should be a prince to rescue us from Harvey."

"Me too. He'll have to wait for next season. So talk to my daughter, and let me know. I've got some savings—I can pay for her ticket."

"Don't be silly, it's my gift. Besides, I am the queen of finding cheap airfare, even late ones. Standby is always good, and there are seats open during the week."

"You're the genius."

Jillian wondered why her sister always said that. She was no genius, and Jana Lee had so much more going for her. "Okay, sis. I'll catch you later." She hung up the phone and slipped it in her shorts pocket. Carly would probably be thrilled to go hang out in Frisco. She'd love the museums and the galleries.

The feel of San Francisco crept into Jillian's memory. It was odd, but she didn't miss her apartment, or the city, or a favorite restaurant, or anything. She didn't even have a favorite restaurant because she ate while she read reports and mostly had the lunchroom caterer send her meals to her office.

Oliver had told her once that this was no way to dine.

These days her favorite thing was a double cheeseburger and a milk shake in Dean's truck or one of Dean's amazing stir-fry dinners at the picnic table on the deck.

Dean pulled Jillian into his arms and wrapped her in his warmth. The steel fire pit they'd bought and positioned on the deck was crackling, and flames teased the night sky. A waning moon rose red-orange across the bay.

He'd promised himself he wouldn't get too attached to his fly-by girl, but moments like these were making it difficult. They'd made a deal to enjoy the time they had with complete abandon. They'd certainly done that.

Her hair smelled as sweet as apricots. He breathed her scent in and leaned his cheek against her head. They were both fresh from a shower—a very interesting shower, and dressed in clean clothes.

He liked having her against him in their favorite rickety lounge chair. She sipped a glass of white wine they'd bought together. He'd been teaching her about cooking, and she'd been teaching him about wine.

Carly had gone up to pack and get some sleep. He thought it was a great idea for her to go see her mom. It sounded like a fresh start would be a good thing for them. The fire took the night chill off so well that Jillian pushed the blanket off her shoulders and used him for a pillow. He and Jillian were such night owls these days, trying to squeeze as many hours as they could into the time they had left.

"Comfortable?" he whispered to her.

"Very," she answered. "Thank you for teaching me how to relax, Dean."

"My pleasure. I learned it the hard way myself, as you know."

"Do you miss building ten houses at once and being the big boss?"

"No. I don't miss the person I was then. I found a good outlet with sculpture."

"You *are* good with your hands." She snuggled against him. "When do I get to see your place, Dean? We've been so focused on this house I can't believe I haven't made you take me up on your hill."

"Let's get Carly to the airport and see where we end up."

"What? No plan? No schedule?"

"Shocking, isn't it?" he reached for his own wineglass and leaned over for a sip. They unbalanced a bit, and he shifted back level, wrapping his arms protectively around her. They fell into a silence he loved. He loved to sit by the fire and have her next to him. He loved the way she was finally letting herself be in present time.

All her worries were about what was going to happen, what might occur—all future based.

He'd tried to show her that, and somehow, after days of unraveling her tightly wound defenses, he'd succeeded.

Now she could feel what it was like to watch the fire flicker in the moonlight and hear the lapping of the waves against the bulkhead. There was a rhythm to all of that, and it could take you to a very good headspace.

But against his own best advice, Dean was having a whole lot of thoughts about Jillian's leaving on Friday. Future thoughts. Would he ever see her again? Should he go to the city and continue this adventure? What would happen to them in her world?

He felt the pain of loss. The loss of moments like these. She was an amazing woman. Her mind was sharp, her body made him ache for her, and her responsiveness to him made it hard to concentrate on getting normal things done. He knew that would wear off or at least reach a more normal level later, but right now it was glorious.

Unfortunately, he had to go home tonight and leave this happy scene. God, how he was going to miss her.

He thought about Trina and the aching emptiness he'd had after she died. One of the reasons he hadn't taken Jillian to his house was this odd sense of her stepping into Trina's territory. But now he wanted nothing more than to bring the two parts of his life together and have Jillian in his space, sweeping the old memories away like the whirlwind that she was. He could keep Trina in a special place in his heart forever.

He sat back and closed his eyes. He didn't want to let Jillian go.

18

Swap, in the Name of Love

Gloria Kissinger paced the hall between Bret Sears's cubicle and her own. Now that the goods had been delivered, where was the fallout? Where was the shouting match between Jackson and the fake Jillian Tompkins? Where was the great scene of fake Jillian packing her bags and being booted out of her fancy office, along with the real one? Where was the memo advertising for a new comptroller for Pitman Toys?

Surely Jackson wasn't as dense as to not put two and two together? She snorted a laugh to herself; *two and two together*. Good one. Twins humor.

Gloria crossed her arms and huffed. Maybe he *was* that dense. After all, men thought with their little brains, not their big ones. She'd just have to make it clearer to him.

Every girl in the office knew that when her time was up with Jackson, there'd be no getting by Olga Reyes. She guarded the gate to Jackson's office like a lioness and knew a lame excuse from ten paces away.

Gloria would just have to think of a *good* excuse. She'd find her moment.

Carly was coming to San Francisco! Jana Lee felt like Christmas. She should go out and buy her a present and wrap it in pretty girl wrap. Or maybe they'd go shopping together for some fancy San Francisco clothes. Of course Carly would have to be able to use them for school in the fall.

Always the practical mother, wasn't she? Jana Lee poured herself a cup of hot tea and sat back behind her sister's desk.

She was marking time by half-hour increments now. Seven o'clock couldn't come soon enough. But now that she'd put the wheels in motion to have Carly brought here, she started to work herself into a snit about the entire thing. What would her daughter think of her being here and lying like this? What kind of an example would that be?

A bad example. Sure, she'd had good motives, but so what if she'd done it out of pity for her sister? It was one thing to talk to Carly about this whole switch thing on the phone, and another to have her here in the middle of it. Maybe this wasn't the best idea.

But she missed her. Her mother's instincts had kicked in, and she felt like her daughter should be here with her. She'd had this sort of tickle in her mind about something just not being right, and if Carly was here with her, that would take care of one part of her worry. A fifteen-year-old on the loose in the summer with a rogue aunt had definite potential for disaster.

Jana Lee remembered visiting Uncle Cyril and Aunt Doreen in Medford, Oregon. She and her sister were about seventeen. When she thought of that summer, the faint memory of her first taste of gin always wafted back to her. All summer they'd hung around the Holiday Inn hotel swimming pool where Doreen had tended bar. Doreen had let her drink gin and tonic on the rocks when no one had been looking. Jana Lee remembered how she'd fallen madly in love with a cute boy named Terry Kjornes, who was all of nineteen at the time.

Of course Jillian had fallen madly in love with him too, but Terry had picked her, something Jana Lee had been extremely grateful for. She'd been so grateful that she'd let him go all the way with her in the backseat of his car on a dark, hot summer night.

Jana Lee felt a little smile turn the corners of her mouth upward. It was good that her memory of that moment was forever linked with a great guy like that. She probably should have married that boy; he was one of the nicest boys she'd ever met, and the most *amazing* kisser.

How different her life would have been if Terry Kjornes had ridden up to Seabridge, Washington, in his red GTO and insisted they get married. That was the summer that Cyndi Lauper kept singing "Time After Time" on the radio. *Lovesick* was what she'd been that summer. Until fall—then she'd stopped writing him and gotten back to her regular high school life. He'd gradually stopped writing her, too.

Which just goes to show you that aunts weren't always the best babysitters.

And hey, she might be *lovesick* about Jackson, but come the fall, she'd find a job and get back to her old life.

She sipped her hot tea, which she'd stirred into submission, and thought about that. Find a job. She liked that idea. But what in the world would she do in Seabridge? She'd have to go to the city to get a job with any future. And that would leave her daughter parentless in those evening hours.

She couldn't picture that. It wasn't what she wanted for Carly. But maybe she didn't have a choice. She could just take a low-level job in town until Carly graduated from high school. She slurped the rest of her tea down and looked at the clock. Tick tick tick. She could hardly wait until she saw her daughter. She had so much to talk to her about.

She could show Carly the design department. Her daughter would love that. Carly would like the drawing boards and ideas pasted up all over the walls. Jana Lee liked the way the place was cluttered with ideas. Sometimes it was nice to be surrounded with colorful inspiration.

On the other hand, she could really see why Jillian liked her soothingly minimal office and home. The whole less-is-more thing was working. She felt very relaxed at Jillian's apartment, with nothing out of place. Carly would be interested in the art pieces Jillian had collected, and the guest room was very comfortable—Jana Lee knew because she'd slept in it over the weekend, watching two late movies on the TV in there, since Jillian didn't have a television in her bedroom.

Jana Lee picked up her teacup and returned it to the tray across the room, by her very cool tea station. She should make herself useful for the rest of the day so she'd stop thinking about Carly's arrival every minute.

In her attempts to be more "Jillian like" she'd scrounged a tight-fitting beige skirt and a fresh white tailored blouse out of the closet. It was a good thing the white blouse had a stretch element to it; otherwise she would have burst a button. The skirt did too, but not enough to make up for her more ample rear end and waist. She shimmied it down a touch and undid the top button by the zipper. It would hold, and no one would be the wiser. The side benefit was she could breathe.

Jana Lee smoothed back her new perky short hair and glanced in the pretty mirror Ollie had hung up for her. A little lipstick wouldn't hurt, but none of that red stuff of Jillian's. It came off on her teeth. A nice melon color would work. She opened the cupboard and grabbed her own makeup bag.

Before she could smooth her Moody Melon on, the intercom made some really static sound that made her jump out of her skin, like a radio without a station. Then her office door flew open. Not creaked, not slid, not even glided. It flung. The door actually hit the doorstop on the wall and bounced.

Jackson Hawks was on the other side of that door, with fire in his eyes. Jana Lee truly considered fainting, since she was going to anyway. But she wasn't a fainter. Moms didn't faint.

"What?" she yelled.

He looked for a moment as if he wasn't sure what words to choose. Then, instead of speaking, he strode directly over to her and took her by the shoulders. She dropped her Moody Melon lipstick, and it rolled away.

Jackson grabbed her up like he was going to tango. All she needed was a red rose in her teeth.

He backed her up against the counter, tipped her chin with his hand and stared into her eyes.

"I love you, that's what, I *love* you."

Then he kissed her hard. He didn't stop either; he kissed her like he didn't notice she'd put her arms around his neck and was kissing him back. Somewhere in the fog of reality Jana Lee heard the quiet click of the office door closing. Bless Oliver. And as for Jackson, as far as she was concerned, *bring it on.*

Jackson ran his hand down her neck and kissed the flesh revealed by her open blouse. There was a ripping sound, and the first button of the blouse popped violently across the room. Wow, great angle.

It must have shocked him for a split second. He jerked back, then seemed to take that button as a sign. He slid his mouth lower, over the ample top of her breast, which seemed to be straining in the too-tight bra she'd borrowed. She gasped as if she'd been dipped in hot wax when he reached up and freed her breast from the brassiere in one quick movement; when his mouth covered her, she made a very unusual sound. It was the sound of complete, unrestrained pleasure sizzling through her body.

She also heard the quick ripping sound of her skirt zipper splitting open. The skirt slipped off and hit the floor without Jackson's help at all.

* * *

How nice of her skirt to depart. It must be fate. There she was in pink bikini panties and pink high heels. Just like he'd imagined. Just a blouse and some bits of silk left to toy with.

He felt a smile cross his lips, and he kissed her surprised mouth. Her eyes were as wide as full blue moons, staring right at him. He glanced up from teasing her breast with his thumb and saw her become even more aroused.

Actually, it was sexy to have her watching him touch her. He felt the slippery silk of her panties and ran his hands across her full backside. She was so, so sexy. But this counter was all wrong.

He picked her up in his arms and carried her over to the desk. Jackson perched her on the edge, reached behind her and swept the contents of the desk onto the floor with a crash.

He needed room. He'd come in here to straighten a few things out between them. And Jackson was determined to straighten them out *all* the way this time.

And much to his delight, she wasn't arguing anymore. She had her arms around his neck, and he kissed her all over those soft lips of hers, soft as a summer peach. He slowly unbuttoned the rest of her blouse and let the heat of his mouth scorch the silky tips of her nipples, first one, then the other. Her head leaned back, and a moan rolled over her that he could actually feel. He flicked the back of her bra, and it fell off. Her bareness was stunning.

She was quite beautiful. Like an artist's model, nude and round and silky soft.

She greedily unbuttoned his Brooks Brothers button-down blue-and-white-striped shirt and rolled her hands down his bare back, his chest, and over his arms. She wrapped herself around him, and he pressed into the sweet, burning heat between her legs. Those panties of hers were all pale pink and lace and wetness. He felt his body go into second-stage arousal, and her big, blue eyes registered the fact that she was aware of that.

He took the moment he needed to free himself from his nicely pressed gray slacks. Only his own silk boxer shorts and her pale pink lacy panties were between them now.

Somehow, things got a little more heated after that. She kissed him slowly and sweetly, running her tongue in tantalizing circles around his own. He put his hands on her full behind and lifted her slightly, strategically, until he could feel her lose control even more. She pressed herself against him. Her breath was jagged and sweet with excitement.

He could feel her desire for him ready for the taking. He didn't know how, but he had to have all of her. He wanted to see those blue eyes of hers drunk with the pleasure he was going to give her, and he'd barely gotten started with that.

He slowed down and smoothed his hand over her cheek, then kissed her softly. Jackson felt like he'd waited for this moment a long time—not just this last week of battling but for perhaps his entire life. He was going to make love to a woman he had truly let himself fall in love with. She'd pried him open like a can opener. There was nothing left for him to keep from her.

"Wait, wait, Jackson." She tried to talk through his sweet, soft kisses. He had her lower lip in his mouth. She put her hand on his arm and shook him.

"Oh God, *what?*" he groaned with pleasure.

"There is something really important I need to tell you. I can't let you . . . you need to know." She stumbled over her words. There was no way she could let him do this thinking she was Jillian.

"What is it? Tell me." He leaned back and put his arms around her waist. "Is it important like . . . for our health?"

"Not really. I'm completely fine. It's just that I think you should know more about me."

"What about you? No, don't tell me. I don't care. I'll love you anyway." He put his mouth on her bare shoulder and kissed her.

She was shocked by what he said. He didn't care! He would love her anyway! So shocked that she hesitated just a moment, then grabbed his silk-boxer'd hips and pulled him into her. He made a movement that drove her wild. She had to have him, secrets be damned. She was going to be crazy for once in her life and let this man who was obviously in love with her give her the pleasure she wanted so badly.

He leaned back and moved his fingertips over the slinky panties, right over her most vulnerable spot. Right where she wanted him to. Jackson slid back the fabric and slid his fingers into her. She grabbed his shoulders and let herself fall into the sweet, uncontrollable movement of his touch. His mouth on her breast, his fingers stroking her, she arched against him and disappeared into the pleasure until the heat ignited her and she pushed against him, hard, and harder.

As soon as she'd regained the tiniest sensibility she wanted him all. She *must* have him inside her. She shoved him away for a moment, stood up and took off the pink silky panties. He held her and helped her and whispered, "Leave on the high heels." She practically had an orgasm right there, again.

Jackson let his silk boxers drop, then made sure he was protected. He'd wanted to take longer, but she was crazy with heat. She barely let him finish before she ran her fingers slowly and tantalizingly over his erection until he was ready to lose his mind. He wanted her. He ached for her. Her touch drove him crazy. Jackson looked in her eyes and knew that they both had to have each other right that minute. They could make love a dozen times in the next week and take hours, but this time, it was now or never.

She slid herself over him, and, with the most beautiful, loving motion, he joined her, deep inside, together in a tangle of emotion and pure sexual need. He kept his eyes open, and she did too. She looked so beautiful that he lost himself in watching her. Those eyes were telling him how to move and what each touch did to her.

She danced against him, he pressed his thumb against her heat, between them, until she cried out and vibrated around him once, then twice, and he heard her cry, "Oh, *Jackson*" through the fog of his own sensations.

He felt the soft leather of those shoes against his back, her pink high heels. He dove deeper and lost himself, and let her pull him harder again and again until he yelled out loud and let go, swirling in her wet, amazing, hot body until he could hardly move. His thighs shuddered. He crushed her against him and felt every moment of her soft, voluptuous skin mingling with his own.

She held him like she understood everything he'd ever felt or wanted. He breathed her in and let himself be intoxicated by her scent.

For the second time that day, the office door slammed open. Jana Lee let out a true scream, not the scream of pleasure she'd just finished with.

She tried to hide her nakedness behind Jackson. Jackson discreetly repositioned them both.

"Oh, isn't this cozy." The voice was female.

It had never occurred to Jana Lee that Jackson might be *married*. Oh my *God*, she hadn't even asked him! That would just figure. She peeked over Jackson's shoulder and saw a perky-looking blonde with very strong bare arms, who looked like she was ready to take them both on. She stood there, hands on hips.

Jackson turned himself quickly to face her. She was sure getting the full Monty there. He shielded Jana Lee at the same time. "Where the *hell* do you get off barging in here like this?"

And where was Oliver when she needed him? He must have stepped away from his desk just long enough for this crazy woman to make her entrance. And hadn't he locked the door? Jana Lee was thinking fast. She did that in a crisis. Obviously this woman had followed Jackson. Maybe she was stalking him. She held up a set of keys and jingled them in the air with a mocking smirk.

"Before you wet your whistle in yet another Pitman employee, maybe you should know she's *not* Jillian Tompkins."

Oh God, not like this, not when she was just about to tell him herself! Jana Lee leaned her forehead against Jackson's back in misery.

"Get out of here, Gloria. You have no idea what

you're talking about." Jackson's voice was calm, but firm.

"Oh, yes I do, you're just too dense to see it. I sent you plenty of clues, but it looked like your willy wasn't listening." She pointed to his bulging shorts, which he'd now slipped into. "She's Jillian's twin sister, Jana Lee Stivers, you idiot. Looks like you've finally been screwed yourself, Jackson. How does it feel having the crap you've dished out all these years come back and hit you in the face?"

Jana Lee felt Jackson's body stiffen. She rested her hands on his shoulders and pressed her cheek on his back. That would no doubt be the last time she felt his warmth. Tears slid slowly down her face.

"Get *out*, Gloria," Jackson yelled this time. Jana Lee looked up long enough to see Gloria stare at him, then turn and leave, slamming the door behind her. Then she heard some really nasty, loud words coming from the other side of the door. Oliver must have come back to his desk.

"You lied to me." Jackson didn't even bother to ask her if it was true.

It wasn't a question, it was a statement. Yes, she had lied to him. He was putting on his clothes, not looking at her.

She wiped her eyes with the back of her hand and stayed sitting on the desk. The fact that she had no top on didn't even enter into the picture.

"Yes, but my sister was having a nervous break-down. I had to help her. She loves this job, she loves working here. She just needed a *break*. Besides, I was just about to tell you. Then you said you didn't care, that you'd love me anyway." She heard her voice start to crack. She would *not* sound pathetic.

When Jackson had jerked his pants on, buttoned up his shirt, tucked it in and fastened his belt and zipper, he stood for a moment and looked at her as if he was taking in every tiny inch.

"Jana—Lee." That was all he said. As if he were trying to learn it. But the tone, the tone was disdain.

Her old anger rose up twenty times stronger than it ever had. She grabbed her blouse and pulled it on herself.

"Oh go ahead, run away. That's your style, isn't it? Don't stick around and hear anyone else's side of the story. That's what I bloody get for helping out my stupid sister. I should have known better than to get mixed up in this. And why she'd want to work for an arrogant jerk like you is beyond me, let alone ask me to *warm you up* for her! Like you could be warmed up. You're a coldhearted bastard, Jackson Hawks."

She marched past him to get her skirt, then grabbed it up and shimmied into it, jerking the zipper up to her waist. "And to think I actually fell for you. I am one first-class fool. Obviously I'm not the first, as evidenced by our little *surprise* visitor!"

She headed toward the door, because damn, there was no way Jackson was going to walk out on her. She'd do it first. She'd walk out on this whole thing. Screw Jillian, screw Jackson and *screw* this whole stupid plan.

But for some reason she felt a little tipsy, like the floor wasn't even. She looked down to see if the carpet had rippled, or if she was stepping on some leftover item of clothing, but no, the floor seemed to be rolling all on its own. She grabbed for the edge of the counter. She looked up and saw the large center light fixture swaying back and forth.

There are moments in life when things get turned upside down and nothing prepares you for what to do. Jana Lee was definitely having one of those moments. She screamed and held onto the countertop. Ceiling tiles fell down around her and she could see the windows buckle.

Jackson grabbed her and dragged her underneath the desk, much to her protestations.

"Shut up, will you? It's an earthquake. This is San Francisco. Didn't your sister warn you things get crazy here?" Jackson scrunched next to her, holding onto her so she wouldn't bolt.

"She left out a few details." A ceiling tile dropped on the desk, scattering pieces around them. She yelped.

"Look, it's over now. These buildings are built to withstand a little rattle and roll."

Jana Lee only had one thought—to get the hell out of there, away from Jackson, away from everything. She coughed dust and tried to back out from under the desk.

"Don't!" he cried as he dove for her.

A terrible creaking sound started almost as if it were in slow motion and got louder and louder.

She heard Jackson yell out her name.

Everything went black after that.

Jackson didn't know a thing about her. Not a thing. Except that he loved her. He'd had one stupid moment regarding her rather huge deception. Just one. *God, don't let that be the last moment between us,* he prayed.

He ran beside the gurney and climbed into the ambulance even when they tried to stop him. Oliver had run into the office right after the ceiling had collapsed, and Jackson hadn't heard most of what Oliver had said. Jackson had been throwing debris off Jana Lee.

Oliver must have called 911, and they'd both worked on her, trying to revive her and bandaging some of her surface wounds. Jackson had wanted to pick her up and get her out of the room, but Oliver had stopped him and reminded him not to move her. They'd pulled the credenza across where she lay in case of aftershocks. The last thing Oliver had done before the medics had burst through the door was hand Jackson a cell phone.

He'd shoved it in his pocket and then helped move the furniture aside to make it easier to get to Jana Lee.

The medics had her hooked up to some machines, and Jackson watched as they got her to wake up. He'd never been as glad as when those blue eyes of hers opened. He reached over and took her hand. She was groggy and kept trying to talk, but they put an oxygen mask over her mouth.

He leaned over her. "Don't worry, you're going to be fine, everything is going to be okay. Oliver will call your sister."

She looked frightened and tried to move her arm to push the mask away, but they had strapped it to a splint board. Jackson was pretty sure it was broken. She also had a big, scraped lump on her forehead that had been bleeding but now had a bandage.

He should have stopped her from crawling out. He couldn't believe she'd actually slipped through his fingers. But not in a million years would he have imagined the Pitman building not being safe. The trouble was, if she hadn't been trying to get as far away from him as possible, she'd be okay right now.

Jackson was a mixed-up guy, that was for sure. She'd deceived him. Jillian Tompkins was crazy to have made her sister do this! Jillian could have just asked for a leave of absence. What an insanely misled woman she was to think she couldn't get her job back at Pitman if she needed to mend her

nerves for a month! She'd never even asked him!
Instead she'd guilted out her sister and made her
impersonate her at work. Jackson shook his head
in disbelief at the crazy scheme they'd cooked up.

Jackson thought about the mind of Jillian Tompkins and how she could have convinced herself
that taking a break from the stress of her job
would have meant the end of her career. And most
of all that her career meant that much to her.

Was he like that? Maybe it was time to put
something besides his job first. One thing was for
sure, he wasn't letting Jana Lee Tompkins Stivers
out of his sight.

19

It Must Be Jilly
'Cause Jan Don't Shake Like That

Dean made omelets for their lunch with tomatoes and spinach and all sorts of green stuff he'd made her go pick with him in his garden. He'd mumbled about needing to weed and thank God he had an automatic sprinkler system, because they'd had no decent rain and this was the driest June he could remember.

It was a beautiful garden, with Dean's metal sculptures sprouting all over the place. They were beanpoles, garden gates, and benches. But most beautiful of all were the huge bronze pieces. Women with smooth bodies curled up like sleeping cats, or sitting serenely on rocks. Jillian loved them.

She and Dean had lolled in the sunshine, eating his strawberries, talking about his work. She'd been feeling very off-center all afternoon, but the relaxed meal and relaxed surroundings had helped her forget about it.

They'd brought Monty with them, and he'd been loping around after her like a puppy dog, looking worried. Maybe he wasn't too keen on new places.

Inside, her bare feet felt good on the dark wood floors, and Monty's nails made a click, click beside her.

The floors were so smooth you could hardly see the joint lines. She followed Dean as he showed her some of his fine art showcased nicely on the putty green walls of the hallways. There were smokey landscapes of a very modern nature, and some pure abstract pieces. She knew he was an artist, but the whole house and its contents still amazed her. It was sleek and minimalist, but it still had warmth. Black, putty green, soft ochre yellow, and a wonderful, deep terra-cotta plastered effect on some walls reminded her of pictures she'd seen of Italian houses.

"Your place is beautiful, Dean."

"Thanks. I designed it myself, and my crew helped me build it." Dean gave Monty a scratch behind the ears.

"Carly should be in San Francisco by now. That was the dumbest flight, with a stop in Portland, but last-minute beggars can't be choosey. I'm just glad we got her down there. Oliver said he was going to book Pops to drive Jana Lee out to the airport. Pops is our company limo driver. Won't Carly be surprised when her mother picks her up in a limo?"

Dean was unusually quiet. He was giving her a tour of the house. She followed him into his office. A large, amazing abstract painting dominated the study. A sleek credenza against one ochre wall had a collection of cat-sized sculpted pieces in dark bronze, but they weren't pussycats. They were beautiful, smooth nudes, like the ones in the garden.

"Wow. That's not who I think it is, is it?" She pointed to the large canvas.

"Kandinsky. Believe it or not, it was done in 1913. That always amazes me."

"Incredible. And those?" She indicated the bronze collection.

"Those are mine. They're actually studies for larger pieces."

She examined one very closely, touching the sleek, curved casting. "Dean, you are very talented. You should give up all building-related jobs and do art full time."

"I did give up building. You brought me out of retirement, remember, Jillian? Come here."

He held out his open arms, and she walked right into them. For a moment, she forgot all about what they were talking about. Or *not* talking about.

"And I took you away from commissioned work to help me remodel a house?" she asked.

"Not really, I didn't have anything going at the moment. Just ideas."

"When is the last time you did a show?"

"I finished a show two summers ago. I've done some big commissions since, and that has kept me busy."

"What do you do up here, all alone with your clay and melted metal?"

"I need lots of headspace. But I do have assistants that come and help when I have to cast a large piece. I use lost wax process for those, which is very weird and time consuming and involved." He smoothed her hair around her ear with his fingertips. Monty Python thumped his tail against them and circled like he wanted in on the action.

"Silly dog." Jillian looked up at Dean. "You are so much more than my handyman."

Dean laughed. "And you are so much more than the lady I thought hired me." He kissed her softly.

"When are you going to start a new project?" she asked.

"It's just about time for me to get back to work—after your project is done, of course," he answered. That vagueness in him returned. He looked past her.

"Can I see your studio?"

"Sure."

"Brrr, I'm chilled." She wasn't sure why, but the same feeling she'd had earlier crept over her.

Maybe she was coming down with something. She snuggled closer and laid her head on his chest. "Show me your studio, and then we can go out and sit in the sun. Or lay in the sun." She eyed him suggestively. "The mountains look like you could touch them from your back patio."

"I didn't turn the heat on and warm it up in here. Sorry." He flipped on a gas fireplace inserted flush in the wall. It was so smooth that she'd hardly noticed it, but there it was, surrounded with black granite with a stainless steel firebox. Extremely cool. Dean had amazing taste. Taste like hers. She imagined herself living up here on his mountaintop. It was so, so quiet. It was such a stark contrast to the city.

"You should see my apartment in San Francisco. You'd like it." She looked up at him and knew right away something was wrong.

"Jillian, I don't know how to make this transition. I don't know how to go from making love to you every chance I get to putting you on a plane and saying good-bye Friday. Going to the airport today, I could feel it."

No guy had ever been that honest with her in her entire life. "I don't know what to say, Dean, but I'm glad you want to talk about it. I-I feel the same way. As a matter of fact, nothing could make me happier than never going back to that job." She felt emotion break over her. She pulled away from him and sat down in his office chair, a familiar position for her. She leaned her head into her hands.

"Do you mean that?" he asked.

"I say it, but I have no idea what I'd do with my life. I have never allowed myself to think past the next meeting, or the next trade show or the next season's line-up. I'm not kidding when I tell you that this past week has been the best time I've ever had. You even turned a project I was making stressful into an adventure."

"We've got something special here, Jillian. It's not perfect, but it would be a shame to let it slip through our fingers."

"We could see each other, I could fly up on weekends."

Dean leaned against the wall across from her looking *so* good. He'd changed in the days they'd been together. Something around his eyes had softened. Without his even saying anything, she knew the answer to what she'd said about weekends. Dean Wakefield deserved more than her weekends.

The ring of the phone punctuated the silence that hung between them. It was so close to Jillian that she jumped and grabbed the receiver. Monty barked.

"Jillian Tompkins," she said. She looked up at Dean and put her hand over her mouth. Oops, she'd just answered his phone, and she'd answered it office style. He was amused, until he saw her face go white and heard her gasp.

He stepped nearer and handed her a pencil and paper—whatever it was, there'd be details. A hard fist of adrenaline punched his gut. This didn't look good.

She was nodding and saying yes, and scribbling things on the paper. When she hung up the phone she put her hand over her mouth, trying not to cry.

"My sister is in the hospital. They had an earthquake and parts of the ceiling hit her. She has a concussion and a broken arm." She didn't make it through the entire last phrase, but he understood. Dean gathered her up and let her sob against his chest.

"We'll fly down," he said. "I'll go with you."

"I can't tell you how much that would mean to me," she choked out. "I feel so, *so* bad, sending her down there. And Carly is at the hospital. They must all hate me. That was Oliver, he tracked me down from Carly's information—my cell phone must not have a signal up here. Carly thought of you, and they found your number. Oliver booked me on a late flight. I'll have him get you a ticket too."

"Fine, we'll settle up with that later."

She was sort of babbling, and he took her hand. "Let's go. Your cell will kick in as soon as we drop down a few miles. We'll pick up some clothes for you and take Monty to a kennel. We have a whole lot to do."

"Dean, we'll talk more about us. I'm so sorry."

"Don't be sorry. I love you." He kissed her softly, holding her close.

"I love you too," she whispered back.

As Dean's truck came around the corner to the beach house, Jillian screamed as she clutched the dashboard rim. This just couldn't be happening. He cursed and swung the truck into park. Jillian could hardly get herself to open the car door. The air hung heavy with smoke.

Dean, on the other hand, got out like a shot and ran. He ran straight into the mess, with firemen still stomping around in their big boots, raking through piles of what was formerly the deck of Jana Lee's house.

She felt a huge wave of panic hit her. Oh, God, not *now*, she had to think. But all she could do was whisper, *"Thank you, God."* Thank you that Carly wasn't here, and that the dog was with them. Monty was whining something fierce. She took some deep breaths and calmed herself down enough to slide out of the car and leave the dog inside, despite his extreme protests.

She ran over to where Dean was talking to a guy in full gear. He had his visor pushed back on his head.

"Glad you showed up. We didn't know who to call. It's not as bad as it looks, the garage is intact, and we were all happy to see no one was in the house. The interior has severe smoke damage, but it was mostly the deck."

"What caused it?" Jillian asked. Dean came to hold her.

"You're not going to believe it, but it was lightning. There was a thunderstorm last night. With the heat lately and all, a kind of thermal inversion. It hit the tree with the old TV antennae mounted to it. The tree split, part of it hit the deck, and that was that. Considering the age of the house, well, it's been pretty dry this month. It could have been way worse, folks."

Dean turned to Jillian.

Jillian couldn't even speak. She'd burned up her sister's house. Her sister, who was lying in a hospital bed.

The fireman went on. "They're going to want to talk to you."

"Look," Dean said. "I know this is going to be hard to believe, but the owner of the house is actually in the hospital with a serious injury—in San Francisco. We were just coming here to get some things before we caught a ten o'clock flight."

"Man, when it rains, it pours. Well, come over to the truck with me and we'll take your information down. Insurance, and all that."

"Insurance? I have no idea." Jillian sounded hysterical.

Dean pulled her over to him. "We'll go look for it. I saw a metal box marked Important Papers in the garage."

"Look at all your pretty work, Dean, just up in smoke."

"Hey, it had a bad layout," he joked. "We'll start over." He gathered her into a hug. "Damn, this hasn't turned out to be the best of days, darlin'."

"I can't even think straight. I heard the thunder last night but didn't think anything of it."

"Let's go talk to the fire marshal. Jillian, we'll make it through. Just take one step at a time."

She'd cry, but somehow it wasn't even available to her. Her whole body felt numb. Her heart was beating like crazy. Dean held her and rubbed small circles of comforting touch into her back.

"Okay, let's do this," she said.

They spent a half hour talking with the officer, who said that, considering the circumstances, he'd let them fly to San Francisco and they could deal with the house later. He recommended a cleanup crew. Dean said he had his own, not to worry. The fireman seemed to know Dean, and that made things easier.

Jillian left her card with her office number. They'd saved portions of the house, which still had all its walls standing. Because of the neighbor's call, the garage, with all of Jana Lee's belongings in it, was untouched.

All the family photos and books and things that Jana Lee would have truly suffered over were in there.

Her house, however, was a different matter.

"I feel so odd leaving this mess," Jillian said as they walked away from the fire marshal's car.

"I'm going to call my old foreman and have him round up the guys that have been working here. They'll start cleanup, take what's in the garage and put it in locked storage so we won't have to worry about anything else while we're gone," Dean said.

"You are a very resourceful man." Jillian smiled a crooked smile at him. "I'm afraid this is all going to hit me later. I'm so worried about my sister and niece that this is actually at the bottom of the list."

"Let's go look for the insurance policy and I'll make some calls. I resurrected my cell phone just for you," he said as he held it up.

"Wow, caveman joins the twenty-first century."

"It was a symbol of my old life. I know this sounds odd, but I enjoyed myself fixing your sister's house up. I wouldn't mind rebuilding it. I've changed. I think I can handle doing small projects without becoming a neurotic control freak."

Jillian couldn't sort anything out right now. She

had to take small steps, like Dean said. She headed for the garage, and Dean helped her find the metal box her sister had covered in flowered contact paper.

"At least we could find it easier," she laughed. The paper they needed was there, and they returned to the firemen to talk about logistics.

She had nothing but shorts and T-shirts, one set on, one set in the overnight duffle she'd taken up to Dean's. But clothes were hardly important now. Monty was going to have to do some kennel time, and he was mighty upset about it. He leaned on her as if he knew.

In hours they were at the airport, with the horrible mess of Jana Lee's house in the hands of Dean's crew. Oliver had given them an extra reservation number over the phone. The flight was only half full, and the stewardess, seeing the shape that Jillian was in, let them sit together.

Jillian ordered a double bourbon on the airplane and closed her eyes against thoughts and images of her sister in the hospital and the smoking pile of rubble they'd left behind.

"It's not your fault," Dean said, watching over her.

"Intellectually, I know that I didn't make an earthquake hit San Francisco, but I'm not so sure about the house. Maybe God was getting me back. I feel responsible for the entire mess." She raised her hand slightly to catch herself from bursting into tears, because if she started crying, she'd never stop.

Dean pulled her close. "God did not send lightning down to hit the house. He sent you to me."

20

Romancing the Twins

Jackson figured as long as there wasn't an actual husband waiting in the wings, he'd seen it all at this point. The Tompkins family, up front and real. For one thing, he was now doing his best to keep an eye on a very emotional fifteen-year-old girl who, Oliver said, was Jana Lee's daughter. He could sure see the family resemblance. She'd spent the entire evening with her mother till they'd made her leave and Oliver had taken her home to his place.

Jillian Tompkins had come in the middle of the night in a pair of white shorts and a Hard Rock Cafe T-shirt. Her hair was crazy and she smelled funny, like smoke. She'd only nodded a hello, as if ignoring him would hide the fact that she'd played hooky from her job for two and a half weeks—including the week she'd legitimately taken off as sick leave.

But it hadn't seemed to matter to him when he'd watched her rush to her sister's side, and seeing the two of them crying their eyes out had been pretty touching. Jana Lee wasn't sleeping much anyway. They'd been checking her constantly, and every time he'd jerked awake she'd been staring at him, wide-eyed.

He'd spent the entire night sleeping in a chair next to her bed, despite the medical staff's trying to remove him. He could be a real hard-ass when he needed to be. And he needed to be with her no matter what. He needed to tell her he loved her and hear her whisper to him that she loved him too.

Now it was morning, and the place was getting very busy. As the light cracked through the blinds, he straightened himself up and looked around. What had roused him this time was the sound of Jillian Tompkins and Carly Stivers coming in the room. Carly greeted him warmly and thanked him for staying with her mom through the night.

Jillian had a tall, muscular guy in tow, who shook Jackson's hand and said he was Dean Wakefield.

Jackson recognized Jillian very clearly as herself, dressed in her own chic black clothes, and much cleaner than before. The three of them, the daughter and two sisters, started talking, and the tears were flowing, mostly out of Jillian.

Once he saw her in the light of day, he truly could not believe he'd fallen for their trick. They were completely different people. Jillian was pretty, but it was Jana Lee's spark and creativity and heart that had made him notice the existence of a Ms. Tompkins at all. He wondered how he'd *ever* missed the fact that Jana Lee wasn't Jillian.

Of course he'd had limited exposure to Jillian— just one mistletoe moment and a few end-of-the-table meetings. He'd avoided her at best, ignored her at most, and just hadn't taken her fully in. It made him think hard about the packages people come in and how their hearts are so individual. The soul, the spirit of Jana Lee was so much more attractive to him.

Wow, he was very, very tired and getting way too philosophical. He stepped into the hall just to give them some privacy and clear his head.

Jana Lee. It sounded like a country singer. He laughed. Him and Jana Lee. And a daughter makes three. He ran his hand over his hair and stared at the beige hallway walls. He'd always planned on having children, but he'd sort of missed the boat.

He leaned against the wall outside the door. No matter what other surprises came up, he knew he wanted to give Jana Lee a great big chunk of his attention. He wanted to see where it would all go. He couldn't lose her now. The image of Jana Lee lying on the floor of that office with debris all over her had kept playing in his head all night. He rubbed his forehead.

"Rough night, son?" The voice of his father was so close that it startled him. His eyes flew open. He could hardly believe it. His father, his mother, his brother Marcus and his wife Nan were all coming down the hall.

For the first time in over twenty years he did the oddest thing. He threw his arms around his father and held him close for a moment. The odder thing was, his dad was right there with him. He felt his strong hands pat him on the back. Then he let go, and each member of his family crowded in for a really surreal moment of group hugs. Jackson was practically overcome. His brother slugged his arm after he hugged him and said, "Hey, man," in that brother way, which helped make him laugh a little.

"How did you know?"

"A section of Pitman Toys caves in and I hear. I'm sorry I didn't come last night, but it was very late and the nurses said she was sleeping when I called. They said we'd be limited to visiting hours. I'm a little confused about some of the details, but the fact that a friend of yours was hurt matters a great deal to your mother and me.

"Jackson, I'm so proud of you for looking after Miss Tompkins like this," his mother said. She held his arm and put her cheek on his shoulder.

"It's not exactly Miss Tompkins, it's her sister. She was visiting. We're doing a new toy line based on their old characters, if you read my reports, Dad. So don't be too surprised, her sister Jillian is in there, and they are identical, except for the broken arm and bruises. I'll fill you in later."

Jackson left out some details, but who cared about all that now? These crazy women were too hard to explain anyway.

"Besides, Mom, Jackson is sweet on her," Marcus blurted out.

"Nice one, Marcus." Nan rolled her eyes.

Dean stepped out of the room just in time to hear that.

"Hi, I'm Dean Wakefield." He extended his hand to Jackson with a smile. "I came in with Jillian."

"I'm Jackson Hawks. This is my family—my father, mother, brother Marcus, and his wife, Nan."

Dean shook hands all around. He certainly was a personable fellow, and he had a strong handshake. "Jackson, I think you and I have a few things to talk about. I'll be in the coffee shop for an hour or so. I haven't eaten breakfast, and Jillian refuses all offers of food. Join me when you get a chance. No hurry." Dean delivered his speech, gave Jackson a nod, then departed down the hallway.

Jackson figured Dean Wakefield knew the entire score and could probably enlighten him further. He smiled at his family and took his father in to see Jana Lee. One at a time, the nurses kept yammering. But this hospital room was a hotbed of happenings.

All Jana Lee could think about was what would have happened to her daughter if she'd actually been killed in that collapse. This, along with her sister's return, had made her an emotional mess, although the amazing sight of Jackson by her bedside all night long had given her a whole lot of hope.

She was determined to be strong and get out of here fast. She pulled herself up, and Carly propped pillows behind her.

She also had the distinct feeling that her sister had something to tell her but didn't want to worry her.

"Is the dog okay?" she asked.

"Sure, sure, we put him in a private doggy kennel that treats them like movie stars. He wasn't too happy at first, but he'll be rolling in dog biscuits before you know it," Jillian answered, but she kind of glanced away, and she and Carly exchanged a few interesting looks.

"Look, sister, I might have a busted arm and a bump on the head, but I'm not stupid. Whatever it is, just spill it. And as you know, they're letting me out of here in an hour anyway. They've had twelve hours of my time and my head is fine, so no more lounging around. You know I'll find out anyway." She had a hell of a headache, but she was itching to take charge and put some order back in her crazy life.

"Mom, don't worry, we'll be fine." Carly patted her hand.

"Fine from *what?*" Her voice hit a high note. Jana Lee stared at the two of them.

"I sort of burned your house down," Jillian said. She then proceeded to throw her face into the blankets at the end of the bed and weep.

Jana Lee thought she might throw up. She thought of her family pictures and Carly's baby things—treasures she'd probably lost forever. Funny enough, she didn't care about the house that much. She clutched her daughter's arm. Thank God Carly hadn't been there.

"Mom, Mom, all our stuff was packed up in the garage and that didn't get touched. Lucky, huh? And no one was hurt. Monty was with Aunt Jillian at the time."

"*Lucky?*" Jana Lee stammered. "Well, I guess that was lucky, in some respects." Maybe it was because so much had happened, maybe it was because Jackson Hawks was in love with her—for some reason, now that she knew nothing truly horrid had happened, she found it rather funny. Jillian had really screwed up big this time. Jana Lee laughed and kicked at Jillian's head with her foot. "Buck up, sister, tell me what happened. Did you try and cook?"

Jillian sat up, looking rather shocked, and Carly

handed her a pile of tissues. Jillian blew her nose. "The fire department said it was lightning."

"Lightning? I get hit by an earthquake, and you get hit by lightning? I'd say Mother Nature must be pissed at us!"

There was a second of silence, followed by laughter.

Jana Lee could only laugh a little because it made her head hurt. She leaned back against her pillows. "Wow, Jillian, the old place is gone."

"You had good insurance, though. Dean read through your policy and said the rebuild would be covered nicely. Did I tell you Dean used to be a big housing contractor?"

"Good insurance. Well, hell, that's good." Jana Lee reached for her daughter's hand and pressed it to her cheek. "The most important thing is that we're all alive and well and safe. We'll figure the rest out later."

"You're coming to my place. I called Oliver, and he's bringing the limo over." Jillian sniffed again and wiped off her face. "I'm *so* sorry, Jana," she choked as she started crying again.

"Okay, we've shed enough tears for today. Help me out of this bed. I feel a giant draft in the behind region." Jana Lee threw off her covers and took Carly's arm.

"You go, Mom!" Carly said. Jana Lee felt a twinge at having taken so long to understand how much her daughter wanted her to come alive and take charge. She'd been so dormant for the past two years.

She got her balance and went to get dressed. She knew from having a baby that if you acted ready to go, they usually put the big stamp of release on your chart and booted you out the door. Heck, these days they threw you out before the ink was dry on the forms.

Jillian had been smart enough to bring Jana Lee some casual clothes—sweats and a tank top she could squeeze over the purple cast they'd set her arm with. As Jillian helped Jana Lee get into her clothes, she thought about the house. Oddly enough, she wasn't as upset as she should be. "By the way, Jillian, your office is a disaster, and I've pissed off Jackson Hawks so badly you might actually lose your job, so I guess both of us are in the same boat."

Her sister gently maneuvered the tank top over her cast.

"Oh *well*," Jillian said, then laughed.

Jana Lee was glad she'd made Jillian laugh.

"However," Jillian said, "I don't think Jackson is an issue. From what I've seen, he hasn't left your side for the last twelve hours. I'd say there was some serious stuff going on there."

"Guilt, no doubt. His building fell on me. He probably thinks I'll sue him."

* * *

"She burned Jana Lee's house down?" Jackson was incredulous. Dean snorted his coffee laughing.

"No, no, it was lightning."

"You have to wonder about all this, don't you? Sounds like a bad movie of the week," Jackson said.

"Hey, right now we're *living* a bad movie of the week," Dean replied.

"These two are trouble, that's for sure. What's the daughter like?" Jackson asked.

"Really good kid. Are you serious about Jana Lee? Don't mess with a mother, my man. The kid gets hurt."

"Weirdly enough, I am serious about Jana Lee. I had to have a ceiling fall on her to figure that out, but there you go." Jackson put his empty cup back on the saucer and wiped his side of the table with a napkin. "What about you?"

"At this point I have no idea how it will work, but I've never met anyone like Jillian Tompkins. As I said to her last night, the best plan I can come up with is to take one day at a time."

"Can women do that?" Jackson looked dubious.

"Not sure." Dean grinned.

Jackson rang the doorbell and tapped his fingers against the doorframe. No switchy, twitchy twin was going to put him out in the cold. He'd spent the bulk of the day surveying the damage to Pitman Toys, meeting with insurance stiffs and talking to his father. They'd gotten more than a few things straightened out. He had a whole lot of that to do—straightening out Jana Lee, and her sister too. Jillian opened the door.

"Jackson?" She seemed surprised.

"Move it over, sister, I have business." He marched past her.

"Oh, come right in, you're just in time for dinner." Jillian said that nicely, with an edge.

He ignored her and followed Jana Lee's voice. She was in the kitchen with her daughter, Dean, and—surprise—Oliver. Jackson greeted each one by name.

"Could I steal you for a moment, Jana Lee?" He wanted a private moment. He went right up close to her and wrapped his arm around her waist. She tried to wriggle away, but he guided her out of the kitchen. "Got a bedroom in this place?"

"There," she pointed. Helpful little minx.

"Well, shall we?"

She wasn't sure what to expect from Jackson, and she felt a little scared of what he might say. She turned to protest this little meeting, but he backed her into the room, holding her good elbow.

"First, Ms. Jana Lee Stivers, I'm very sorry about your broken arm." He kissed it. "It was rude of that earthquake to interrupt our quarrel, and even more rude of Gloria whazzername to interrupt us just before the earth moved. But the earth had already moved for me, *before* Gloria came in.

"Worse than that, I reacted like a fool to your so honorable confession of truth. I'm sorry."

"You were going to leave me naked on a desk." Jana Lee tried to cross her arms awkwardly, but he uncrossed them as he wound his arms around her waist and kept backing her up.

"Actually, at the end there I think you were doing the leaving. I've thought about this a whole lot. We need to get past this whole thing where you did your sister a favor, and stay focused on each other. I know who *you* are, whether I had your name right or not. *You* are the most amazing, colorful, strange girl I've ever met. You have a great mind, and those lips are yours alone." He leaned in and kissed her quickly.

Jana Lee was trying to cling to her new take-charge thing. "You don't *really* know me. I have a daughter."

"And from what I hear, a charcoal house. I did a whole lot of thinking last night watching you in that hospital bed. There is no way I'm going to let you vanish out of my life. I can't promise things will work out between us, God knows. Your daughter might hate me. You might find out I snore."

"I also live in Washington. That's rather major."

"If you had a job, would you consider a move?" He was so close to her she couldn't think. His wonderful scent was making her dizzy. Or was it the concussion? She moved backward out of his arms and ran around the other side of the bed. He leaned over the silk coverlet and smiled at her. "Going somewhere?"

"Don't make me run, Jackson, I'm not supposed to joggle my head."

"You can stop running, Jana Lee. What do you think of my idea? How about coming to work for Pitman Toys as one of the design team? You obviously don't know your cost ratio differential from your elbow."

She sat down on the bed.

"What about Jillian's job?"

"She can certainly keep it; Jillian is very good at what she does. And Pitman will throw in some therapy, because anyone who thinks they can't take a leave of absence to regain their personal sanity is just plain crazy. We're not that kind of company."

"I don't know, Jackson. I'll think about it. Carly has school and friends."

"Discuss it with her. And one more thing . . ." He vaulted right over the bed and took her in his arms. "You're going to need some bed rest." He kissed her neck. "And tender loving care." He kissed her temple. "And I'm just the man to oversee that project." He lowered her down on the bed and kissed her with the most convincing, heart-stopping kiss she'd ever received.

"I love you, Jana Lee," he whispered.

"I love you, too, Jackson."

She forgot all the crazy thoughts dancing in her head and let Jackson kiss her. Nothing felt as good as Jackson kissing her. The rest of it could wait.

Dinner was served, and Oliver was cooking. Jillian's very handsome Dean had been a great assistant in the kitchen. They'd decided on a seafood linguini dish earlier and had had the market send over food, because damn, this cupboard was bare. What *did* that girl live on?

To Oliver, the course of true love had never seemed as rocky as it did with this bunch. He stood in Jillian's kitchen and listened to the chatter of a little clutch of people who were beyond clueless. The universe had literally rearranged their lives, but none of them had caught on—no house, no office, new men, a daughter who loved art and would adjust well in a big city like San Francisco.

Of course it remained to be seen if Jackson would make a good stepfather, and if Jillian could give up her high-stress job and become Mrs. Dean Wakefield. Oliver tossed the Caesar salad and snickered to himself.

"Dean, could you pop the cork on those two bottles of wine? Jana Lee shouldn't be the only one with something to dull the pain."

"I hear you." Dean opened drawers until he

found a corkscrew and went about his assigned task.

"Don't you find it interesting that the very things that held each of our sisters in her rather rutlike, stuck place are now gone with the wind? Or the lightning, as the case may be?"

Dean looked at Oliver while he twisted the corkscrew. "Kind of weird, isn't it? Seeing them together is very enlightening. They are very similar. More so than they think."

"Getting to know Jana Lee after years with Jillian, I'm inclined to agree with you." Oliver grated fresh Parmesan cheese on top of the salad. "I've been thinking about what the next step might be."

"I'm sure open to suggestions," Dean said.

"I think a trip, all five of you, including Carly, the daughter. But not just any trip—a cruise. Something where you're stuck together and have nowhere to run."

"What about the house in Washington?"

"That will take some planning, and really, do you want to start reconstruction right away? You could draw house plans at sea. It is a joint project, after all."

"I see your point. A cruise. I see."

Oliver could see Dean's brain sorting through all the possibilities and ramifications of that idea.

"What about Jillian's job?"

"I hate to be immodest, but I can handle it. After

you've been someone's assistant for as long as I've been Jillian's, there is no aspect of their job you aren't familiar with." Oliver picked up the appetizer trays. "Shall we? A little wine and antipasto will certainly lighten things up in there."

Dean picked up the two bottles of wine, which probably should have breathed more, but hey, breathing is overrated. A cruise with Jillian sounded like heaven. They'd certainly be able to sort things out in a calm, quiet environment. It would be great for all the girls. Oliver was a genius.

Dean walked into the dining room and set one bottle at each end, then joined Jillian at the table. They were deep in it about the structural aspects of Pitman and what had made the ceiling cave in. Dean poured Jillian a glass of wine and passed the bottle around.

"I think a toast is in order," he said. Everyone got very quiet and stared at him, probably wondering what there was to toast to, considering the recent disasters that had befallen them.

He waited till everyone had a glass except Jana Lee and Carly, who were both drinking water. He raised his wineglass. "Here's to the two best looking sisters I know, and their ability to switch, bother and bewilder us all. If it weren't for that, we would have never found our way to each other."

Jackson looked like he was in complete agreement; Jana Lee and Jillian looked at each other and laughed. Carly cheered.

"Now, what say you all go on a cruise to oh, Hawaii?" Oliver said.

Dean laughed at the dead silence. Then the sisters started in, the daughter joined, Jackson bounced replies back. It was chaos. Dean looked at Oliver and noticed he was enjoying himself a great deal, swigging wine and stacking crostini and sun dried tomatoes on his plate. Oliver was a devil, that was for sure.

Epilogue
One Year and a Few Months Later

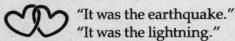 "It was the earthquake."

"It was the lightning."

"It was the cruise. A double wedding at sea. How could you beat that?"

"No, it was rebuilding this beach house."

"It was the Little Princess dolls, and all those royalties."

"What about finding out Harvey the Dragon was doing superstore grand openings in your own county and he was the scary clown Jillian saw? That was a real shocker, wouldn't you say?"

"Scrapbook moment for sure."

"I'd say getting *knocked up* takes the cake, wouldn't you, Dean? And you better say yes," Jillian said.

"Yes, yes! It takes the cake. You win, Jillian." Dean balanced baby Benjamin by his chubby little waist and Jana Lee watched the baby drool and gurgle as Monty Python came over to nuzzle Dean in a rather low-level display of dog jealousy. "Of course that would refer back to the cruise," he teased. He handed Jillian the baby and went off to mind the barbeque.

It didn't matter whose opinion they took about which event had brought them together or shocked them all out of their former lives—they were together again.

Jana Lee was amazed to see the beach house done up like this. Where there had once been a plain, rather characterless beach shack, there now stood a two-tiered beauty with decks and balconies and views out every window. She loved the two master bedrooms and the huge combination art studio/ bedroom for Carly on the very top, plus the extra guest room on the main floor for stray friends. The best part was the modern state-of-the-art everything—wiring, plumbing, kitchen, and lighting. It was now the perfect no-stress getaway for both couples.

Jana Lee sat back against the comfortably upholstered chaise next to her sister. She'd laughed at everyone doing their usual round robin. It was hard to say who had come up with the idea of making the beach house their joint vacation house, but she thought it might have been Oliver.

Good old Ollie, the voice of reason. Oliver, who was now bugging her about packaging costs and safety standards the way Jillian must have bugged other people. Oliver, who had learned to barbeque like a champ, even though he'd never tried it.

"Hey, Ollie, how's it coming?"

"A few more minutes, Princess Jana Lee, you can't rush these things."

Ollie had brought his partner to the grand opening of their beach retreat, and they'd been cooking up a storm along with Dean for the last three days. Thank God someone in this family could cook, because Jana Lee and Jillian and Jackson were pretty pathetic. Carly, on the other hand, was learning from her new uncle Dean, and had turned into quite the babysitter as well.

Carly had taken to San Francisco like a champ, and the most amazing thing of all was watching her with Jackson's family, who just lavished her with acceptance and affection—and two boy cousins. Jackson's mother was pretty overindulgent with the designer dresses, and teas at the St. Francis, but she liked to show her only granddaughter off. Once in a while she tried to take Marcus's boys, but they were better suited to soccer match picnics so far.

Carly loved her arts high school and planned to stay in the city for college after she graduated.

It was pretty sweet that their first official social event as a married couple had been the remarriage of Jackson's parents. It was strange, but Jana Lee felt like Carly had contributed to that reuniting somehow.

Jillian noticed her sister off in the clouds. "What are you thinking about?" she asked. Knowing her sister, it was something business related. "Don't forget what I taught you. Set it all aside when you take vacations. And these vacations are mandatory from now on."

"Sister Jilly, I am the ultimate balanced woman. I have a yoga class every evening to work the kinks out. I swear I wasn't thinking about work."

"Oh, so now that you're the thin one, you can rub it in?"

"I told you that extra twenty-five pounds would be murder to take off."

"It's all Dean's fault. He cooks too well and too often."

"Plus he got you pregnant. I was thinking about you with the baby stroller, and the giant pile of diapers, and having a hard time keeping a straight face, really. Who would have figured."

"Oh, just because you've got your big design job and wear real clothes now doesn't make you such a hot shot. I've been there."

"I invented casual Fridays at Pitman, you know. Even Ollie has been known to put on a well-tailored retro forties shirt. Why didn't you listen to him long ago? That man knows his stuff." Jana Lee put her finger where Ben could grab it.

"I was an idiot, or so my therapist tells me," Jillian said.

"Dean made you see a therapist?"

"Dean *is* my therapist. He's cheap, and his best advice is to work in the garden, play music and sleep as much as possible. Particularly when baby Benny is napping. He spoils me."

"Jackson too, he never lets me go to work on weekends, and we're out of there by *five*, can you believe it? He says life is too short. The town house looks so good now you wouldn't believe it. Oliver helped me pick out furniture and fabrics, and his mother helped me turn it into less of a bachelor pad. She's a good woman."

"It's so cool for Carly to have a family like that." Jillian got all choked up. "We wasted too many years, Jana."

"Eh, we were just lost, and now we're found. Now if Dean could just teach Jackson to cook, we'd be all set," Jana Lee said.

"You may get your wish!" Jillian pointed, and they giggled together watching Dean instruct Jackson on the fine art of corn on the cob.

"I guess we're happy little princesses now," Jillian said.

"I guess we are," Jana Lee agreed, and she

leaned over to give her sister a kiss on the cheek. Benjamin grabbed a handful of her hair and held on for dear life. Their laughter filled the salt sea air of Seabridge Bay with happiness.

Who wants to be cold anyway? Start the new year right with these sizzling new romances coming in January from Avon Books . . . and you'll be feeling the heat in no time.

An Unlikely Governess by Karen Ranney

An Avon Romantic Treasure

Beatrice Sinclair, forced to accept a post as governess, never expects to be tempted by the seductive pleasures Devlen Gordon offers her. While she strives to draw her young charge out of his shell, she must also confront the passion she soon feels for Devlen . . . but is he her lover—or her enemy?

Sleeping With the Agent by Gennita Low

An Avon Contemporary Romance

Navy SEAL Reed Vincenzio must eliminate Lily Noretski . . . by *any* means possible. Lily is as beautiful as she is dangerous, and in possession of a devastating weapon. He must win her confidence, find the weapon . . . and put everything on the line for a woman he soon loves but cannot trust.

The Bride Hunt by Margo Maguire

An Avon Romance

Lady Isabel Louvet is a kidnapped bride, stolen by a Scottish chieftan to warm his bed! But she is rescued by a feared warrior of legend—the brave hearted Anvrai d'Arques. Isabel's fierce spirit stirs his passion, her touch makes him wild. And her love will set him free . . .

A Forbidden Love by Alexandra Benedict

An Avon Romance

The Viscount Hastings is the most scandalous man in all England! So when he discovers Sabrina, a Gypsy in danger, he spirits her away to the most *unsafe* place in the land . . . his bed. He longs to join her there, but instead vows to uncover the secrets this beautiful woman hides . . .

Avon Romantic Treasures

Unforgettable, enthralling love stories, sparkling with passion and adventure from Romance's bestselling authors

Avon Romances

the best in

exceptional authors and unforgettable novels!